U.U. Bund.

A

Tales of the North Coast

Tales of the
NORTH COAST

The Beautiful
and Remote North Coast of Scotland
from Melvich to Tongue

GATHERED AND WRITTEN BY

Alan Temperley

AND

The Pupils of Farr Secondary School

ILLUSTRATIONS BY THE PUPILS
UNDER THE GUIDANCE OF

Elliot Rudie

AND WITH A FOREWORD BY

James Scotland

THE RESEARCH PUBLISHING CO.
52 LINCOLN'S INN FIELDS · LONDON

*The publisher acknowledges the financial assistance of the
Scottish Arts Council in the publication of this volume.*

© ALAN TEMPERLEY, 1977
2nd Impression, September 1977
ISBN 0 7050 0045 1 (hard-back)
ISBN 0 7050 0046 X (limp)
Printed in Gt. Britain for the Research Publishing Co.
(Fudge & Co. Ltd.), London.

Acknowledgements

Our thanks are due primarily to the hundreds of local people who, by so readily telling us the old stories and giving us the information we required, have made this book possible. In a very real way the book is theirs. More particularly we would like to thank Mr. D. Macleod, recently retired Headmaster of Farr Secondary School, without whose continual support and assistance the book would never have been written; Mr. K. Henderson, Headmaster of Farr Secondary School; Miss C. Mackay, Farr; Miss J. and Miss I. H. Mackay, Farr; Mrs. I. Ross; Miss J. Slaven; and Mr. J. Barlow. Our thanks are due also to the Scottish Arts Council for their generous financial assistance; the Saltire Society of Scotland; the late Sutherland Education Committee; and Professor J. MacQueen and the School of Scottish Studies, Edinburgh. We would like to thank Messrs Secker and Warburg for the extracts from Mr. John Prebble's *The Highland Clearances*; Messrs Routledge and Kegan Paul for the extracts from Dr. Ian Grimble's *The Trial of Patrick Sellar*; William Collins and Sons Limited for the extracts from Dr. T. C. Smout's *A History of the Scottish People 1560-1830;* the School of Scottish Studies, Edinburgh, for the extracts from Dr. Eric Richard's *The Mind of Patrick Sellar*; and The Reader's Digest Association Limited for the quotations from *Folklore, Myths and Legends of Britain*. In conclusion we would like to acknowledge the hand of many past pupils whose work, long forgotten by themselves, has been such a help.

Contents

Contents *(Continued)*

Contents (Continued)

9

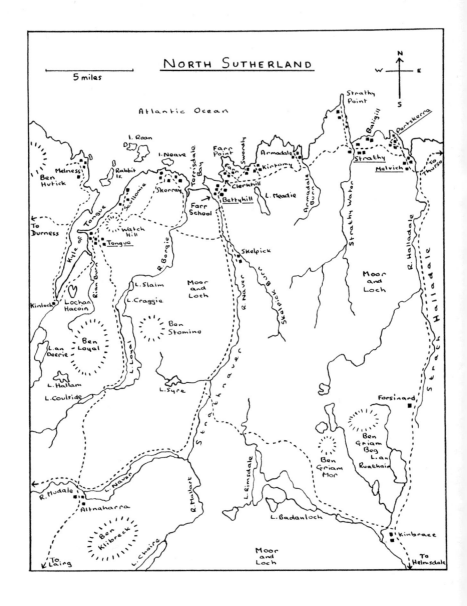

NORTH SUTHERLAND

5 miles

Atlantic Ocean

N
W — E
S

Strathy Point

Baligill
Portskerra

I. Roan

I. Neave

Farr Point

Armadale

Swordly

Kirtomy

Strathy
Malvich

To Thurso

Ben Hutick

Melness

Rabbit Is.

Skerray

Tarrsdale Bay

Clerkhill
Bettyhill

Farr School

L. Meadie

Armadale Burn

Strathy Water

R. Halladale

To Durness

Eilean nan Ron

Watch Hill

Tongue

R. Borgie

Skelpick

Skelpick Burn

Strach Halladale

Kinloch

Lochan Hacoin

L. Slaim
L. Craggie

Moor and Loch

R. Naver

Moor and Loch

L. an Deerie

Ben Loyal

Ben Stomino

L. Loyal

R. Naver

Forsinard

L. Hallam

L. Syre

Ben Griam Beg
L. an Ruathair

L. Coulside

Strach Naver

Ben Griam Mor

R. Mudale

R. Naver

R. Mallart

L. Rimsdale

To Lairg

Altnaharra

Ben Klibreck

L. Choira

L. Badanloch

Kinbrace

Moor and Loch

To Helmsdale

Foreword

Almost thirty years ago, when I was beginning my teaching career in Martyrs' Primary School, Glasgow, I inherited Primary V; as lively, devious, good-hearted, uncontrollable, shrewd, stupid, poker-faced, generous a collection of ten-year-olds as you would ever meet — in short, an average class. Casting around pretty desperately for something to catch their interest, I noticed the name of the school, and asked them if they had. "Well, who were the martyrs?" They didn't know, but they were impatient to find out, and in no time they were scouring the Townhead, the oldest district in the city fortunately, to find out why it was the Head of the Town, whose castle was mentioned in Castle Street and so on. Nothing new, of course, but I would not have believed how much social history was turned up by thirty-odd unacademic youngsters, how quickly, and how thoroughly, and how long it held their interest.

Alan Temperley's book raises the same process to the creative level. With these Tales of the North Coast his pupils have built a memorial to a way of life long dead. Some of these their teacher has turned into genuine short stories — try 'The Seal Maid', for example, or 'Emily Macintosh and the Tinker' — but most of them remain unpolished, not chiselled into the shape Maupassant or Maugham or O. Henry taught us to expect. They are in truth 'tales', anecdotes told round a peat fire in the long dark evenings when people had to make their own entertainment.

Not all of them are the unchallenged property of Strathnaver: people from many parts of the Highlands and beyond will recognise, 'The Carrying Party', 'The Minister's Wife', 'Resurrection in Clachan Churchyard' and of course 'The Seal Maid'. But that merely stamps them as folk tales. The fairy tales are genuine relics of a Gaelic culture; some of the ghost stories raise the authentic *frisson*, notably 'The Phantom Cortege' with its horrid precognition, and 'The Lonely House'. Most of them combine to give us the 'feel' of history, of what it must have been like to live in Strathnaver two centuries ago, when it was several times more populous than it is today. It would be hard to find better material for a history lesson than 'Killing a Sheep'. And the illustrations, of course, provided by the children are delightful.

11

A way of life now vanished, and we know, alas, when it went. Alan Temperley's last section brings the Clearances before us with an uncomfortable jolt, especially when he is quoting from contemporary observers: it is difficult to read unmoved Donald Sage's account of his last service. This is a rich historical record, the kind of collection that could be made — will be, I hope — by pupils all over Scotland. But it is more than that: it is a first-class read. I salute Alan Temperley, and the boys and girls of Farr.

James Scotland

Preface

Seals, battles, shipwreck, fairies, rogues, the evil eye: the tales in this volume have been gathered from a remote necklace of villages on the north coast of Sutherland. They have all, with the exception of five*, been gathered orally from the people of the district.

The region concerned is the thirty mile stretch of coastline running between the beautiful Kyle of Tongue and lonely Strath Halladale. It is a region in itself, bounded to the west and south by empty moors, to the east by the low, flat lands of Caithness, and to the north by the Atlantic Ocean. It is a country of long, low hills, the occasional mountain, lochs and salmon rivers, rocky headlands, and some of the most lovely beaches in Britain. The climate is severe, but it is the wind and wild emptiness that make it so, for the sun shines through the summer, when the meadows are thick with wild flowers and the nights so short that it scarcely grows dark; and in the winter the frosts are light and there is comparatively little snow. The villages are small; a church, a shop, a village hall, and a scattered population of anything from twenty to three hundred people.

Historically the district is part of the old province of Strathnaver, which covered the whole of what is now north and north-west Sutherland. It is the country of Reay, the land of the Mackays, and even now more than a third of the people who live in the district bear that surname. Today the hills and empty straths are a rich hunting ground for ornithologists and students of botany and geology; and historians and archaeologists find much to interest them in the many remains of earlier settlements and raiders — mesolithic clearances; neolithic shell-middens; bronze-age hut circles; iron-age brochs; norse-type castles; long-houses, cists, cairns, and the burned out remains of the nineteenth century evictions — all still lying there on the hillsides.

Originally the tales, which are all traditional, were gathered by the pupils of Farr Secondary School and myself when I was their teacher of English. It seemed a pity that so many excellent stories,

*Dhruim na Cupa; The Jacobite Gold in Lochan Hakon; Emily Macintosh and the Tinker; The Piper Who Loved Horses; The Clearance of Strathnaver.

handed down over the years, should be simply forgotten: already few people knew more than half a dozen, and we in the school were ideally situated to make a collection. Our intention was to print them privately for sale to the people of the area and tourists. The scheme never came to fruition, however, though we put in a great deal of work upon it. When I left the school three years ago I took over the collection myself, and have since then re-organised and re-written it and added six or eight tales that were told to me later. Almost all of the children's work has been incorporated, however, and the shape of the majority of the tales is just as they were originally written. Under the guidance of Mr. Elliot Rudie, Principal Teacher of Art at the school, the present generation of pupils has produced all the illustrations. We have included the names of no individual students since over the years so many, in their different ways, have been involved in the book's production.

I think the stories fall into two main categories, those which are true, or can reasonably claim to be so, and those which are fanciful. Often enough, of course, a story in this latter group may have its foundation in fact, and there are all sorts of permutations in between. Where one of the accounts obviously falls into the 'true' group, we have done all we can to ensure that the facts are correct. Where it falls into the 'fanciful' group, we have not embellished it more than the telling of the story requires. It would be easy for anyone to take the skeleton of a traditional tale and use it simply as the spring-board for his own imagination: we have sought to avoid this completely, since it would negate the honesty and whole point of the collection. Where there was more than one account of a tale we have tried to give a key version, sometimes combining facts, sometimes omitting them. We hope that we have not offended anyone by the inclusion of a tale which has more truth to it than we realise. We wish to stress that this is a collection of traditional stories as they were told, and is not intended to be anything more than that.

Farr Secondary School is a small comprehensive school of one hundred secondary and sixty primary pupils situated in Bettyhill, at the mouth of the River Naver. The children travel in daily by buses from the villages round about. It is a lively establishment and an important part of local village society.

We have three reasons for limiting our collection to the district between the Kyle of Tongue and Strath Halladale: it is, as I have observed, a distinct region of its own within the county of Sutherland;

the children, who come from every corner, know it personally and in great detail; and whilst general volumes of Scottish tales abound, we are not aware of any intensive collections from such a small area. A danger, of course, in making such a compilation, is that a few good stories will be used to support a welter of the second rate. We believe that this is not the case here, and one of our hopes is that we might encourage other districts to make similar collections.

With the recent deaths of one or two of the older members of the villages, some of the stories contained in this volume would already have been lost. Before the First World War the collection would have been many times as long. With the passing of Gaelic as the conversational language, the shattering social impact of radio, television and modern transport, and the ever-accelerating dilution of a strong but limited culture brought face to face with the rest of the world, the old ceilidh stories are ninety per cent forgotten already.

In making our collection of Scottish tales before they are lost altogether, we have many eminent historical precedents. Today, increasingly, people are becoming aware of the speed of change and impermanence: a mood and need is growing for stability and simplicity. There is a move back to the country; for reasons other than financial people are growing their own vegetables; intelligent young men and women are doing their best to follow and revive the work of the old craftsmen; libraries are being more widely used then they have been for many years; there is a great vogue for tales of rural life and the old days; on both radio and television the B.B.C. is devoting more time to the simple telling of stories. And in these days when so much is being laid bare before us by the scientists, astronomers and television networks, another human need is revealing itself in the growing interest in things that are mysterious and strange.

Tradition, the countryside, the supernatural, a simply told story: these are the basic ingredients of most of the old tales. And so it is, with some trepidation, that an Englishman and a hundred young Scots present a selection of the local stories for your enjoyment.

Alan Temperley

HISTORICAL TALES

Donald Sailor

In 1786 Donald Mackay of Armadale was twelve years old. He was a lively, imaginative boy, 'bha fiamh ghair, a ghnath na gnuis' (a smile ever on his countenance), as he was remembered throughout his life. He had received no formal education and so was not able to read or write, but since that was the position of the majority of people in those days, it was no great necessity. You did not need to be able to read and write to run a croft or work on the fishing boats, and Donald was growing up to take his place in the crofting community. During the summer months when the cattle were out on the hills he worked as a herd boy, and during the winter he worked with his father on the farm.

One day in the summer of 1786 Donald was waiting for the postman to come back from Thurso on his weekly journey to Kirkiboll (Tongue). He had entrusted the man with a shilling to buy a pocket knife for him at the shops there. A shilling was a lot of money to him, and he had wanted a pocket knife for a long time. But as he lay on the hillside watching the road, two figures appeared in the distance and slowly drew towards him. Idly he watched them, then when they were quite close they spotted him and came over to speak. They were two sailors from one of MacIver's boats from Lewis that had been wrecked in Portskerra a few days earlier, and now were making their way to Loch Eriboll to join another boat belonging to the same company. They were not sure of the road and asked the boy in Gaelic if he could direct them. As he stood to point the way the men looked him over, talking between themselves in a strange tongue, which was probably either English or Lowland Scots. Then they offered him two shillings if he would actually walk the road with them as far as Farr (Bettyhill), and put them right for Kirkiboll afterwards. The cattle were quite safe and gladly Donald agreed, they seemed pleasant fellows and doubtless had stories to tell to an adventurous youth like himself. Besides, two shillings was a fortune to a boy of that age.

17

By the time they reached Farr he was bewitched by the men's conversation, and when they offered him a further two shillings to continue with them as far as Kirkiboll, he gladly agreed. He had been there several times to visit relatives, and knew the road well.

By the time they reached the village the evening was drawing on. Donald received his four shillings from the men and, though he was very tired, was preparing to set off home, for the nights were quite light enough for walking, when they suggested that it would surely be better if he put up at the inn that night and walked home the following morning. They were most hospitable, and he agreed. He was given good food and drink and a clean bed, and the next morning was fresh and ready for the long walk back to Armadale. For a while he chatted to the sailors, and again became fired with the tales they had to tell; and so, when they suggested that he might walk the road with them to Eriboll, for a whole four shillings more, and maybe even see over the ship, he agreed. If they took the ferry across the Kyle it was only nine or ten miles, not all that far for a boy accustomed to walking: he would be able to return to Kirkiboll and his relatives the same evening.

By the early afternoon they were dropping down the hill towards the loch, a deep sea-inlet nine miles long and over a mile wide, ringed with rocky, heather-covered mountains. The ship, a neat little sailing vessel, was anchored just off shore. When they reached the water's edge they shouted across and a boat pulled out from the ship's side to take them aboard.

Donald was shown everything, and was entranced. He handled the wheel and explored the decks and climbed aloft with the sailors. Then he was taken below, where he was given food and plied with strong drink and kept talking for a long time. When at last he climbed back on deck they were under way. The mouth of Loch Eriboll lay behind them, the sails were set and the ship was just beginning to rise and fall on the waves of the open sea. Donald pleaded to be put ashore, but the sailors just laughed at him and told him to keep out of the way.

Back at home in Armadale his parents were distraught. They hunted the hills with all the men and women of the village, and enquired in the whole area round about. They heard of the boy with the two sailors, he sounded like Donald, and they managed to trace them as far as Loch Eriboll. A ship, they heard, had left that day, but the name of the ship and its destination were a mystery.

19

There was no more they could do but ask people to enquire. A year slipped by, but no word came of their now thirteen year old son.

As for Donald, once he had thrown off his distress he found life on board to be none too bad. He was of a naturally cheerful disposition and quick at picking up the work, and like any boy enjoyed the excitement of travel and seeing new places. The ship was not, of course, exclusively employed in smuggling, but it seems that almost as often as not when they travelled across the North Sea, some part of the cargo was not declared on their bill of lading. This skirting of the law added a certain zest to the already roving seamen's lives and, of course, considerable profit. They carried anything, travelling between Rotterdam and Liverpool, Copenhagen and Dublin, Bristol and the Isle of Man — anywhere there was a cargo to pick up and trading to be done. In Lewis they traded gin and brandy for herring, which they cured themselves. Skye and the Outer Isles seem to have been the centre of a fairly active liquor traffic, and using various ports in the islands as bases they traded up and down the west coast.

It was in their main port, Stornoway, that two years after he was stolen away Donald managed to find a man to write a letter to his parents. At last he was able to tell them what had happened and that he was alive and well. However he made no suggestion as to how he might be rescued or attempt to reach home again himself.*

When he was nearly sixteen, the ship was sailing along the north coast past Thurso and the captain thought it a good opportunity to fill up the water butts, so they anchored in Thurso Bay and a boat put off with a number of small barrels on board. Donald was one of the rowers, and as they drew towards the quay he spotted some men from Armadale in another boat close to them. In great excitement he shouted across and they shouted back, recognising him. The other sailors turned the rowing boat and sped back to the ship in the bay. They hoisted the boat aboard and set sail at once. This was

*The people who tell this story, and the book written about Donald Sailor, suggest that it was quite impossible for him to escape from the ship, that he was a permanent captive. However it seems to me that it would have been a comparatively simple step for a young man so spirited and resourceful to have slipped ashore somewhere in Scotland during what was to become a seven year captivity, and make his way home again, had he so wished. These protestations seem to be an attempt to whiten a character in no need of whitening. Life on board ship was colourful and lively, almost certainly much more so than the crofting life he lived with his family in Armadale, and he preferred, at least for the present, to remain where he was. Certainly a while after he did eventually reach home he longed to be away at sea again, and commented later that "were there a road to Stornoway, I would . . . have taken the journey with great delight."

the second and last time during his seven years' absence that Donald's parents had news of their son.

He finally made his escape in September 1792. By this time he was nineteen years old, a hardened sailor and probably bearded. He had switched ships the previous winter and so was sailing with a crew who knew less of his history. Again they were sailing along the north coast of Scotland and put in for water, but this time, as fortune would have it, they anchored once more in Loch Eriboll. Possibly because of its associations, possibly because he was so near home, Donald decided that it was time he left the ship, and quickly made plans. Clearly he could not ask for his wages (fifty shillings a year), but he did have clothes and possessions that he was reluctant to leave behind. When no-one was observing him he slipped down to the cabin and put on as much as he could without attracting attention underneath his seaman's clothing, and filled his pockets. Then he was ready. Taking his place in the rowing boat beside an older sailor, who was also called Donald Mackay, they rowed to the shore. When the barrels were filled they placed them in the bottom of the boat and then Donald Sailor told the older man to climb in and he would push off. He did so, suspecting nothing; then Donald very quickly pulled away the two oars and shoved the boat hard out into deep water.

For a moment or two the older sailor, who could not swim, was at a loss, then he sent out a great cry to the ship, "D'fhalbh am balach bho thir mor!" (The boy from the mainland's away!)

Donald called out to him, "Beannachd leat a' Dho'nuill!" (Goodbye, Donald!), and took to his heels up the hillside.

When he looked back at the ship another boat was being lowered, so he kept going, roasting under so many clothes. Topping a ridge about three-quarters of a mile from the loch, he dropped for the first time out of sight of his pursuers and found himself in the stubble of a cornfield. When they came chasing after him they would expect him to be much further on. Very carefully he pulled a sheaf away from the end of a stook and crawled inside, panting and streaming with sweat. Ten minutes later he heard the sailors come running past. They were gasping and cursing him. He lay where he was, and in a little while they returned. He recognised the voices as they called out to each other. When all was quiet once more he lay still for several minutes longer, then cautiously moved the sheaf aside and crawled out of his stook. The coast was clear. Twilight was falling.

21

Down below him the two ship's boats were alongside. He watched as they lifted them aboard, weighed anchor, and the white sails puffed out. Like a swan the graceful little ship moved down the darkening loch and out into the open sea. Free at last, with seven years of shipboard life behind him, Donald made his extra clothes into a bundle and set his face towards the hills.

He slept on the hillside, and in the early morning arrived at his relatives' house in Kirkiboll. The following day he walked home, and cresting the rise in the late afternoon saw his father's croft lying below him in Armadale. It looked no different, it was impossible to think he had been away for seven years. But as he drew towards the house and saw his father working at the barn he saw how all too true it was. He was greyer, older. The crofter looked up and saw a strange young man approaching, fair-haired, bearded, his face tanned and healthy. He did not recognise him. Donald asked if he could have a bed for the night: it was a not uncommon request in those days when people travelled on foot.

"Certainly," his father said, "but I will have to speak to my wife."

They went inside and Donald was given the best chair. When his mother came into the room she saw the young man sitting there, but said nothing.

Then Donald could not restrain his feelings. "Oh, mo mhathair!" he cried. "Nach eil sibhe gu'm aithneachainn?" (Oh, my mother! Do you not recognise me?)

There is much more to his story than that, but we will leave Donald the Sailor at his joyful homecoming. The whole of his later life was punctuated by colourful escapades which probably were the result of his restless and high-spirited nature as much as his roving years at sea. He married and had a family and his descendants still live in Bettyhill and Swordly.

His story is fully told in a book entitled *Sketches of Sutherland* by Mr. Alexander Mackay, which was, I think, last published in 1889.

Dhruim Na Cupa

In 1427 Angus Dhu*, Chief of Mackay, was in Inverness. He had been summoned there by James I along with all the other Highland chiefs, for James was determined by one bold sweep to subdue these troublesome men and rid himself of a nuisance. Some were arrested and executed, some banished, and others, of whom Angus Dhu was one, were compelled to give up their sons and heirs as hostages. The lives of these young men depended on their fathers keeping the king's peace and presenting to him at least the face of unquestioned loyalty. They were taken to court to be 'civilised' and educated so that when they came to take their fathers' places a more acceptable and obedient rule might spread across the Highlands.

Angus Dhu was not so young as he had been and the time was coming when he would be looking to his heir to shoulder some of the burdens of leadership. For at that time Angus Dhu was second in power only to Donald, Lord of the Isles, in the three northern counties. By his largely enforced but advantageous marriage to Donald's sister, Elizabeth, he had inherited lands which greatly extended his power and influence. The whole of the Mackay territory was called Reay, and its centre was in Tongue.

Even then, in the fifteenth century, the Mackays and the Suther-lands had been enemies for a long time. Robert, Earl of Sutherland, through Angus Dhu's association with the Lord of the Isles, com-manded now only a fraction of the Mackays' power, but when Donald died, and his successor Alexander was placed under a ban, things took a decided turn in his favour. He was most anxious to gain for himself some of the new lands which had come to Angus by his marriage, and now looked about for allies who might be persuaded by self interest to work for his own good. He found such a man in Angus Murray of Pulrossie.

To understand his place in the story we must look at three other men, all brothers, who are also very important. They were cousins of Angus Dhu and named Thomas, Neil and Morgan Mackay. When Angus Dhu inherited the lands from the Lord of the Isles, he life-

*Angus Dubh: Black Angus.

23

rented huge areas to these three cousins: Thomas took Strath Halladale, Pulrossie and Creich; Morgan the whole of Strathoykell; and Neil all the Ross-shire lands. Now Thomas was being troubled by raids into Strath Halladale by Mowatt of Caithness, and hearing that Mowatt was travelling south he pursued him and slew him near Tain. The remainder of Mowatt's troop took refuge in St. Duthus' Chapel, but the infuriated Mackays set fire to the building and burned them all to death. The atrocity was reported, Thomas was declared an outlaw, and all his possessions and lands were seized. Angus Dhu refused outright to bring his relative to 'justice', but Thomas's own brothers, Neil and Morgan, agreed to hand him over into the hands of Angus Murray of Pulrossie. In this they were tempted by two factors: first there were the lands belonging to Thomas and now confiscated; and second, and perhaps more significant, there were the two daughters of Angus Murray of whom they were both enamoured and later married. They betrayed their brother into Angus Murray's hands, he was escorted to Inverness and executed. All three, Angus Murray, Neil and Morgan received their reward.

On account of the potentially dangerous situation, in 1430 Angus Dhu's son and heir Neil, (not to be confused with the treacherous Neil), was transferred from the court in Edinburgh to a prison on the Bass Rock. Because of this he became known as Neil Bhass. His return was uncertain, Angus was older, and the question of succession was not to be avoided. Now Angus Dhu had a younger, illegitimate son, named Eoin (Abrach) Mackay*, who had been reared by his mother's family in Lochaber. Obviously his succession was questionable, so despite him Angus's two cousins, Neil and Morgan, were persuaded to press their own claims to the chieftainship. Angus was too wise and well informed not to see that these were claims with a threat not far behind them. For Morgan and Neil had been pushed into making the claim by Angus Murray, backed by the Earl of Sutherland. An outright refusal was dangerous in the prevailing situation, so Angus Dhu tried to buy them off with gifts of large areas of land. In younger days, before his son was imprisoned by the king, such a claim would have warranted a fight to settle the matter, but now he was bound to keep the king's peace. The offer was rejected absolutely, and to his astonishment he learned

*Eoin Abrach: Ian (or John) from Lochaber. See 'Ian Abrach'

24

that Morgan and Neil were preparing a great army, determined to claim their 'just' inheritance with the sword.

Angus Dhu could command no allies. Part of the army now preparing against him were his own men from his own lands, life-rented to Thomas, Morgan and Neil. In their turn they were backed by Angus Murray and the Earl of Sutherland, and had strong connections with Caithness who were no friends of Angus Dhu.

The old chieftain summoned all his leaders and his young son Eoin Abrach to a meeting in Tongue. The whole situation had patently been contrived by his enemies, and now they had to prepare to meet a force which must certainly be much greater than their own. Spies were sent down into Sutherland and information began to filter back. A situation was chosen near Lairg for the gathering of the clans, a day was settled for the invasion. But which route the invaders would follow was known to only a few, and Angus Dhu could only guess. It seemed not unlikely that they would follow the direct route from the south, cutting across the lower slopes of Ben Loyal. With this in mind Angus Dhu went out himself to seek a position where a small force could meet a larger to best advantage. He soon found it in the place called Dhruim na Cupa (the ridge of the cup), about two miles south of Tongue. However it was by no means certain that they would follow this route and so he positioned scouts high on the southern slopes of Ben Loyal to watch the surrounding country. For days they waited.

Meanwhile from all across the Reay country the men gathered. Individually and together they must have been an impressive sight. Their dress was a jacket of strong cloth coloured dark red with a native dye, kilt of the Mackay tartan, thick hose and brogues of skin to which the hair still clung. On their heads they wore the flat Highland bonnet, decorated with the clan crest and at least one eagle feather. Their fighting arm held a sword with heavy hand guard, and the other arm and fist supported the thick, hide-covered targe or shield. All men of an age would be bearded.

The watchers on the mountain saw the invaders while they were still far away, tiny insects, a shadow of men moving across the moor. Messengers ran down to Angus Dhu: there was no longer any doubt, they were taking the direct route.

The Mackay commanders positioned their troops. In close formation the main body was assembled high on the slopes of Dhruim na Cupa. One detachment moved far down the pass through which the enemy must advance, and concealed itself in a copse on the slopes of a gorge. Now Eoin Abrach and the other commanders persuaded Angus Dhu to retire to the top of the ridge and watch. Reluctantly the old chief agreed and relinquished command to his gallant young son. Possibly the greatest leader and warrior the Mackays had known, his days of valour were past.

For hours they waited. The men lay on the hillside.

At last the enemy appeared, a force of nearly fifteen hundred clansmen, marching in desultory order around the lower slopes of Ben Loyal. The leaders strolled in front; clearly they were expecting little opposition. Then they saw the Mackays far above them. They came on through the pass, climbing all the while, and drew closer to the still ranks of the Mackays. One of the invading leaders cried out, "Tuiginn ceannlaigh sinn na laoigh," (Come on, we will soon shackle those calves*). A man of Mackay called back to him, "Thoir an aire ort fhéin, is docha gu leum na laoigh ro ard dhuibh," (Look out for yourself, the calves may jump too high for you to handle them). Then those in front ran on. They were too hasty. They had no plan of battle, they arrived out of breath from climbing the long slope and tired from the march. They were cut down in their dozens by Eoin Abrach's disciplined men. Then more and more Sutherlands poured up the slope, fighting resolutely, and the battle grew hot. "Throwing away the encumbering kilt and plaid, the combatants set to in their shirts, hewing at one another with two handed swords and murderous battle axes, each determined to win or die." † But the attacking Sutherlands had not seen the large detachment hidden in the gorge, and as the last of the invaders ran by they leapt out and attacked them with great ferocity from the rear. They were taken completely by surprise and now, having neither orders nor adequate leadership, began to go to pieces. They were taken in front, on the flank and in the left rear, and though they fought on with their accustomed bravery it was not enough. Their leaders were slain, among them Neil and Morgan Mackay, the pretenders, and Angus Murray, and there was nothing left for their troops to do but flee.

---

*A play on words. Ben Loyal is called in Gaelic 'Beinn Laoghal': 'the calf-like mountain' or less precisely 'the mountain of the calves', referring to either cow or deer calves. The Anglicised 'Ben Loyal' is a simple corruption of this Gaelic: it has nothing to do with loyalty.

† Rev. Angus Mackay: *A History of the Province of Cat*. The *Metrical Chronicle* also speaks of the ferocity of the fighting.
"Was neuir sene in na dais beforne
So cruell counter sen that God (His Son) was borne."

Hotly pursued by the fierce and triumphant Mackays they fled up the slope towards the northern summits of Ben Loyal. They were hunted down and killed, even, it is claimed, to the last man, who died at Ath-charrie.

This final survivor, it is said, was making his way through a quiet glen not many miles away when he met a man of Reay who for some reason had not been able to join his clansmen.

"How did the battle go?" he asked the fleeing soldier.

"I'm the only Sutherland left," came the reply.

"Then you won't live to tell the tale," cried the fierce Mackay, and drawing his dagger he plunged it into the soldier's breast.*

Despite heavy losses it was a magnificent victory. Angus Dhu, well pleased, came down to look over the field of battle. Eoin Abrach and those commanders who were there took him to view the bodies of his cousins and Angus Murray. As the old warrier stood, contemplating their remains, a Sutherland who was hiding in the

*Though this total destruction of the invading force is popularly claimed, there is an air of poetic licence about it, for there were certainly survivors. They were, however, very few.

bushes nearby, shot an arrow which struck him in the side. Angus Dhu, nicknamed Angus the Absolute, the great Chief of Mackay, fell dying. The victory was complete, but the sorrow was great.

The battle, which took place in 1433, became known later as 'the Bannockburn of the North', and for a century there was comparative peace between the Mackays and the Sutherlands. Eoin Abrach, in the absence of his older brother Neil Bhass, took on himself the mantle of chieftainship, which he wore with great distinction. The Earl of Sutherland, furious at his defeat, but unable to do anything about it, despatched assassins to murder the new hero. They came close and Eoin Abrach was compelled to hide. A cave in the hillside below Castle Varrich, at Tongue, became known afterwards as Leabaidh Eoin Abraich (the bed of Eoin Abrach). Many people urged him to claim the full title of chieftain, but he refused, steadfastly maintaining that this was the rightful position of his older brother.

In 1437 King James I was murdered at Perth, and shortly afterwards Neil, with the assistance of a kinswoman, who was married to Lauder, the governor, managed to escape from his prison on the Bass Rock. He was twenty-four years old, and for ten years had been the king's guest. Immediately he returned to Sutherland and assumed his title as Chief of the Clan Mackay.

Eoin retired to a seat in Achness in Strathnaver, where he became the sire of a sept of the clan known as the Abrach Mackays and renowned, even among these warriors, for their fighting prowess. It was one of his sons who eventually hunted down and killed the Sutherland who had shot his grandfather, Angus Dhu, after the battle of Dhruim na Cupa.

An early account of the affair was written in the reign of King James VI, although not published until 1764. It is entitled *The Conflict of Druimnacoub*. Most of the facts are as we have portrayed them, but it paints a slightly different outcome to the battle itself.

They encountered at Druimnacoub, two miles from Tongue — Mackay's chief dwelling-place. There ensued a cruel and sharp conflict, valiantly fought a long time, with great slaughter, so that, in the end, there remained but few alive of either side. Neil Mackay, Morgan Mackay, and their father-in-law (Angus Murray), were there slain. John Aberigh, having lost all his men, was left for dead on the field, and was afterwards recovered; yet he was

28

mutilated all the rest of his days. Angus Dow Mackay, being brought thither to view the place of the conflict, and searching for the dead corpses of his cousins, Morgan and Neil, was there killed with a shot of an arrow, by a Sutherland man, that was lurking in a bush hard by, after his fellows had been slain. This John Aberigh was afterwards so hardly pursued by the Earl of Sutherland, that he was constrained, for safety of his life, to flee into the Isles.

Footnote: For many centuries the land of the Mackays was passionately and valiantly defended against the Sutherlands and other invaders. Thousands of clansmen gave their lives for it. At length, it is sad to say, the great wealth of the Earl of Sutherland enabled him simply to buy it. Lord Reay, Chief of the Clan Mackay, having given his money to the Protestant cause, was forced to recoup it by selling a parcel of land. It was followed by others, and in 1829 the Earl of Sutherland was able to complete the purchase. The Mackays, of course, remained a clan, with a chief, but in 1875 the 9th Lord Reay died without an heir, and the title passed to the Dutch branch of the family, who had stayed in Holland after fighting on the continent with Gustavus Adolphus during the Thirty Years' War. The title remains in Holland today.

Killing a Sheep

Uisdean pressed his face against the crack in the barn door. The old ewe's feet were tied now and his Uncle John was trying to hold it still on the table with its head and neck over one end. His father had the knife in his hand.

"Uisdean! You come away from that door this minute. I told you!"

He looked around. His mother was standing in the kitchen doorway.

"Now away down and get me another bucket of water!"

He turned away from her and pressed the side of his face to the crack in the door again and peered through. Thick blood was pumping in a stream into the big bowl at his father's feet. He had never seen so much blood. Suddenly he did not want to watch any longer and ran to the kitchen door and picked up the bucket.

When he got back from the well his Auntie Jean was carrying the bowl of blood across the yard. In the kitchen his mother was chopping some onions into a dish for making the black puddings.

"Can I go and watch now?" he said.

His mother nodded. "It's dead now, poor beast."

It was gloomy in the barn. His father, in waistcoat and checked flannel shirt, the sleeves rolled back from his brown forearms, was stripping the skin from the dead animal. There was a hot, fleshy smell from it. At length the fleece hung clear and he snipped it away at the neck, leaving the head still woolly.

"Hang it over there," he said, handing the fleece to the boy and pointing. Carefully Uisdean hung it across the wooden shaft of the plough, the wool underneath.

"Where's Uncle John?" he said.

"He's away," his father replied. "He just called in to help me with the killing. You need two for that."

Then his father was feeling at the beast's stomach. He found the spot he wanted, pushed in the knife and ran it from end to end. All the innards spilled out on to the table. Some fell off the edge and trailed down on to the dusty floor of the barn. Then he was reaching among them and inside the carcass, picking out the heart, kidneys and intestines and putting them in another bowl beside him. When he got to the liver he examined it carefully, looking for fluke and disease, but it seemed clean enough and he put it in with the rest. In went the stomach too, and he laid the pink lights on one side for the dogs. Then he was scraping the fat from inside the carcass.

At last he was done and Uisdean carried the reeking bowl across to his mother and auntie in the kitchen. When he got back his father had cut off the head and was cleaning up the carcass. When he was satisfied he took it through to an outhouse and hung it from a rafter, bluish-pink and still warm.

"Why don't you hang it in here?" said Uisdean.

"The smell might blow through to the byre and frighten the animals," his father said. "Look, you take this head across to your mother and bring me that pail under the bench."

They shovelled what was left of the sheep, which wasn't much, into the bucket and buried it behind the midden. Then they tossed a couple of buckets of water across the barn floor and scrubbed it with a stiff broom to get rid of the blood and the smell. Then they went in and had a cup of tea. His father said he needed a whisky too.

His mother and Auntie Jean had turned the intestines inside out and scrubbed them clean. Now they were lying, bleached and white, in the bottom of a bucket of salty water. In one bowl his mother was mixing the blood with onions, fat, salt and pepper to make black puddings. When it was ready she pulled a length of intestine from the bucket and pinned one end shut with a sliver of wood, binding it tight with a figure eight of string. Then she took a ladle and poured

31

the thick mixture in, making a long, black sausage. When it was nearly full she pinned and tied the other end and reached for another length of intestine. Meanwhile his Auntie Jean was making white puddings, mixing oatmeal, onions, fat, salt and pepper, and packing it into the larger intestine: these puddings were much fatter. They did not have enough wooden pins and she was having to use a hen's quill instead. When they had finished Uisdean tied and blew up the remaining lengths of intestine into long balloons and hung them to dry in a corner of the kitchen. His mother would use them for white puddings when she wanted them.

After that it was time for dinner. In the afternoon Uisdean went to the house of a friend who had a new puppy and they took it down to the shore. They arranged to go ferretting the next day.

While he was away his mother cleaned the sheep's head, removing the eyes and brain and singeing off all the white hair with a hot poker. When it was clean she put it to boil in a pot on the kitchen range. They would have broth and potted sheep's head. The black puddings simmered gently on the other side of the fire. Every so often she leaned forward and prodded them with a long knitting needle to stop them from bursting.

Uisdean's birthday, November the fourth, was only a week away, so she took the chance to wrap up a navy blue pullover she had knitted for him. Then she took out the bottle of ink and wrote a birthday card.

In the evening, while Uisdean and his father were out repairing a stone dyke, she made haggis. She chopped up the heart and kidneys and mixed them with oatmeal, onion, fat, salt and pepper and packed them into the sheep's big stomach. Then she tied the ends with string and it was ready for boiling. The other stomach she cut into lengths of tripe, scrubbing and scraping the rough insides until they were creamy white and spotless. She liked a little tripe herself, but her husband and Uisdean refused to touch it. They had the haggis next day for dinner, with potatoes and turnip; it was very good, spicy and hot.

When the carcass had been hanging in the outhouse for two or three days his father took it down and salted it away for the winter. First he split it right up the backbone and then cut away the various joints. When that was all done he lined the bottom of the half-barrel with rough salt, and having rubbed every piece of meat thoroughly with salt, packed in a single layer. He covered it over with more salt, making sure that the gaps were filled, and packed another layer of mutton on top. Soon it was all salted away, all except one piece of meat they would be eating over the next couple of days.

It would last them till March. There was no butcher, but plenty of rabbits, fish, salt herring, eggs and the occasional hen, so they did not go short. Most of the mutton would have to be boiled, it was the only way of getting all the salt out. Uisdean had been eating it for the last twelve years and his father for the last forty. They were both strong and healthy: it was good food.

The Jacobite Gold in Lochan Hakon

By March, 1746, the fate of Prince Charles Edward Stuart and his tragically loyal Jacobite followers was, in retrospect, sealed. For three months he had been on the retreat. The support he so desperately needed from the people of England and Scotland was not forthcoming, his troops were deserting in their hundreds, the weather was bad, they were poorly clad and ill equipped, his quartermasters were grossly inefficient, and he had to all intents and purposes run out of money.

In the middle of the month King Louis XV dispatched the sloop *Hazard* from Dunkirk with in excess of £13,000 in gold coin (English coin and louis d'or) for immediate delivery to Prince Charles at his headquarters in Inverness. She was commanded by Captain George Talbot, and escorted by a detachment of more than a hundred French, Irish and Scottish Jacobite troops. In addition she carried arms and stores.

It was a treacherous voyage. Soon after leaving Dunkirk the *Hazard* was engaged by English privateers and had to run to Ostend for safety and repairs. Then, keeping well away from the east coast, since King George's troops, headquartered at Aberdeen, were also being supplied by sea, she set sail up the east coast for Inverness. Turning west, well out from the Moray Firth, Captain Talbot was then assailed by British warships, stationed there to blockade the port of Inverness, and had to turn north once more and make a run for it. He was pursued by the English frigate *Sheerness*.

During the night he managed to snatch a lead, which the frigate quickly cut down in the hours of daylight. Turning west through the Pentland Firth, Captain Talbot picked up local fishermen who volunteered, for handsome payment, to pilot him further west.

As they reached the middle of the north coast the *Sheerness* was not far behind, and drawing closer all the time. The two pilots, drawing on their local knowledge, advised Captain Talbot that if he were to turn south into the Kyle of Tongue, his sloop's shallower draught would enable him to sail into waters where the *Sheerness* could not follow. Once there, though he could be blockaded, his superior numbers of fighting men would enable him to fight off the *Sheerness's* sailors, and march south with the Jacobite money, overland to Inverness.

Captain Talbot took their advice, and swung south into the mouth of the Kyle of Tongue. They did not take sufficient account of the state of the tide. As the *Hazard* drew west towards the Melness shore, seeking to follow the main channel, she drifted on to a sandbank and stuck fast. The *Sheerness*, sailing swiftly in pursuit through the Kyle Rannoch between Island Roan and the mainland, drew close.

The *Hazard* was port side on to the *Sheerness*, which enabled her to fire repeated broadsides at the frigate. In that attitude, however, she presented the maximum target for the frigate's vastly superior guns. The outcome was inevitable.

Three hours later the *Hazard* was hopelessly crippled. Her rigging was down, water flooded into the holds, most of the guns were out of action, and there had been very heavy casualties. The *Sheerness*, however, was unable to come alongside and capture the vessel because of the shallow water and still greater number of troops aboard the *Hazard*.

Darkness fell and the tide turned. As it swelled the *Hazard* slowly and sluggishly floated and swung in towards the shore. Captain Talbot directed her towards the nearest beach. When she finally settled there were still eight or nine feet of water inshore, and it took several hours, for they were still under heavy fire from the *Sheerness*, to transport the gold, arms, wounded men, and enough provisions to support them on the long march to Inverness, to the beach. Leaving the most severely wounded men with clansmen who had gathered on the shore, the remaining soldiers and sailors, under Captain Talbot and Colonel Michael Brown, set off southwards down the western shore of the Kyle of Tongue.

They were in Mackay territory, and the Mackays did not support the Jacobite cause. They must have been confident, therefore, in their numbers and their gold, to have stopped only an hour later at the largest house in the district. There they were able to rest for a while after the battle, fortify themselves with food and drink, and obtain valuable information and even a guide for the first part of the journey south. When they set off once more it was the early hours of the morning, and by the time they arrived at the head of the kyle it was nearly midday.

35

Meanwhile news of their progress had been sent across the kyle to Tongue, the seat of the Chief of Mackay. Officers from the *Sheerness*, too, had come ashore to Tongue, and were exhorting the leaders of the clan to assemble a force and march south to intercept the Jacobites. While it was still dark a large body of clansmen set out and prepared an ambush near Lochan Hakon above the head of the kyle.

Wearily in the early afternoon the Jacobites toiled up the rough slope above the river. Ahead of them reared the high, many-peaked ridge of Ben Loyal. Suddenly, from their left, the hidden force of Mackays came sweeping down the hillside towards them. Tired, in disarray, the mixed Jacobite troops scattered. Some bearing the gold, determined that it should not fall into Government hands, ran to the shore of Lochan Hakon and flung their treasure into the deep water. Others fled, trying to outstrip the Mackay troops, but were soon overtaken and captured. A few gathered together and prepared to offer resistance. There could only have been one outcome to such a battle, had it been engaged, and Captain Talbot, having seen his men shot to bits by the *Sheerness* only hours before, quickly surrendered.

They were marched north to Tongue and taken aboard the *Sheerness*. Shortly afterwards she set sail with them to the Government headquarters at Aberdeen, and several weeks later they were transported to a more permanent captivity in the jail at Berwick Castle — where one hopes that their treatment was more humane than that meted out to many of the Jacobite prisoners.

Nearly all of the gold was recovered and used to swell the coffers of King George, and the *Sheerness* received a fine bounty of prize money. Of the uncertain sum that was flung into the loch, and one or two caches which it is claimed the Jacobites made near the Kyle

36

of Tongue, there are several unproven stories. One hears of a shepherd's family which suddenly became very wealthy; of a hill on their route which is known as the 'mound of gold'; of much secret searching, which produced one or two louis d'or and some bottles of French brandy; of a cow accidently retrieving a golden coin from Lochan Hakon in the cleft of its hoof.

What is certain is that none of the gold reached Prince Charles Edward Stuart in Inverness, even though upon hearing of the disaster he sent a band of his best men north in a vain attempt to recover something of what was lost. And for the Jacobites even worse, the great Loch Arkaig treasure, their final hope, vanished in the west without trace a few days later.

On the 16th April, 1746, less than three weeks after these proceedings, the Jacobites fought their last, desperate battle on Culloden Moor near Inverness. The gallantry of the Scottish soldiers could not survive the combined incompetence of their leaders and power of the English guns. They were needlessly massacred, and when they fled, ruthlessly hounded and butchered by the Duke of Cumberland's men. New regulations were imposed. It was the end of the clan system and the old Scottish way of life.

The Farr Stone

There has been a religious settlement at Clachan, below Bettyhill, since time immemorial. Certainly in early Christian times there was a priest's cell there, and probably more than that, even a monastic settlement with a wooden chapel and graveyard. The date of this, for reasons which will emerge later, would probably be some time around the eighth century, shortly after the earliest priests arrived and felt they needed the sanctuary of Island Neave.*

For twelve hundred years the settlement has followed the fluctuating fortunes of a Christian church in the Scottish Highlands: Viking raids, clan attack, the breakaway of the Protestants, the foundation of the Church of Scotland, the Disruption in 1843, reunion with the United Free Church in 1929.

The church which at present stands upon the site is a fine, four-square building of the Telford style. The last service held there was more than thirty years ago, during the Second World War. After that the church fell into disuse: the dust gathered, part of the ceiling fell, the walls peeled, small holes began to appear in the roof. Gone were the great days when it was the focal point of the vast parish of Farr, with a splendid manse and a glebe that consisted of some of the best agricultural land in the area; when the Reverend David Mackenzie railed at his poor flock from the magnificent pulpit, exhorting them to submit meekly to the evictions as divine punishment for their sins.† By 1965 the church authorities were considering removing the roof to avoid paying rates: the church seemed consigned to its fate. Since then, however, after a slow start, it has found a new lease of life as the Farr Museum of local history, which is now becoming known as the Clearances Museum. A great deal of money has been spent on repair and redecoration by the new local authority, so that once more the church is in immaculate condition, a white, rectangular building set above the beach, with long, paned windows, slate roof, and neat little bell-tower. Local and Highland enthusiasts have been

*See 'Eilean Neave'.

†See 'The Clearance of Strathnaver'.

most vigorous in collecting and preparing the implements, artifacts and relics for display. At the moment the museum is in its infancy, but in view of the extraordinary amount of interest that the idea has generated it seems certain to flourish.

In the graveyard surrounding the church, exactly ten yards from the middle of the west wall, stands the Farr Stone. It is a grey stone, six feet in height, twenty-six inches broad, and nine inches thick, rising from the soft mossy grass of the graveyard. It is covered with lichen, pale green, brown, white and yellow, and little clumps of spring flowers have been planted at the base. It faces due west.

The traditional story of the stone's first appearance is that one day, centuries ago, a strange vessel arrived in the late afternoon and anchored in Farr Bay. Though the people examined the ship from the shore, they had no idea where it came from, and did not dare to venture closer. The following morning it had gone. Later in the day they discovered the new stone in the graveyard, twice as big as anything that was there previously, and covered with a most complicated and beautifully executed pattern. Clearly it had been carried

39

in during the night, though how the sailors had handled a stone of such dimensions in a small ship's boat, and carried it across the quarter mile of rough dunes and beach was a mystery, for investigation revealed that it went fully six feet into the ground as well.

Farr Stone is a Celtic monument of some distinction. The pattern, now, is so far worn away that though you can distinguish it sufficiently to get an indication of its splendour and intricacy, the casual observer will probably be somewhat unimpressed. When one considers the length of time it has stood, however, subjected to the weathering influence of the winter gales, frosts and salt sea air, it is still a remarkable monument. Though one would wish, of course, to leave it in its original position, it seems a pity that something is not done now, even to the extent of removing it to the museum, to preserve what remains, before it becomes a plain, blank, slab of rock.

Until comparatively recently the carving was very distinct. It was described by the Reverend Angus Mackay of Bettyhill at the turn of the century as 'magnificent'. "Whom it commemorates," he wrote, "we cannot say, although it is called Clach Fhearchar, Stone of Ferchar, but it conclusively proves that the culture of those early times was broad and that their piety was intense. The man who designed and executed this monument, and the men who could take pleasure in it, were neither rude nor unlearned, for on every line and feature of its beautiful grey face are carved refinement, culture, learning."*

The stone is a typical example of the early embossed style of Christian use of pagan decoration, which places it quite firmly in, or around, the eighth century A.D. The cross is carved in high relief above the surface of the stone, and the central whorl quite heavily embossed upon that. It is definitely not a Viking stone, for they were more simple, and did not use the decorative key patterns. The Vikings, in fact, were at this time themselves being influenced by such monuments as the Farr Stone, and taking the decorative ideas back with them to Scandinavia. When the patterns returned, some time later, they were quite distinctive.

Even allowing that the soil is sandy the fact that the stone is set so deeply into the ground suggests that it was once pagan. There is no decoration on the back as was often the case in early Christian years, when pagan stones were re-carved on the reverse side with Christian symbols. In many cases, of course, as with the cross itself, the

*Rev. Angus Mackay: *A History of the Province of Cat.*

symbols were the same. Possibly, therefore, the pagan stone, facing west, was simply re-carved on the face, the sculptor removing the old pattern as he chipped away the rock to leave the cross and whorl standing out in relief. This would be quite in keeping with the practice of Christian settlements springing up on the sites of old pagan ones, one religion simply replacing the other. This view is supported by the proximity of the Columban settlement on Island Neave. Almost certainly the two were for some time closely connected, and since the island community was the parent body, the existence of the stone on the shore suggests that it was there already, and consequently pre-Christian.

The precise function of the Farr Stone is uncertain, but in view of the fact that it undoubtedly marked something important, two possibilities seem to emerge. It could be the gravestone of a great or widely respected chief. It could also, and possibly in addition, have been a stone erected to show that here was a religious settlement, be it pagan or Christian, centre of learning, or small monastic community.

Farr Stone has been standing for twelve centuries. The church beside it has a long history. When they are digging new graves in the churchyard now, the shovels are unearthing skeletons which have been in the earth for nobody knows how long. As you walk through the graveyard you cannot be unaware of the people and the history all about you. 'Now' becomes a mere moment in the slope of time, and most certainly not the end. The wind blows in from the sea as it has for the last ten thousand years.

In Need of a Job

It was the early years of the nineteen thirties. Down in Glasgow the queues of quiet men stood raggedly along the pavements outside the employment exchanges. The factories and shipyards had been closed down: those men who landed the few poorly paid jobs that existed were the lucky ones. To ease the pressure the government and local authorities created what work they could. The Sutherland County Council pursued its policy of reconstruction along the poor moorland roads. To augment their gangs of local men and tinkers they regularly sent for squads to Glasgow, for the drop out rate in the rough conditions they had to endure was high.

The men who travelled north were not always accustomed to such work. Some had never handled a shovel in their lives. Desperate for work, they took whatever they could get; told lies about their previous experience. The authorities handed them travel warrants, one-way to the work site, pushed a few forms into the filing cabinet, and forgot about them. After that the men were on their own. They were often ill-prepared, clad in shabby suits and thin mufflers, light shoes — occasionally even patent leather as they wore their way to the end of what lay in their cupboards at home.

The work of reconstruction on the road at Drumholliston (across the open moor to the east of Melvich) which took place at that time has been described as the last of the local 'bad' jobs. For the men who were new to the work it was insupportable. Their soft hands blistered within the hour, their unmuscular arms ached unbearably, and in addition they had to avoid the continual surveillance of the foreman and timekeeper, for if they were seen to slack there were plenty of other men to take their places. Sometimes they sat in quarries, breaking the lumps of rock into two inch metal with light, incessant hammers; or they levelled the new roads; or dug out the boggy peat with shovels that hung like lead in their hands. In only the most severe of weather did they stop work, and then they were not paid. The wind and rain blew in from the sea across the shelterless heather, the mud and bogs squelched underfoot. In the winter the frosts came, with snow and sleet.

The weather was not always bad, of course; on fine summer days labouring on the open moors must have been quite pleasant, and for many men it was the work to which they were accustomed. For a long time, however, Drumholliston seems to have been exceptionally bad. One foreman on the job was so hated that, we are told, a plan was conceived to have him murdered, which even progressed as far as the digging of a hole a little distance across the moor to get rid of his body. For men accustomed to working in offices, and living at home, the situation must have been intolerable.

At night they retreated to wooden huts, heated with bogies (small, straight-sided stoves). They hung dripping clothes from strings strung across the roofs and flung themselves on their plain beds. Usually they did their cooking on a hot-plate at the end of the hut, or possibly in a small room divided off for the purpose. If they were unlucky enough to be in a dirty hut there were the lice to contend with as well, and some slept naked so that the beasts would not infest their clothes.

Unused to such conditions many men stayed no more than a few days, and others who would have stuck it out for a while longer were dismissed arbitrarily. The timekeeper, sometimes walking around the site with a leather pouch like a bus conductor's at his waist, would see a man resting and pay him off on the spot. Some were sacked within three or four hours. With the rate of pay at six shillings a day, and eightpence an hour, they found themselves two hundred and fifty miles away from home with no more than a few shillings in their pockets. There was no waiting on for a few days for a lift: when a man was dismissed, he went.

One cold January day several men who had quit the job on Drumholliston and been dismissed, set out to make their way home to Glasgow. The shortest route was west to Bettyhill, and then south down Strathnaver to Altnaharra and Lairg. They walked all day and may well have been given a lift part of the way since they reached Altnaharra in the evening and it is a distance of more than forty miles. It was dark when they arrived; they were wet, and dirty from the work they had been doing, and some of them were rough individuals. When they asked for shelter for the night they were refused, but at length were given the use of a barn.

One of them was ill. He had been coughing all day and from time to time the others had had to wait while he sat down for a few minutes to gather the strength to continue. During the night he grew worse.

43

Clearly a fever was on him. It was terribly cold: they pulled the bits
of straw about their feet and tried to keep warm.

In the morning they were a worn and shivering group of men.
Their comrade who was ill was a problem. He should have gone to
his bed, but there was nowhere for him to go. They felt that the doors
of the villagers were closed against the likes of them, for the wandering gangs of labourers, commonly known as tramps, had bad
reputations. He solved the problem himself by insisting on going
with them. It was best to get moving; he was not as bad as all that.
Once more they set off into the bitter January weather.

It was snowing slightly, and a withering wind blew into their faces
as they made their way along the strath at Vagastie. Time and again
they had to wait a few moments to let the sick man catch them up.
The snow thickened, there was no shelter. Then they were climbing
up the long hill at Crask, the worst for snow in that part of the
country, and out across the open moor. They had covered twelve
miles and were at a bend in the road just at the crest of the moors

when the sick man collapsed and lay unconscious in the thick covering of snow. His work mates gathered around. Within a few minutes he was dead.

They did not know what to do. But there was little they could do. Laying him decently at one side of the road, and marking the spot, since the snow would soon cover him up, they walked on, and when they came to the first houses, and later Lairg, told the people and the authorities.

He was found where they had laid him. Whether he was taken home to be buried in Glasgow, or laid in the paupers' graveyard near the poor house at Bonar Bridge is not known, but a pile of stones was raised to mark the spot where he died. This, along with that whole stretch of road, has become well known as the Tramp's Cairn. Today the road gangs keep the cairn tidy, and travellers and holiday makers, passing the spot swiftly in their smart cars, can see it standing beside the road, a memory of days when life was by no means so easy.

Maol Ruadh

If you drive half way up Strathnaver and halt your car on the Skail corner, you will find a little rocky bluff just ahead of you, and to your left a thin grove of birch trees standing in a bog. Twenty yards away, just beyond these twisted, mossy trees, is what appears at first sight to be a jumble of rocks lying at the edge of the flat valley floor. If, however, you cross the stile and skirt around the bog, you will find that it is the remains of a little dwelling. The roof and walls have fallen away, and the moss of centuries has covered them so thickly that now it looks as if the house was deliberately sunk into the ground. The inside is clear, however, fifteen feet long and a little over six feet wide. The remaining slab walls are about two feet high, and a stone projecting from each wall in the middle divides it into two rooms, with a door in between. Two leaning birch trees grow from the brink. A low circular mound two or three yards away marks the remains of the old surrounding wall.

The dwelling is known locally as 'the temple'. It is believed to have been, in the seventh or eighth century, the Strathnaver home, or 'cell', of the Red Priest. He was a follower of the great Saint Columba, one of the missionaries who went out from Iona to spread the Christian message across the Highlands. Through his constant journeyings he became well-known, and was commonly referred to as Maol Ruadh, the bald, red-headed fellow — very likely through having shaved his crown into the priest's tonsure. Later he became known simply as Sagart Ruadh, the Red Priest. The fact that his hair was red possibly implies that he was a Celt. It may have been he who built the well-known priest's cell at what is now Applecross in Wester Ross: and Amulree, the little village in Perthshire, is believed by some to be an Anglicised corruption of 'A Maol Ruadh', the Red Priest's Ford, so perhaps he was there, too.

He was killed, it is said, and probably by the Vikings, at the entrance to his little cell in Strathnaver. Certainly the Vikings sacked Iona and made many forays into the Southern Land, looting and killing, at the same time, so it seems quite possible.

He was buried about half a mile down the strath. His grave is marked by a crooked stone about two feet high, rough-hewn, and with a plain cross cut very deeply into it. It is situated to one side of what has certainly been a burial area, a slightly raised circular mound twenty yards across. The lesser stones, smothered by the growth of centuries, stand up around it like mossy lumps. The burial area is quite unmarked and unfenced, just standing there in a big field on the flat, glacial floor of the valley. The River Naver flows just beyond its eastern edge, about fifteen yards from the grave stone of Maol Ruadh.*

Travelling in the north a little before his death, Maol Ruadh is said to have prophecied that Strathnaver would be depopulated, and then re-populated once more when the river waters reached his grave: or that the people would be driven out for their sins, but allowed to return when his bones were washed to the sea. Old sayings linger, and at the time of the Strathnaver clearances it was recalled. Workers from the House of Sutherland found that the course of the centuries had brought the channel of the River Naver very close to the grave and, knowing something of the strength of Highland superstition, are said to have actually built an embankment around the spot to save it from flooding. Their work was wasted, however, for in an after-snow spate, described later as 'a great flood', the embankments were washed away and the grave was submerged.

*It would be dishonest not to allow that the stone with a cross could simply mark the burial area — though tradition for centuries has had it otherwise; and that a Red Priest is also reputed to be buried at Applecross.

47

Strathnaver was, of course, depopulated at the time of the clearances in the early nineteenth century, and then partially re-populated between 1900 and 1903.

The following nineteenth century verse, of regrettably uneven quality, was written by a gentleman who signed himself 'Duthaich MhicAoidh' — The Land of the Mackays.

'Then sweep, Naver! sweep, for the dark clouds are hov'ring
Tow'ring in masses on corrie and steep;
Tear the Red Priest from his fern-shadowed cov'ring
And bear him away to the sonorous deep.

Then softly shall stream the red beams of the sunset
Over Strathnaver when peopled again,
And the glory of peace for poor hearts shall be won yet
And they who are sad shall yet sing love's refrain.'

Three Fishing Tragedies

It was only after the clearances in the early nineteenth century that men began fishing to any extent along the north coast. Driven from the fertile glens to the half-barren coastal strip, they turned to the sea as a source of food and employment. The coastline was rugged, with few adequate harbours, the weather stormy, the sea-currents swift and treacherous. As an industry fishing never achieved the importance in the north that it did on the east and west coasts of the county, although as a livelihood it continued developing right up until the First World War, since when it has declined. Always the open boat was used, and there were many tragedies. The three stories which follow are representative. Each, after the manner of the times, has been commemorated by a lengthy memorial poem which unfortunately it is not possible to include in this collection.

THE EXCELSIOR, THE LIVELY AND THE DIADEM

On the twenty-fifth of June, 1890, a severe storm swept across Scotland. Fifty-one deaths were recorded as a direct result, the greater proportion through drowning at sea. Of these, twenty came from the north of Sutherland; seven from Melness, and thirteen from Portskerra and Melvich. If you consider the size of these villages, it was a disaster of the greatest magnitude. For example, almost *all* the fit and young men of Port Vasco, the particular clachan in Melness which crewed the *Excelsior*, were taken at a stroke.

During the summer months, when the weather could be more trusted, the fishermen worked further away from home than usual. Their open boats, up to forty feet in keel, were sailed and rowed to the fishing grounds. A normal crew consisted of about six men, with three more on shore. While the boat was away fishing, those on shore, possibly older or less fit, sold the fish that had not been sent away immediately, sometimes smoking or salting it as the season or the market required: when the boat came in they were needed to haul it up the shore, for there were few natural harbours in the north of Sutherland: and while the fishermen rested they cleaned the fish and repaired the nets. Wives and children helped as well.

Then, as now, most of the open boat fishermen did not swim and had no safety equipment. Their boats, heavily ballasted for stability while they were sailing or hauling the nets, would not float if they were swamped. Consequently the men relied entirely upon their excellent seamanship and judgement of the weather for safety. Tragically, it was not always enough.

The boats lost in the storm of June 25th, were the *Excelsior*, from Melness, and the *Lively* (WK866) and *Diadem* (WK894) from Portskerra. Their names alone make poignant comment.

An appeal on behalf of the relatives of the twenty men lost was launched by the Glasgow branch of the Clan Mackay Society. It makes pathetic reading. After a statement of the situation, (seventy years after the evictions the government was still wondering whether it could partially finance the erection of a harbour at Portskerra), the Appeal lists the men lost and their forty-one dependents. The following are representative:

Drowned	Age	Dependents
George Stuart	20	Only support of an infirm widowed mother and widowed sister.

Drowned	Age	Dependents
Robert Mackay	32	Wife and three children under five years.
William Macdonald	30 ⎱	Brothers — father, very delicate;
George Macdonald	28 ⎰	mother, do.

These are the only two sons, and the parents have nothing but the walls of the house, and are really most destitute.

Donald Sinclair	47	Two sisters.
Hugh Macdonald	31 ⎱	Brothers — father, in weak health, and mother; four sisters, two not strong.
William Macdonald	28 ⎰	
Hugh Macdonald (Big Hugh)	46	Widow, mother-in-law, sister-in-law; aged mother (widowed by husband drowning).
Robert Mackay	35	Wife and three children under five years.
Angus Gunn	20	Father and mother alive, but in a very needy condition.

Such was the poverty of the times, and such the impact upon two little fishing communities.

THE DROWNING AT KIRTOMY IN 1910

On the morning of Saturday, the seventeenth of December, 1910, five men from Kirtomy set out to bring in their creels for the Sabbath. They were John Walter (Mackay), whose Orkney boat the *Rival*, they sailed in; his nephews Murdo and Vhatie (Mackay); a man named Neil (Mackay); and John Pring (Mackay), always known as Johnnie Pring, an orphan who had been brought up by a good woman of the village. It was a grey, uncertain morning, and John Walter did not like the look of the weather. Already the wind was strengthening from the north-east and there was a moderate sea.

The *Rival* was an open boat and they had to sail her against the wind to reach the spot where their creels were lying on the far side of Kirtomy Point. They were not the only Kirtomy boats out that day: two more were doing the same thing around Farr Point, two miles to the west. They had been fishing around the headlands because the lobsters stay well out during the winter months.

The creels, weighted down with stones, are quite heavy, and a good load of them puts a boat far down in the water. So the *Rival*, by the

51

time they had finished their work, was an altogether more sluggish boat; added to which, she was never very good in a heavy sea.

While they were working the wind was backing through north into the north-west and strengthening all the time. By the time they were ready to return it had become a full gale and the sea was rising. The two boats at Farr Point had the wind square on the port quarter and were able to make a fast run home before things got too bad. People in the village expected the men in the *Rival* to run south-east before the wind into Armadale Bay, and not attempt to tack back into Kirtomy against such a sea and such a wind. Whether the younger men of the crew had their way, being perhaps more impetuous and less experienced than John Walter, no-one knows; but as the other two boats were being dragged, none too soon, from the foaming seas at the shore, the *Rival* was spotted coming around the headland more than a mile away.

People hurried around to the Aird (the hillside) to the east of the bay to see how she was faring, and found that the situation was none too good. The boat was tacking to and fro against the wind and making very slow progress. The spray was flying from the tops of the waves and sometimes she would disappear altogether in a deep trough.

An hour later they had brought her right to the mouth of the bay. By this time, even if they got to the shore no-one knew how they were going to land in the huge seas that were pounding on the rocks; but it was a problem they never had to solve. The crew had thrown a lot of the creels out on the way down, when they saw how things were going, but the *Rival* was still heavy in the water. Probably she had shipped a lot of water, too, and that was keeping her low.

When she went, it was by no half measures. A big wave swept up and broke clear across the side of the sail. She went down like a stone.

Everything was lost for a moment, then the watchers on the shore saw two little figures clinging to an oar, one at each end. They were recognised as the brothers, Vhatie and Murdo. None of the crew could swim, but in seas like that, clad in boots and heavy fishermen's clothing, there could be little swimming anyhow. Murdo was washed away from the oar and disappeared, but Vhatie hung on for more than an hour. His wife was among the people watching. There was nothing they could do to help. Then he, too, was gone; the surface of the wild sea was empty.

The next day was Sunday, but not everyone went to church. The sea had calmed sufficiently for men to venture out with grapnels, rowing to and fro to see whether they could find any of their drowned friends on the bottom of the bay. One body was recovered, that of Johnnie Pring, hooked up by the sweater. The other four were never seen again. On that stretch of shore even if the sea did bring them in they would have lain under the steep ledges of rock in deep water.

As for the *Rival*, she was washed back across the Pentland Firth by the tides, and broken up on the rocks of Orkney.

Quite often a tragedy of this nature is used by people of more imagination than veracity to hang other tales upon. It may seem thoughtless and even heartless, but it is understandable, particularly in the context of Highland life with its tradition of ceilidhs and story telling. Death and disaster are the very stuff of folk tale and legend. At least two stories are attached to the sinking of the *Rival*.

I.   In the late morning of the day following the storm, while the boats were dragging the bay, a Kirtomy man went up to the top road to give a message to a friend who would be passing that way. As he was waiting a stranger came walking along the road. He paused, and together they looked down the glen towards the village.

"Did they find any of the bodies?" the stranger asked.

The villager shook his head. "No," he replied.

"Nor will they," said the stranger. "None but the lamb."

For a few moments they chatted, then the man turned, nodding goodbye, and continued his journey along the road. The villager never saw him again, and no-one knew who the man was.

However his strange words were remembered. The only body to be recovered was that of Johnnie Pring, the youngest of the crew.

II.   Shortly before the tragedy an elder of the kirk who lived in Kirtomy had a strange dream. He dreamed that he saw a ship on the land, always a sign of trouble ahead. It came sailing up the road through the village. As it came to John Walter's house it paused, and a little boat went up the path to his front door, then returned to the ship. It sailed on. As it came in turn to the houses of Johnnie Pring, Murdo, Neil and Vhatie, the same thing happened. Then the ship just sailed away up the road, and he dreamed no more.

THE PORTSKERRA DISASTER OF 1918

At 9.40 p.m. on the twenty-second of August, 1918, a severe gale swept in across Portskerra from the north-west. Before midnight

seven men of the village were drowned and many more very lucky to be alive.

The herring were good, and that evening seven boats from the village were out fishing in the bay. It was calm, but the fishermen needed to have their wits about them, for out of the stillness sudden squalls drove in with drizzle, then as quickly they were gone and all was quiet again. By late evening a fine rain had set in, but there was still no sign of the gale that was to come.

The nets were out, the boats lay on their drifts. Thirty men rested, waiting for the tide to slacken. Suddenly, with no warning, a strong wind began to blow out of the north-west. Within minutes it had become a full gale and the sea was rising. Some tried to haul their nets, others turned and made straight for the shore, leaving the nets behind.

Across the Pentland Firth at Orkney, the trawlers patrolling the naval base at Scapa Flow turned and made for shelter.

In the village the women and the children and those men who were not away at the war felt the wind and went out to see that the boats were safe. None of them was in yet and already the shore was wild. In the storm and the just-dark all was confusion. A lot of people went down to the Melvich Sands, and in the next hour three

boats managed to fight a way in through the huge breakers. They were the *Daisy*, *Annie Jane* and *Vine*. The crews waited with the other villagers.

Then a fourth boat was spotted, swamped and wallowing, mixed up with the breakers at the mouth of the River Halladale. Her nets were so tightly bound about her that they had to be cut away. This was the boat belonging to the mill family Fraser. The crew of four were all drowned. Among them were a father, his brother, and his fifteen year old son.

Three boats, the *Kathleen*, the *Julia*, and the *O. M. Pritchard*, were still on the water, hidden in the darkness. It was hours before the village got news. The *Kathleen* had been driven by the storm beyond Bighouse Head and come in at a little bay further east. The *Julia* went even further, to Sandside Bay at Reay. In two and a half hours of darkness and storm the fishermen managed to keep her off the cliffs and guide her through enormous seas to safety. They said they could never have done it by daylight. Finally there was the boat named the *O.M. Pritchard*. Despite all the efforts of the crew she was driven on to the wild rocks of Bighouse Head. Three of the crew were drowned. The fourth, Hugh Mackay, was twice washed up on to the rocks and then swept back into the sea again. On the third occasion he managed to catch hold of a rock and hang on with the water breaking right over his head. Somehow he made his way through the turmoil to the higher rocks, scrambled around the base of the cliff, climbed it in the darkness, and made his way across the moors to Bighouse and the village. His family believed that he must be dead and were mourning him as he walked into the house.

Almost as quickly as it had arisen, the storm slackened, and by breakfast time a dead calm had fallen over the coast. The waves subsided, the sea flattened to a gently moving sheet of glass. A lady topping the rise above the village with her children, and looking down over the bay, commented upon the beauty of the morning and the wonderful peace and stillness of the scene. She was soon to hear what had happened, and in those conditions find it unbelievable.

Such an event was not uncommon fifty and a hundred years ago, and now is only a story; but to the people involved and one small Highland village it was a tragedy as great as the whole world war.

Fifty-nine years later the *Vine*, never refloated, lies buried in the sand somewhere along Melvich Beach: the *Julia* is still in use, sailing out of Scrabster.

56

Eilean Neave — The Saint's Island

If you go to the harbour at Skerray you will see Eilean Neave facing you just off shore. It is a small island, about half a mile square. The summit is crowned with fine grass and it is ringed with rocks and splendid cliffs, particularly the massive Red Crag that plunges sheer into the sea at the western end, and the wicked confusion of black precipices on the seaward side. It is separated from the mainland by a strip of water about two hundred yards wide known as the Kyle Beg (the Little Kyle). If you want to land on the island it is easy to row a boat up the Kyle Beg and turn into a beautiful, sheltered and deserted beach of white sand. The water is crystal clear and as cold as ice.

The word 'neave' is Gaelic for 'saint' or 'holy'. Island Neave was a small but important religious centre for perhaps as much as two hundred years. It is also called Coomb Island: this is probably a corruption of Calum, the Gaelic equivalent of Columba. The name originated many centuries ago.

When Saint Columba brought Christianity to Scotland in 563AD, missionaries moved out from the island of Iona to attempt to convert the people who lived on the mainland. When they came to the north the inhabitants seemed wild and fierce, and being rather frightened of them, the missionaries crossed to Eilean Neave for security. You can still see the marks of the priests' cell, a green circle in the grass with slightly raised edges, mossed and grown over centuries ago.

Since the island has no water the missionaries had to cross frequently to the mainland, and there is a well nearby, above the Skerray Pier, which is still known as Fuaran Chaluim Cille (the Well of Calum the Church-builder). Nearby, too, is a patch of land known as Iomair Chaluim Cille (the Rig of Saint Columba).

One of the leading missionaries from Iona was named Cormac, who certainly sailed along the north coast, and it may have been he who founded the religious settlement on the island. This is supported by the fact that four miles inland is Loch Cormaic, and an old story has it that one of the priests, visiting the shore, was surprised by a

57

group of pagans, who abhorred the teaching of the missionaries. Being cut off from his boat he had to flee inland. At the loch he was overtaken, and repeatedly crying out the name of his leader, was murdered, and his body mutilated.

At the time of the priests the people on the mainland were not

allowed across to the island even for the services, but gathered on the hill opposite to hear the preacher, who shouted across the Kyle Beg. This place is still known as the Cnoc a Phobuill (the People's Hill).

Finally, almost certainly, the island was sacked by the Vikings.

Today the crofters take their sheep across to the island by boat, and leave them there for the summer pasture.

The New House *

During the summer holidays Douglas worked with his Uncle John and a man named Murdo, carting load after load of stones from the quarry and the ruins to the place where they were going to build the new house. They began to take stones from the old broch too, but the minister and the police got on to them and they had to stop it.

By the time school was starting again the pile was enormous, fine big stones all grey and pink and speckled white, and smeared with earth.

"Surely that's enough," Douglas said, standing back and wiping the dirt from his hands against the sides of his trousers.

John shook his head, squatting on his heels and pulling the old black pipe from his pocket. "Did you never hear the old saying? 'If you're building a house the first thing you do is get a pile of stones as big as you think you need. When you've finished, you make another pile the same size. After that you get half as many again, and then just maybe you'll have enough.' "

They worked on through the autumn, and at the end of October his father came home from America. Hamish Mackay was a mason, and a whole gang of them went over to work there for the summer. It cost just five pounds to travel steerage and cook your own food. Normally he buried his tools out there to keep them safe through the winter, but this time he had brought them home with him for there was work to be done. He had not seen his new baby yet: with a pretty wife and four children waiting for him, he was glad to be home.

For the last three years they had been living with Hamish's brother John and his wife in the old family home, but John had a family of his own now and it was time Hamish was getting a place for himself. The last time he was home they had chosen a site on the hillside, just at the foot of the common grazing.

When Douglas came home from school the following Monday they had already cleared away the topsoil and were down to the pan,

*In telling this 'story', a certain liberty has been taken with regard to the dates. Few logs were excavated from the peat moss after 1850, whilst men did not start spending their working summers in the United States until about 1870.

59

the hard gravel base upon which they would build. The brown rectangle of earth looked tiny, far too small for a house. A long, heather-covered hillside, dotted with rocky outcrops and a few clumps of whin and bracken, stretched up behind: in front the ground fell away through thin birch trees to the river, then climbed again to the distant summits of the moors. The patched grey sky seemed very big, and close. Douglas helped to sort out the big rocks they would use as foundation stones, projecting beyond the upper walls all round the house. His father and Uncle John trimmed them with their masons' hammers and rolled them into place. Murdo and another local man, who were being paid, did the labouring.

By the end of the week they were nearly finished and Douglas went off with the horse and cart to the blue clay pit half a mile up the valley. The smooth clay, lying in a hollow of the limestone rock, cut like cheese, shovelful after shovelful. When the men were ready they watered it down into a sticky grey mud, mixed in pebbles which had been carted from the river, and used it as mortar. In time the clay dried out just like cement. It was a great skill selecting the correct stone and setting it accurately the first time.

They worked until it was dark. When they returned home Douglas carried a slice of clay in the bottom of a bucket for his aunt. She would water it down and use it as whitewash: she wanted to whiten the wall above the fireplace, for the peat smoke made it dirty very quickly.

The frosts came late that year and by the time they woke one Saturday morning to find the ground white with a heavy hoar frost, the six foot walls and high chimney ends were as good as finished.

Douglas poked his head out of the curtains across the front of his box bed to see his father pulling on his trousers and boots.

"Just the job," he was saying. "We'll go out to the peat moss and see what we can find. Come on, Douglas, Jimmy; time you were up."

Douglas jumped down and pulled on his own trousers and boots and a jacket, and went through to the next room for his breakfast.

It was cold and clear out on the moors. The crisp white ground crunched under their feet. They were looking for wood. The few ancient birch trees that straggled up the hillsides above the river were no good for building, though some people used them as couples in the roof, selecting them so that the natural twist could be laid to the ridge, following the curve of the thatch. But beneath the ground, perfectly preserved in the peat, lay the fallen remains of the great old

Caledonian Forest. Where the pines lay close to the surface the frost did not lie, either because of the oil or the warmth in the wood. Suddenly Hamish turned off to the right. "Aye, well there's one," he said. He had a bundle of sticks in his hand and pushed a couple through into the soft earth, marking the line of the dark streak in the frost.

By the middle of the morning the frost was going, but they had marked four trees and Hamish was well pleased. They dug them out during the next week, sawed them into logs, and dragged them over to the peat road with the horses. Then they loaded them on to carts and took them down to the sawing house, the 'tigh sabhagadh', a long, narrow rectangle of wall. They laid the log along the top and cut it into planks and couples and joists with the huge, two-handed frame saw, one man standing above and the other below. Even though every bite took out an inch of wood, it was a long job.

They fastened the couples together at the apex with wooden pins. When they were ready they hoisted them into position and pinned them again, to timbers which had been built into the walls.

Christmas came and went. In January there was snow, but it lay only for a few days: and then there were gales, but Hamish had particularly chosen a spot in a ripple of the hills where they were sheltered.

In between the couples they nailed wooden spars, and in the hour or two of daylight when he got home from school Douglas was sent out to help where they were cutting duffets (divots), known as 'sgrathan', for the roof. For this they used a flatter spade, a broad cross-blade that was pushed by a bar across the chest and pared a slice of turf from the ground. They were working on a patch of hillside where the heather had been burned a couple of years before and grown in short and thick again. The duffets were egg-shaped and about thirty inches or three feet long. In the middle they were three inches thick, tapering away to nothing at the edges. If the ground was wet they let them drain for a few days before taking them home on the cart. Then they laid them on the wooden spars of the roof, heather to the inside, like big slates, starting at the eaves and working up to the ridge.

When he was bringing in the corn the previous autumn, John had filled the whole end of the barn with sheaves of straw. Now they brought them out and began the thatching, starting at the eaves again and working up to the ridge. John had thrashed the corn very thoroughly so that not too many grains would be left to germinate and grow green on the roof. When it was finished they threw a length of herring net from side to side and secured it with long, home-made ropes, which they fastened to pegs high up in the wall. This rope was called 'siaman', and was twisted from any combination of heather, roots, straw and reeds.

By the middle of March the outside of the house was finished. A neighbour who was a joiner had made the door and small windows, and fitted them while they were working on the roof. It was a rush, for Hamish had arranged to work again in the United States during the summer. But he changed his mind. His wife, Mary, was expecting another child and there was a lot to do yet to the inside of the house. They would manage.

At the beginning of June they moved in. Mary had kept big peat fires burning at each end, and although the wooden linings and inner partitions were hardly started, the blue clay floor and inside of the house were quite dry and they all had beds. Like many women, she spread dry sand on the floor to be sure it stayed dry, for the damp always tended to rise from the ground below. Perhaps Hamish would fit a casy floor of stones embedded on edge in blue clay, or even Caithness flags, sometime in the future. You could still see the heather on the inside of the roof, but there was no hurry to fit a ceiling, some people even left them like that. A ceiling was warmer for the winter, though, and Mary had unpicked some good sacks and sewn them into two neat pieces of cloth. Jute ceilings would do fine for the present. Already the vegetable garden was planted, up on the hillside the peats were cut, and Hamish had decided where he would build the byre and barn when he was ready.

The land was not his own, Hamish would still have to pay cottar's fees. But so it was that Douglas's father provided a home for his wife and children. Another little house was added to the scattering of crofts on the side of the hill.

E

HISTORICAL
EMBROIDERIES
and LIGHTER TALES

Ian Abrach

Traditionally, Ian Abrach, founder of the sept of the Clan Mackay known as the Abrach Mackays, was the illegitimate son of the great fifteenth century chief Angus Dhu (Black Angus).

The story begins a year or so before his birth, at the house of Tongue, traditional seat of the chief of the Clan Mackay. Among the many servants of the house was a dark-haired girl, a Cameron from Lochaber, and it seemed to Angus Dhu's wife that her husband particularly favoured her, and she became jealous. Whether Lady Mackay had just cause for her feelings at that particular time is uncertain, but the girl was young and beautiful, and in the light of what happened later she may well have been right.

One night, during a period when the chief was away on a deer-hunting expedition, the servant girl had a strange dream, and the next day, being rather simple and innocent, told it to her mistress. She had dreamed that she was sitting upon a hill near the head of Strathnaver. Close beside her a spring came bubbling from the ground and flowed away down the strath, growing bigger and bigger as it went, until the whole valley was flooded with its waters.

The significance was not lost upon Lady Mackay, however, and finding some small fault in the girl's work, she was summarily dismissed.

The girl was very hurt. To the best of her knowledge she had never given cause for offence, and she felt that if the chief had been there she would not have been so casually and harshly treated. As she began to make her way home she thought more and more about it, and her Cameron spirit roused itself. She would not meekly submit

65

to the injustice: she would go beyond her mistress and appeal to the chief himself.

A day or two later she arrived at the camp in the Reay Forest where Angus Dhu and his companions were hunting.

The chief was astonished to see the girl in such a remote area, and so far from Tongue. His first thought was that there must be some private trouble at home, but soon the girl, partly angry and partly distressed, was pouring her tale out to him. He was as puzzled as she was, until he heard about the dream. He felt sorry for her, but there was little he could do. He could not take the girl back with him to Tongue and expect his wife to make her welcome again. She was tired; the best he could do, being perhaps less cautious of dreams than his wife, was to offer her shelter for the night and a protector for her journey homewards in the morning. She accepted the shelter of his own roof.

Secrets will out, and it was not long before Angus Dhu's wife got news of the affair, and that, worse still, the servant girl was with child on account of it. She was a superstitious woman, for they were superstitious times, and determined that she would do her utmost, short of physical harm, to prevent the child from being happily born. She sent for a spae-wife (a wise woman, almost a witch), who knitted a magic garter for her. While she wore it, the spae-wife assured her, her husband's concubine could not be delivered.

Naturally Angus Dhu soon knew about this, but argument only made matters worse, and he could hardly tear the garter from his wife by force. As the time drew on for the baby to be born he became increasingly anxious about it, and hunted in his mind for some way of helping the girl in her difficulty. The arrival of a traveller from the Lochaber district gave him the idea he needed. He collared the man as soon as he arrived, whispered a set of instructions in his ear, slipped a coin into his hand, and pointed him towards the kitchen.

When they heard he was from Lochaber, the servants were naturally all agog to hear. Had the Cameron girl had her baby yet? The man took a deep draught of the ale they had given him, wiped his mouth with the back of his hand, and casually observed that she had, indeed, given birth to a fine son just the day before he came away.

Lady Mackay was even more on tenterhooks than her servants for whatever news the man had brought, but she could not display it so publicly. It was not many minutes, however, before her maid brought her the information. She flew into a passion, tore the uncomfortable garter from her leg, and hurled it into the fire, declaring that it was no good believing in witchcraft any more. The garter burned up in a shower of sparks, the spell was broken, and at that very moment the Cameron maid in Lochaber gave birth to a strong, healthy son.

Eighteen years later, or so, a dark young man by the name of Eoin (Ian or John) Mackay, appeared at the House of Tongue. He claimed to be this same child, reared by his mother's family in Lochaber. Enquiries justified this claim, and the darkness of his looks bore undoubted witness of both his father's and his mother's appearance. Angus Dhu accepted him as his son, though Neil (Bhass), his older, legitimate son, was heir to the chieftainship.

Ian Abrach (Ian from Lochaber), as he became known, was soon a firm favourite throughout the clan. He displayed his father's boldness, excelled at athletic sports, and was a brilliant fighter with the sword.

A legend is still told of his arrival at Tongue House. Angus Dhu, seeking to test the young man's fitness to become his accepted son and a leader of the Clan Mackay, demanded that he should go across the causeway to the nearby Rabbit Islands and challenge, in hand to hand combat, the leader of a band of wild outlaws who were giving him trouble. Even as the words were out of his father's mouth Ian Abrach strode from the house. He crossed the Kyle of Tongue and made his way to Ard Skinid, just across the water from the Rabbit Islands. For days he waited until the tides were low enough for him to make the crossing. As soon as they were he waded over the long causeway with the water to his waist, and called out the leader of the brigands. This was a Goliath of a man, greatly feared in all the district round about. To begin with he laughed at the young man, but he did not laugh as they began to fight. It was a long, long battle, ranging from the seashore to the summits and crags of the island. At length the leader was overpowered by the young fighter, and slain. Ian Abrach, who had come all alone, looked around the circle of brigands which surrounded him, and cut off the dead man's head. Again he waited for the tide to fall. Though wounded and exhausted he made his way straight back to the House of Tongue. His father, with several of his clansmen and the servants, heard of his approach and gathered to meet him in the hall. The young man strode proudly in through the front door holding the fearsome head by its wild red hair, and flung it across the hall floor. Angus Dhu embraced his son.

67

In another tale of his arrival which is still told in the district, Ian Abrach did not come north of his own accord, but was stolen by his father, who with a band of fierce Mackay warriors fought a way south to fetch him from his mother's family in Lochaber. On their return to Tongue House the boy, who was twelve years old, was hungry. A servant sat him at the head of the great banqueting table and fetched a huge salver of venison and another of game, both beneath heavy silver covers. As the boy lifted the cover above the haunch of venison, his father released a wolf, which had been kept half starved in a closet close by. With a great snarl the huge grey creature flung itself forward upon the boy and the salver of meat. Before it could reach him, Ian Abrach plucked the dirk from his belt, and as it sprang leaped aside and drove the blade deep into its flank. Dying, the animal skidded across the table and fell to the floor. Moments later it lay still. His black eyes fierce, Ian Abrach looked hard at his father for a full half minute, then sat himself at the table once more and proceeded with his meal.

That is legend. What is fact is that soon after his arrival the young man was called upon to show all his Cameron and Mackay powers of leadership. The year was 1433. The Reay country was being invaded by the Earl of Sutherland with a numerically vastly superior force. Angus Dhu was growing old, his son and heir, Neil, was imprisoned by King James I of Scotland on the Bass Rock. Bound to keep the king's peace, Angus Dhu had no allies. Ian Abrach took command of his father's troops and, at the Battle of Dhruim na Cupa on the slopes of Ben Loyal, the Sutherlands were routed.*

At the conclusion of the battle, Angus Dhu, who had been kept safe on a ridge during the heat of the fighting, was killed by the arrow of a Sutherland hiding among bushes nearby. Ian Abrach assumed the chieftainship. He wore the mantle splendidly, but though he was pressed to claim the position permanently, no-one knowing whether Neil was alive or dead, or would ever be permitted to return, he repeatedly refused. He asserted that his half-brother would undoubtedly return and that he was only holding the title in his absence. Four years later Neil escaped from his prison on the Bass Rock and returned to the north. Ian Abrach resigned the chieftainship to him and retired to Achness at the head of Strathnaver.

*See 'Dhruim na Cupa'.

For the excellence of his service, Neil bestowed upon his brother, in fee, all the heights of Strathnaver, from Mudale to Rossall, on both sides of the river. Soon Ian married, and his branch of the clan became well-known as the Abrach Mackays, famed for their excellence of character and prowess in war.

Within a hundred years the descendants of young Ian Abrach had married and multiplied until they were spread through all the glens and across the hillsides of Strathnaver. The dream of the Cameron servant-girl was fulfilled.

Loch Mo Naire

"Mo-nair is a Celtic, pagan, demi-goddess frequently to be met with in medieval Irish literature."* A small loch which bears her name is to be found beyond Skelpick, five miles upstream from the mouth of the River Naver. Right up until the last years of the nineteenth century she was paid her devotions by the superstitious people of the district who prayed and bathed there on the first Monday of every Quarter.† It is possible that the River Naver, which is close by, and can be traced back as far as Ptolemy, who called it on his map the Naberus, was originally named after this goddess. Her name, however, is so like a Gaelic phrase, commonly used in the old days, that the best known story of Loch Mo Naire is quite different.

The loch lies at the north end of a large area of flat ground known as Dunvedin Haugh. Five hundred yards away stand the ruins of an old fort or 'doun' and here, it is claimed, in the eighteenth century, lived a harsh factor to the Duke of Sutherland by the name of Sir Robert Gordon. ‡ Now one day a poor old woman from Skelpick had gone to see Sir Robert to ask him a small favour. She was a well known local character who possessed a healing stone or talisman that had cured many people and was quite famous. When Sir Robert heard her request he flew into a rage and called the old woman a witch. The factors had often more power than they could handle and had no need to bridle their tempers. Sir Robert threatened the old woman with dreadful consequences unless she handed the talisman over to him. She absolutely refused and fled from the house. He pursued her down the haugh, but she had quite a long start and only when they were right at the loch did he catch up with her. She was determined that he should not have her precious stone and as he went to grab her she flung the talisman far out into the grey loch crying out, "Mo naire, mo naire!" (which in English means "For shame!" or "Shame on you!") and calling a curse on the name of Gordon.

* Dr. Henderson, one-time lecturer in Celtic Studies, University of Glasgow.
† Rev. Angus Mackay: *A History of the Province of Cat.*
‡ Not to be confused with Robert Gordon, the old tacksman, who gave accommodation to Patrick Sellar at the time of the evictions.

70

Previously the stone had cast a spell upon the water in a bowl which the patient had to drink: now it was found to be so powerful that it charmed the whole loch. Soon it began to gain a wide reputation.* People travelled from as far away as Orkney and Inverness to bathe in the healing waters. The magic was particularly potent on the first day of May, although it would work its cure at any time. Sick and old people came with great faith and hope and there are stories of immediate and remarkable recoveries: an old lady who had to be carried there, but was able to walk away; a simple boy whose fits and rages left him; a barren, long-married woman who shortly afterwards conceived a child. There was a ritual that the patient had to follow. He must go to the loch while it was still dark, and at the first streak of dawn strip himself and wade into the water. After throwing a silver coin far out, he should duck three times, allowing the water to close over his head each time, and ask to be relieved of his malady. Then he should dress, and if possible walk sun-wise around the loch, being sure to be out of sight of it before sunrise. During the whole of the time he must speak no word but to the spirit of the waters. Today old coins are to be found in the loch, greatly eroded by the acid in the water; but coin hunters should beware, for it is traditionally said that the man who takes a coin away from the loch will be struck by the disease of the patient who threw it in. Well into this century people were coming to bathe in Loch Mo Naire, just as they still do in the more sophisticated spas of Cheltenham and Bath.

There are one or two variations and additions to the story. Some say that it was not Sir Robert Gordon at all, but simply a thief named Gordon who wanted to get his hands on the stone to make some easy money. Twice he tried to steal it, then finally he threatened the old woman who was so frightened of him that she threw it away when she saw him coming up the strath. In a third account the woman was a gipsy, a travelling healer, who was lodging in the district with a family named Gordon. Seeing the silver in her palm one day the husband of the house tried to woo her and win the talisman from her, but she saw through him and there was a dreadful scene, which led

*"The curative powers of Loch na Naire, 10 miles west of Strath Halladale, have long been famous. Crowds used to gather on its shores on the first Monday in August, between midnight and 1 a.m., when, apparently, the magical properties of the waters were at their height. The tradition may well go back to pagan times: an essential part of the 'cure' was the offering of some gift, such as a coin, to the waters. There was also the suggestion that the ancient May festival of Beltane was just as good a time to immerse oneself, as a cure for all diseases." *Folklore, Myths and Legends of Britain.*

71

to the stone being flung into the loch. In all the accounts the healer was a good woman, and although she took money she never took more than the patient could afford, for it must be the patient's own if the cure was to work. Finally, as she called out a curse on the name of Gordon, the loch would not cure anyone of that name; and later the name of Sutherland was added to it, probably for reasons of local history.

And a sequel to the story. An old woman who lived alone and could not walk had no means of getting to the loch, so she sent a boy with a bottle on the first day of May to get her some of the healing water. She told him to hurry up and waste no time on the way, but going up the river he met some other boys and stopped to play with them. He soon forgot his errand and when he remembered it was too late to get to the loch and back before dark. But rather than disappoint the old lady he filled the bottle from the well at Naver Bridge and brought it back to her. She thanked him and blessed him for his kindness. Then she drank the wonderful liquid, and she swore until the day of her death that it was the only medicine that ever did her any good.

Two Shipwrecks

THE SNOW ADMIRAL

On January 28th, 1842, the British ship *Snow Admiral*, of Sunderland, was wrecked on the rocks of the Beri Geo at Portskerra. It was a stormy night, one of the worst nights that year, and the Norwegian crew of the ship could do nothing about it. The sails were torn, they were driven before the wind, and could only wait until they struck the rocks. There was not one survivor.

The wreck was found the next morning, wedged between high rocks in one split of the entrance — for the mouth of the Beri Geo is divided into two channels by a high stack. The white water was breaking clear across her. The alarm was raised, but it was too late. Ten bodies were found that day. They were taken to the church in Strathy and buried in the churchyard there. Later four more bodies were found, and for some reason they were not taken to the church, but buried above the shore at the head of the Beri Geo. Exactly who the four were is now uncertain: some say that they were the captain and his family, who by some chance had been washed up together; others that they were three children and a member of the crew. It is, however, commonly believed that at least two of them were children.

Today only two gravestones remain, and you can see them on the hillside. The inscriptions have been worn away with the weather of a hundred and thirty five years. More than once, and even in recent years, visitors from Norway have enquired about them and been directed down the track to the Beri Geo.

When the weather is calm and the tide low and the light falling in a certain way, what looks like part of the wreck of the old *Snow Admiral* can be seen in deep water just off shore.

Surrounding the disaster are some later stories. One, which is certainly unsubstantiated, is that on the night of the shipwreck, a flashing light was seen on the headland. Though it is probably not true, this is not so fanciful as it might seem, for it is believed that wreckers definitely were working around the north coast.

73

There is another claim that a ghost in oilskins and sou-wester can be seen walking near the graves at Beri Geo.

A third story pre-dates "Whisky Galore". The main cargo of the *Snow Admiral* was cheese and butter, and a lot of this was washed up on the shore: people ate it for months. But she was carrying a certain amount of whisky as well, and a few small barrels survived the pounding on the rocks. Old Peter Mackay, scavenging among the wreckage, found three barrels far down the shore. He hid them in a little cave nearby. But someone else had seen them too, and when the customs officers came nosing around they got to hear about it. They hurried down to the shore but they were too late, the barrels had already gone. Now Peter Mackay had made the mistake of speaking about them and pretty soon the customs officers were on his trail. By good fortune Peter Mackay saw them coming down the road towards his house and just managed to get outside in time. They spotted him and asked if he could tell them where Mr. Peter Mackay lived. He indicated the house and hurried away. When the customs officers realised the trick that had been played upon them they ran down to the shore after him, but again they were too late. Already the old man had brought his boat around, and even as they watched he was pulling on the oars and bobbing on the waves a hundred yards off shore. From where they stood they could see the three little kegs of whisky sitting on the bottom boards of his boat. In a few minutes he had rowed out of sight around the headland. They never caught up with him, and the men of Portskerra got merry a dozen times over.

Strathy Bay was a tumult in the darkness. The crew of the Norwegian ship *Thorwaldsen* saw the foaming rocks come closer and closer. Twenty-seven of them were never seen again.

Only five bodies were washed up on the shore. They were those of the captain, Hans Berg, and his wife Elenora, and three of the crew. They were buried, as soon as possible, in the top corner of the little cemetery above the dunes at Strathy. The captain and his wife were laid together and, almost side by side with them but a little apart, the three members of the crew. A timber from the vessel with the ship's name painted upon it, reputedly its wooden name-plate, was laid at the head of the grave. Now the wood has rotted away and the grave is unmarked.

Men from the village salvaged what they could from the wreck and even today some of the old houses have timbers from the *Thorwaldsen*, or *Torrivolsen* as it is more often called, as couples in the roof.

More than a century later the figure-head of a ship was to be seen decorating the garden of the Post Office in Bettyhill, and afterwards the garden of another house in the village. In 1965 it was taken to the embryonic museum of local history in the old Farr Church at Clachan. Being uncertain of its origin and representation, the trustees made enquiries of the folk museum in Stockholm. They reported that the figure-head appeared to be modelled upon a self-portrait sculpture of Bertel Thorwaldsen (1770-1844), a most distinguished Danish classical sculptor, and founder of the Thorwaldsen Museum in Copenhagen. He was the son of an Icelandic ship's carpenter, and a later carpenter had carved his likeness for the figure-head of the vessel which was to bear his name. Today he stands on a broad shelf in the Farr Museum, a bluff, visionary figure, cloak thrown back, eyes reaching forward towards new horizons.

Very soon after the shipwreck the superstitious folk of Strathy began making gloomy predictions. "No good will come of those foreigners resting in the graveyard," they said. Nobody listened to them — until one night exactly a year later.

Tim Macleod was walking past the cemetery. The moonlit iron gates made him think of his dead mother and father who were buried there. He turned through them and strolled between the graves to the far corner where he stood for a time, looking over the stone wall to the pale sands and breakers of the beach far below. The night was

unusually still. There was no sound but the soft roar of the sea and the occasional cry of a disturbed sea-bird on the cliffs.

On his way back he crossed the graveyard to visit the grave of his parents. As he stood there he felt there was someone behind him, but looking round saw nothing. Then he looked a second time, and his blood ran cold. There, on the soft moss at the foot of their grave, stood Captain Hans Berg and his wife Elenora. Their bodies were half transparent, and through them Tim could see the stones of the graveyard wall. He stayed silent and watched.

The couple stood side by side, looking out to sea. Her hand rested on his arm. They scarcely moved, though her dress rippled a little as if there was a wind.

They were not there for long. Only a few minutes later they began to slide back into the earth and fade from view. Before their shoulders reached the grass they had vanished. The moonlit graveyard was deserted.

Port na Coinnle

'Port na Coinnle' is Gaelic for 'The Bay of the Candles'. It is the name of a small cove situated near the south-east corner of Island Roan.* The entrance is narrow and the bay is surrounded by high cliffs, save at the back where they subside into a very steep slope of grass. A small jetty is built on to the rocks at the mouth of the cove, with steep steps cut out of a spur to the very top of the cliff. There are great drops on both sides of the path, so that when the island was inhabited the iron safety rail was very necessary. Now the island is deserted, the houses are roofless, the safety rail staggers out over the precipice; but right up until the years preceding the Second World War there was quite a large population and even a school.

This is the story of how Port na Coinnle was given its name.

A Dundee vessel, the *S.S. Onega*, returning from Montreal, was sailing along the north coast when a bad storm arose. Rather than sit it out at sea, the captain took his ship into the sheltered waters behind Island Roan and dropped anchor in the mouth of the Kyle of Tongue. He failed to take account of the effect of the huge waves building up in the shallow water, however, and the ship began to drag anchor. She dragged right into the shallows near Coldbackie, and the waves pounded her to a wreck.

From both sides of the Kyle and Island Roan the people watched helplessly as the *Onega's* lifeboats were carried away and overturned, and the entire crew were swept to their deaths. At great danger to themselves the Highlanders tried time and again to launch rescue boats from Scullomie and Coldbackie, at the mouth of the Kyle, but the seas were too rough and would have swamped the little fishing boats before they had gone a quarter of the distance. When the weather moderated the following day, it was too late.

Bodies were washed up all along the shore, and watchers on the cliffs saw some still swilling to and fro in the water, borne up by their

*The Ordnance Survey map of the area names the island 'Eilean Nan Ron' — the Island of the Seals. It names the bay 'Mol Na Coinnle' — a 'mol' being a stony beach, which is precisely what it is.

life jackets. Boats were launched and, where possible, the dead sailors were picked up.

Over on Island Roan, Mary, the Piper's daughter, was watching the cattle when she saw seagulls mobbing something in the water far below her, and looking closely saw that it was a body. Then she saw another. It was more sheltered there than in Kyle Rannoch, and though they could still not cross to the mainland, the men were able to launch a boat and pick them up. A third body was discovered floating further off.

They took the bodies to the little bay and laid them on the pebbles well above the high water mark. Someone brought a tarpaulin to cover them, both for decency and to keep the sea birds away.

During the night the wind increased again and two men went down to the bay to see that the tarpaulin was still secure. As they reached the edge of the bank above the shore, they stopped and stared. All around the canvas a series of white lights gleamed and shone in the darkness. When they went down they discovered that the light came from phosphorescence in the water that was draining from the bodies and clothes and lifejackets of the dead sailors. It looked for all the world, they said later, as if someone had lighted candles around them.

The citizens of Dundee believed, as was common in those days, that the people of the north were savage and wild. It was said there that the Highlanders had actually fought to prevent the drowning men from coming ashore. Feelings ran very high.

There is no church or graveyard on Island Roan, and it was several days before the sea had calmed enough for the small local boats to take the bodies across Kyle Rannoch to the mainland. They were taken first to the pier in Skerray and then by road to the church in Tongue for a Christian burial.

A song, well-known as 'The Stately *Onega*', was composed locally at the time of the tragedy. It tells of the voyage of the *Onega*, the shipwreck, and the great efforts of the Highlanders to rescue the drowning seamen. For some time it achieved a considerable vogue, and was much sung at ceilidhs right up until recent years. Some time after the shipwreck, when feelings were still running high, the song was overheard by some Dundee sailors at a party aboard ship in Aberdeen harbour. They were much surprised, for by this time the inhumanity of the Highlanders towards the crew of the *Onega* was common knowledge, and even a byword among seamen. From them the news filtered back to Dundee where, in consequence, a full account of the incident was printed in the local newspaper, and the northern fishermen received their due credit.

Irish Dorothy

Irish Dorothy was a camp follower. In the olden times it was common and even customary for a soldier's wife and children to follow him from camp to camp to look after his requirements and keep the family together. She arrived in Scotland with an Irish mercenary force at the time of the Jacobean uprisings. After the battle of Culloden she became a refugee, fleeing from the English soldiers as they pursued their ruthless hunt across the Highlands. Eventually she landed at the Calf Rock beside Loch Meadie in north Sutherland, about four miles into the moor to the south-east of Bettyhill. Bean Eoraidh Eireannaich (Dorothy, the Irish wife) as she became known, found a cave there and made it into a home for her two young sons.

They lived on whatever they could get, often stolen sheep which Dorothy slaughtered herself. On one occasion she met a shepherd on the hillside and invited him in to eat a bit of mutton. The mutton was fine, which was just as well because it was one of his own sheep: he saw his mark on the fleece lying in a corner. But Dorothy and the boys needed more than mutton, so occasionally she had to make a trip to the shop at Clachan, just outside Bettyhill. Doubtless she collected a hen or two on the way back — for the shepherd had also observed brown feathers scattered about the entrance — and maybe a few cabbages or turnips from the fields around the village. Only one of the boys was old enough to walk the long journey with her, so the younger boy had to stay behind in the cave. A piece of half-cooked meat was attached by a string to the child's big toe, they say, to keep him amused in her absence. If he was choking on the meat he would kick and jerk it out of his mouth.

Eventually she just vanished. She was not seen for a long time, and when they went to look for her she had gone.

Today no-one is sure where her cave is. There are a number of caves in the Calf Rock but none, you would think, dry or roomy enough to afford shelter to a woman and her two children in the wild conditions that exist out there. Still, she was desperate whilst we are merely curious: it makes a lot of difference.

The Priest's Stone

If you cross the road outside the Strathy Inn and head straight into the hills, after about half a mile's rough walking you will find the Priest's Stone lying flat down in the heather. From the position of the cross, being situated towards one end with a rough, tapering tail of rock below the foot, it looks as though it was originally erect, but for as long as people can remember it has lain on its back, showing the cross to the sky. It is a sandy stone, both in texture and colour, and covered in skins of grey, green, black, white and tawny-coloured lichen. Clearly it has been damaged and much weathered over the years, for the arms of the cross overlap the edges, and one of the side crosses is almost indistinguishable. It was very deeply carved, however, grooves chiselled around five circles, marking the four points and intersection of the cross, and joined by stocky arms: the circles at the four points are double. To each side of the main shaft there is a small, plain cross. The centuries have laid the grooves wide open, and shallow, like cuts that have been rubbed with salt and left to heal. I measured the stone, which is roughly coffin-shaped, with the span of my hand, possibly even as the old mason did who originally carved it: it is fifty-four inches in length, and twenty-one inches broad at the shoulder, narrowing to twelve at the bottom. The cross is thirty-six inches long. At some time a man has gone up with a spade and dug the heather from around the stone so that now it lies in a shallow, roughly rectangular depression in the lee of a small hillock, a rectangle of grass among the tufts of heather. A cairn of white stones has been built just above it, I believe by boys from Farr School, so that now you will find the place quite easily. As you stand there high above the river on the open moors the view is magnificent, south to the far-off hills, and north beyond the village and headlands to the open sea.

Well, at least that much is fact, and so is the name 'The Priest's Stone' which it has always had in the village of Strathy. But beyond that, so far as we can discover, all is vague tradition and speculation. The Ordnance Survey map shows some of the many cairns that exist in the area, revealing that there was at least one battle; and its situation near the eastern marches of the Reay Country would frequently have been crossed by raiding parties going into and coming out of Caithness. The moors are marked with the grassy tracks of old roads. In the valley at the foot of the long hillside are the remains of many hut circles, sign of comparatively intensive settlement. On the summit of the Drum Hill, between Loch Achrugan and the river, is a rocking stone that makes a loud booming note, and is traditionally said to have been used to give warning of clan attack.

The best that can be gathered from the stories one hears, is that there was, many centuries ago, a pitched battle on the site, and that a priest, fighting on the side of the men of Reay, was killed. Being a respected and holy man, a Christian stone was raised above his grave on the hillside.

Some of the stories are more definite, and their tendency is to claim the grave as that of a chief. In one account it is the grave of a chief who died of wounds after betraying his men at the battle of Fleuchary: rather than take him home with his disgrace upon him, they buried him where he lay. In another account the chieftain was drowned by trickery, caught in a net in a deep pool of the river, and buried on a height of land above the spot. In yet a third account it was the site of a battle between two clans returning home after driving out the Vikings at the battle of Fiscary: their antagonism, stifled so long, burst out, there was more bloodshed, and a chieftain was killed.

There is again the possibility that the Priest's Stone does not mark one particular grave at all. Certainly there has been at least one terrible battle on the hillside, and many men have been killed. If they were buried where they fell, or with their comrades in communal graves, the stone could have been erected with a priest's blessing to indicate a graveyard, and that that region of the hillside was designated holy ground.

Everyone in Strathy knows the saying that if you move the Priest's Stone there will be a thunderstorm. Two boys wrote:

"My cousin and I went up to the grave a short while ago. It took us about half an hour to find it. When we found it we cleared all the lichen from it to see all the carvings on it. There was a big cross with two little ones at the side of it. We did not move the stone as we did not want a thunderstorm. Before leaving we built a mound of stones to mark the place. That night when we were in bed the wind howled around our houses but there was no thunder and lightning."

"One day my cousin, brother and I went up to the grave. My

cousin and I tried to move the stone. After a lot of effort we managed to move it a little, but not as much as we intended because it was very heavy. We tried to lever it up with a bit of wood but it broke. That night when we were all tucked up in our beds there was an awful thunderstorm."

Captain Ivy's Cave

Long ago a ship, fleeing from pirates, found itself on a windward shore in the teeth of a great storm, and being relentlessly driven on to the rocks. There was nothing the crew could do and in the darkness, while the people of the village slept, the ship struck the rocks of Strathy Bay and was soon broken up by the fierce waves.

In the morning the wreckage and many fine pieces of cargo were found washed up along the shore. In among the weed and debris, too, were the bodies of drowned sailors. All were dead, not one survivor to tell the tale — or so they thought.

But Captain Ivy had escaped, and gone to ground in one of the caves along Strathy Beach. Probably he was badly beaten by the waves, but he was more frightened of the pirates who were following him than he was of his wounds. Many years before he had captured a pirate ship, made the crew his prisoners, and given them into custody. Now they were released or had escaped, and were hot on his heels, seeking revenge.

So, while the people of Strathy prepared his shipmates for Christian burial — and collected the more valuable pieces of cargo before the customs could get their hands on them — Captain Ivy stayed well out of sight. He only left the cave when he was quite sure that the coast was clear. It is said of him that he walked backwards, preferring that anyone seeing his footprints should think there was a man inside the cave, rather than that he had just left and was now to be found along the beach. When he returned he walked backwards too, so that then it would appear that someone had just strolled into the cave and gone away again.

A few days later the pirates turned up. They had heard of the shipwreck and come to see for themselves. Their enquiries revealed that no captain had been found, that he must have been washed away to sea with the rest of the crew. They were not convinced, knowing Captain Ivy of old, and set about scouring the shore and the neighbourhood for themselves. More than once they were in the very mouth of his cave, but though they looked, they found nothing. A

85

few days later, satisfied that Captain Ivy really was dead, they went away, and never returned.

It is not surprising that they did not find him, for the cave is well hidden. To find it, you go first to the graveyard high above the beach at Strathy and climb down through the quarter mile of rolling dunes. To the right of the beach, which is one of the most beautiful in the north, you will find a wall of pale cliffs, with stacks and fissures and lovely geos* full of pale green water above a sandy bottom. Running in from the sands are three caves, and the most seaward of them is Captain Ivy's Cave. The back of the cave is piled with smooth white boulders, and little twists in the rock form completely black shadows. One such patch of shadow conceals a narrow, descending crack through which you can squeeze, to find yourself in a little chamber with a floor of dry sand. At the far end, at the base of the rock wall, there is a small hole, and if you lie flat and wriggle, it is possible to squeeze through this into a spacious chamber beyond. This is the cave that was once occupied by Captain Ivy. On the floor stand the stone table and chair where he sat to eat his meals, and against one wall is the flat slab where he made his bed. Normal tides do not enter the chamber and the floor is dry.

Captain Ivy stayed in the cave for many years. When he lit a fire he did so at night, when the smoke could diffuse through the cliff without being noticed. He lived on what he could pick up — whelks, fish, dulse, stolen vegetables, snared rabbits, and the occasional sheep, cleaned and hung to dry and cure in the salt air.

What eventually happened to him no-one knows. Some say he died of frost-bite, others that he drowned or was simply found dead at the mouth of the cave.

Of course some unimaginative people might claim that there was never a Captain Ivy at all, only some poor old eccentric who used to visit the cave in days gone by; and others may say that he is simply another corruption or misunderstanding of a Gaelic phrase. However, true or untrue though the story may be, it has been known as Captain Ivy's Cave for generations, and is locally famous.

*Geo: a rocky inlet.

Castle Borve

The castle is situated on a tiny promontory to the east of Farr Point. If you walk around it now, on the even higher crags, you will probably not notice the ruins. All you will see is a small promontory with a narrow neck. Hundred foot cliffs fall sheer to the water on all sides except for a ragged tail that staggers out to the north. It is undercut by a long and almost flawlessly constructed sea-arch, and the sheep have nibbled the crown of fine grass smooth. But if you go closer you may spot the remnants of walls sitting as firmly today as they have for the past nine hundred years on slopes of seventy and eighty degrees. You have to scramble down a few feet and lean out over the precipice if you want to see them close up. Further on you will find the grassy mounds and ditches which are all that remain today of the castle's fortifications and internal structure.

Forty-five years ago there was a lot more. Just across the narrow neck were the quite recognisable remains of a drawbridge, and further up the ruins of the guards' house and trenches. But a Bettyhill minister of that time, believing that archaeological remains might be found on the site, went there with a lot of local boys and threw all the stones down to the rocks below. They destroyed the ruins and found nothing.

The castle was built, and brilliantly so, by the Norse at the time of their supremacy in Britain. It was constructed as a stronghold for a Viking and his wife by Thorkel, a noted Norse builder of the eleventh century.

There is a tradition that the site was so difficult to build on that the Viking expressed doubts as to whether it was feasible, and Thorkel offered to build it free if any flaw could be found in the construction. When it was completed the Viking and his wife said they were quite satisfied, but the only way to inspect some of the walls was by boat. When Thorkel and the Viking were down in the boat, the Viking's wife hung a thread down the wall which looked like a crack from below. They came back and Thorkel had himself lowered on a rope to inspect it. The rope was cut or dropped, and Thorkel fell to his death on the rocks below.

Another tradition claims that a secret passage was constructed from inside the castle to the shore. Only a handful of men were employed on this, and when it was completed they were disposed of. Then Thorkel was killed, as we have said, so only the Viking himself was left with the knowledge of this secret passage and possible escape route.

The castle passed into the hands of Mackay of Farr during the period of the decline of the Norse power in Scotland. It was destroyed by the Earl of Sutherland in 1555. The history behind this is interesting.

Aoidh Mackay, son of Donald and head of the Clan Mackay, was summoned in 1555 to appear before the Queen Regent (the mother of Mary Queen of Scots) at Inverness, "for that he had spoiled and molested the country of Sutherland during Earl John's being in France with the Queen Regent." He disregarded the command and this same John, Earl of Sutherland, was commissioned to invade Mackay territory. From the start the fighting did not go well for the Mackays. A large detachment soon fell back on Castle Borve, one of their principal strongholds, and were laid seige to by Earl John. Cannons, which had been hauled two hundred and fifty miles north from Edinburgh, were now dragged over miles of boggy, rocky ground to an eminence above the castle,* and proceeded to open fire. The ancient walls, so magnificently built, were never intended to withstand such a pounding: they fell, and the stronghold was taken. The gallant commander, Ruaraidh MacIan Môr, was hanged, then the castle was razed to the ground. Aoidh gathered his men and fought back, but at length he was so beset on all sides that he was forced to surrender. Earl John handed him over to Sir Hugh Kennedy, by whom he was conveyed south to Edinburgh Castle and imprisoned for a long time. During his absence the Mackay lands were governed by his cousin John Môr, who used the opportunity to lead one of the most disastrous of all raids upon the Sutherlands, culminating in the bloody rout of the Mackays at Garbharry. Upon his release, however, Aoidh reassumed his position as chief, and later distinguished himself most notably in the Border wars against the English.

As for the name of the castle, it is almost certainly derived from the Gaelic word 'borbh', which means 'fierce' or 'wild', a most fitting description of its setting and at least part of its history.

*This eminence is still known as Ru nan gunnach (Gun Point).

SUPERNATURAL TALES

FAIRY TALES

The Witch's Romance

Two sisters, who were both witches, lived together in a cottage surrounded by flowers in Borgie. The younger was short and pretty, with fair curly hair and no end of admirers. Often and often she would be sitting by the fire laughing with a young man, or bouncing into the house singing in the early hours of the morning. But while she was pretty, her older sister was beautiful, a tall, slim and stately woman, dark, with a superb crown of gleaming nut-brown hair. Unfortunately though, she was shy, as shy as her sister was friendly, and when any gentleman called to see her she could find nothing whatever to say, and would stammer so much that she had to run around making tea and doing little jobs to try to cover up her embarrassment.

One summer, however, a very handsome young gentleman came to stay at the inn a little distance from their cottage. He was quite the finest young man the district had seen for a long time, and the younger sister was most keen to make his acquaintance. Very soon she did and he was invited home for tea, but strangely enough, as these things sometimes turn out, with him the older sister found no awkwardness at all. As they sat in their little living room she was lively and witty and charming, and so beautiful that no man could have failed to fall in love with her.

For the first time in her life the younger sister was jealous, and when the young man had gone they soon found themselves involved in a quite heated exchange of words. Neither of them was that way inclined, and they were both very upset.

One or two times more he came to the house, but the older witch could see that it made her sister unhappy so she arranged to meet him, so far as she could, in other places. Sometimes, very shyly, she would call at the inn; or they would meet by a clump of trees on the riverbank and stroll down the glen in the twilight.

Normally the older sister did not go beyond her lovely garden in the evenings, unless perhaps to take a breath of fresh air in the fields around the cottage, but now each time she brushed her gleaming

hair and put on her prettiest dress, she could see that her sister was
still unhappy. It cast a slight gloom over her own evening, and she
began to wonder how she could possibly avoid it.

At the time the younger witch had no admirer of her own, and this
was probably at the root of the trouble. Left alone, she went to bed

early, not long after nine o'clock, even while the sun was setting on
those long summer evenings. It gave the older sister the very opportunity she wanted.

Early one evening she announced that she was going to see the
young man no more; he was becoming boring, and starting to take
her for granted. At about five past nine she yawned and said she was
going to bed. For a while she made getting-ready-for-bed noises,
drawing the curtains, opening and shutting the wardrobe door two
or three times, dropping her shoes on the boards at the end of the
bed: but all the time she was really getting ready for going out. When
she was finished she looked at herself in the mirror then threw
herself on to the bed and pulled a light bedspread to her chin in case
her sister should look in on the way to her own bedroom. She did,
and then for a few minutes could be heard getting ready for bed
herself in the next room. The older sister heard her settling down,
and then gave her another ten minutes to fall asleep. (Being witches
they could both fall asleep whenever they wanted with a little spell.)
Then, very quietly, the older sister climbed out of bed, slid the curtains
back and pushed open the window. The cool evening breeze flowed

92

into the room, fanning her cheek and stirring the folds of the chintz curtains.

Then she went and stood right in the middle of the cream and blue rug that lay on the floor. Her big brown eyes were open, and her mouth was forming words. Suddenly she had vanished, and there, in her place, stood a little brown sparrow. It cocked its chirpy head to one side, looking this way and that with bright black eyes, listening. Then, with a whirr of wings, it sprang into the air, flew once around the room and straight out of the open window into the evening air.

The fields passed by underneath, and in less than two minutes it landed on the bank of the river in a quiet, sheltered spot. The next moment the sparrow had gone and the beautiful witch was standing in its place, her dark hair all wind-blown.

So, for two more weeks, she was able to continue meeting her handsome young man. She was idyllically happy, in love for the first time in her life.

Full of the joys of living, the witch would sometimes turn herself into a raven when she had left the house, flying higher and higher, circling, swooping, falling out of the sky with a great rush of wind that made her eyes sparkle and her chest heave with excitement. On other occasions, if she had time, she would become a bee or a field mouse, sipping nectar from the hearts of summer flowers, nosing through the sweet grasses of the hedgerows, so that her evening trysts became journeys of excitement and exploration.

One evening brought it all to an end.

She had left the cottage, as always, an inconspicuous sparrow. Once free, however, she had turned herself into a beautiful brown hare and was slowly lolloping along the side of a field, stopping every now and then to nibble some sweet grass or rub her long silky ears with a paw.

Now it happened that her young man had been out shooting that day and, not realising the time, was late back. Suddenly, as he walked through the fields, he saw a fine brown hare hopping along just in front of him. He stopped, pushed off the safety catch of his gun, and was just raising it to his shoulder when the hare turned and looked at him.

There was something about it that made him pause for a moment, something strange. As for the lovely witch, she was terrified. There stood the man she loved, looking straight at her along the sights of a

93

gun, one eye shut, the other narrowed, ready to kill. Without a sound, almost as if someone had released a spring, she was away. There was a deafening blast behind her, and red-hot fiery pain as bullets struck her in the legs and back and shoulder. For a moment she was bowled over, screaming the hare's cry of pain, but then she was back on her feet again, and running, running, as if her heart would burst.

When she got back to the house she squeezed under the gate and ran through the flowerbeds on to the lawn. A moment later she was a sparrow, ready to fly up to the bedroom; but she could not fly. When she tried to flap her wings they just fell open and she toppled to one side in the grass. Then she became a jackdaw, a seagull, even an eagle, but it was no use, she could not fly at all.

Back in her own shape she called up to her sister to come down and let her in. The tears streamed down her lovely face.

An hour later she was tucked up in bed, heavily bandaged, and her sister made her a drink of herbs to soothe the pain.

The next morning the young man called at the cottage to see if she was alright, for she had not turned up for their meeting. Perhaps, he thought, he had offended her by being so late. It was her pretty young sister who came to the door. With a few words she told him exactly what she thought of him, and sent him away, never to come near that house again. Behind her, leaning heavily against the bannister at the head of the stairs, was her sister. She was in her nightgown, and looked very unwell. When he called up to her to ask whether he could not see her again, she shook her head very slowly, sobbing, and limped painfully across the landing into the bedroom. With a click, the door closed behind her.

Not knowing what he had done to offend her, the young man walked slowly away down the front path. He shut the gate behind him, and looked up at her bedroom window. The curtains stirred slightly, and were still. Two minutes later he had disappeared around a bend in the road.

It was the end of the romance.

The Fairy Foundling

One day a shepherd was strolling along the Skelpick road with his dog, a handsome black collie. Suddenly there was a faint, mewing cry from over by Loch Duinte. His dog left his side and headed towards the loch with a long, loping run. Again the faint cry floated through the summery air. He left the road and walked across the heathery knoll towards the sound. Two or three minutes later he came up to the dog which was standing over a little bundle just up from the water's edge. It was a baby. The little creature was weeping in the most distressing way, its face all red and puckered up. He picked it up, cradling it in his arms, and looked around for the mother. But there was no-one there, so he took the baby home with him.

Nobody ever claimed the child so the shepherd and his wife brought him up as their own. They had a baby daughter already and the two children grew up as brother and sister.

At the age of seventeen the young people realised that they were in love with each other, and their parents were delighted to arrange a marriage.

A grand feast was arranged as part of the celebration. Long trestle tables were set up on the grass outside the cottage. After the wedding ceremony the guests sat down to eat. There was so much food and drink that in a while the musicians became dazed and could play no longer. The young bridegroom was well known as a piper, and taking up a set of pipes that lay beside him, he placed them to his lips.

The guests listened, entranced, to the wonderful, weird music that he played. Never had they heard anything like it; it seemed to put a spell on them and one by one, with a smile on their faces, they fell asleep. On he played until no-one was left awake except his lovely young bride and himself.

The guests woke up to a magically beautiful day; the sky blue with little white clouds, the air full of bird song and the scent of wild flowers, bright butterflies dancing in the sunshine. The young couple had gone. They were never seen again.

95

The Evil Eye

Two neighbours in Bettyhill, a fat old man and a thin old woman, had been enemies for years. When they spoke to each other it was only to quarrel. They were jealous too, and neither could bear to hear that the other one had bought something nice, or got a better price at the sheep sale, and so on.

Now it happened that the old man was very fond of his cow, a gentle, fat creature that produced gallons of rich milk and a fine, strong calf every year. The old woman's cow, on the other hand, was a thin, sickly animal, ill-tempered, and more trouble than it was worth.

So when, one day, after a row between them, the old man found that his cow was sick, blowing and kicking and holding the milk back, he was in no doubt what was wrong with her. The old woman's grandfather had had the second sight, and now she had put the evil eye on his good cow. A right witch she was.

The usual remedies did no good at all, so he went to a woman in the village who knew about these things. She made all the arrangements for him.

At eleven o'clock that night three women came to his house. One of them was fair, with golden hair; one was dark, with hair as glossy as a crow's wing; the third was an old lady, whose hair shone silver in the lamplight. They took a bucket, and each placed something in the bottom. The fair girl put in a wedding ring, for gold; the dark girl put in a heavy black key from the barn door, for iron; and the old lady put in a little thimble made of silver. Then, at the dead of night, they went to the place 'where the living and the dead pass over' — in this case the bridge over the Clachan Burn that leads to the graveyard. There they filled the bucket with water and carried it back to the house. The old man had given his cow no water, so that she would be thirsty. Now they placed the bucket before her in the lantern-lit byre and the cow dropped her head to drink. The silvery water trickled from her muzzle. What she did not drink the old lady poured over the cow's back, to the last drop. During the whole of the spell nobody was allowed to speak a word or make a noise.

It worked. As they poured the last of the water over her back the cow stopped blowing and became calm again. The power of the evil eye was broken.

But in his neighbour's byre the thin, sickly cow began kicking and lowing and tugging at the chain that held it in the stall. The curse had transferred itself to the woman's own beast. Two days later it died.

As for the old man's cow, she lived on to a ripe old age and gave him the best milk in the parish.

Two Fairy Knolls

Strathnaver

CHA CHUM TIGH BHREATUNN RUINN*

All through the summer Millie Mackay of Skerray had been working with a shepherd's family near the little ruined township of Achness, in Strathnaver. She had helped with the housework, the children, the cattle, the sheep — whatever needed doing at that busy time of the year. Now the autumn was coming on and she was due to return home. As part of her wages she was taking with her quite a lot of butter and cheese and some joints of lamb. With her own belongings, few as they were, it was too big a load for one girl, and so her brother Hamish was coming to carry it for her and accompany her home.

It was a fine day and they made good progress, but it is a long way from upper Strathnaver to Skerray and in a while they were glad to sit down on a grassy knoll and have a rest. Millie had prepared some food for them and now she unpacked it. They had not seen each other for some months and there was plenty to chat about as they lay back in the warm sunshine.

Suddenly Hamish stopped talking and sat up to listen. Then Millie heard it too, the faint sound of singing drifting through the air. It was coming towards them and as they listened it grew louder and louder. They could distinguish the voices, it sounded as if there was dancing. Soon it seemed only a few yards away and they could make out the words quite distinctly.

> Cha chum tigh fiodh fiodha sinn,
> Cha chum tigh fiodh sinn,
> Cha chum tigh bhan na slatan ruinn,
> Cha chum tigh Bhreatunn ruinn. †

---

*This story is said to be true. The knoll is situated near the green circle at Carnachy Burn.
†The wood-wooden houses won't keep us,
The houses of wood won't keep us;
The white slatted houses won't hold us,
The house of Britain won't hold us.

They were alarmed and Hamish said to his sister, "It's time we were away from this place. Come away."

Quickly they gathered their bundles and the food together and hurried off. As they left the knoll behind them the sound of the singing grew fainter, and soon they could hear it no more.

THE MAN WHO LOVED DANCING

Sandy Munro's wife was expecting her eighth child. He was fishing for herring in the Minch out of Lochinver at the time. A week before her confinement he set out with his brother-in-law, Jamie, who was also at the fishing, to walk home to Armadale. It took them several days, for they were both fond of a ceilidh and a blether. At length, though, they found themselves walking up the old road in Strathnaver, at the edge of the valley. It was a warm afternoon. They reckoned to get to Bettyhill that night, where there would be a dance, and walk the last seven miles to Armadale the following morning.

Jamie was tired, for they had spent the previous night with friends in Altnaharra, and had not seen their beds before the morning sun was in the sky. Seeing a little hill ahead, with fine long heather, he suggested a rest.

They lay down. The sun was warm on their faces. They would undoubtedly both have slept, and were already feeling drowsy when to their ears came the faint noise of dancing and music and revelry. They sat up. The sound was coming closer. It seemed to be issuing from a small dark cave set in the side of the hill. Quietly they crawled across to the entrance and peered in. Far down, in what seemed to be the very heart of the hill, was a glow of golden-white light, flickering like candle flames. The sound of dancing and merry laughter was loud.

Sandy Munro loved dancing, and was always ready for a bit of fun. Before Jamie could stop him he scrambled down to the entrance. Crouching, because of the low roof, he began to make his way along the dark passage. Jamie could see his silhouette against the distant light. He called him back time and again, but Sandy took no notice. He grew smaller — then suddenly he vanished. One moment he was there, the next he was not. Jamie called and called, but there was no reply. The sounds of revelry grew louder for a moment, and then continued.

It was the evening when Jamie arrived in Bettyhill and reported what had happened. No-one believed him. But when a week later Sandy had still not turned up, Jamie was accused of murdering him. For although he and Sandy were great friends, it was well known that he disapproved of Sandy's carrying on, and his way with the women, when he was married to his sister. Besides, the story of the music and dancing was not to be believed: they had visited the cave — it led no more than a few feet into the hillside. Jamie pleaded for his life. He was given a year and a day from the date of Sandy's disappearance to prove his innocence.

He returned to the cave and made himself a rough hut right at the entrance. All through the autumn and frosty, snowy winter he scarcely moved away from the spot. The spring drew by, and then summer was upon him once more. Soon it was the anniversary of Sandy's disappearance. He had only one day left.

As the rising sun tipped the edge of the moor Jamie became aware of a faint noise. He pushed back his blankets and sat up, listening intently. It grew louder. He heard the sound of music and dancing. Springing from his bed he rushed to the mouth of the cave. It had opened once more: far down the tunnel he saw the gleam of pure light, and heard again the sound of merry laughter. He called to Sandy, and called again, but there was no reply. He dared not go to investigate, for he feared that he would himself disappear. And there was no-one there to witness it. For hours he waited, terrified that the cave would close once more and he would have to return to Armadale alone.

Then, in the middle of the afternoon, just at the time when Sandy had disappeared, the sound of the music grew louder and there was a swelling of happy voices. Peering down the tunnel Jamie saw a mist, a shadow, and then Sandy was coming towards him out of the darkness.

"What's the hurry?" he called. "Could you not wait for me to finish the reel?"

When Jamie told him that he had been down in the tunnel for a whole year Sandy laughed and stretched his shoulders and said that they had better be getting along if they were to have time for a meal and a rest before the dance in Bettyhill that night. But when he reached the village he discovered how true it was: and when he arrived in Armadale the following noon he found himself the father of a fine sturdy boy, just one year old.

The Carrach

The Carrach is a fairy knoll that stands above the Swordly Burn a few hundred yards from where it flows into the sea. It is covered with heather and commands a lovely view across the moors and out beyond the cliffs to Swordly Bay and the open horizon.

THE SWORDLY MILL

Once upon a time an old mill stood on the bank of the Swordly Burn. It was a fine building of old, weathered stone, with little windows, green doors, and a big wooden wheel that turned and turned in the chuckling mill race. It stood just below the Carrach, on the far side of the stream.

The miller was a hard-working, simple sort of man. He lived alone, though no-one knew why, for he was a pleasant-faced, strong fellow, not yet middle-aged, and well liked by everyone for his perpetual good nature. Although he had little money and few possessions, and his food was of the plainest, he was content.

One night, as he was washing after a hard day's work, a fairy from the Carrach called at the mill house. She was out to make mischief.

101

She walked straight in without knocking, and after watching him for several moments began poking and prying about the room, opening the cupboard doors and rummaging through the drawers. Then she sat down at the table and began asking him question after question of the most impudent and personal nature. At last he grew tired of it and turning his back on her proceeded to wash himself as usual. She was annoyed at this and told him that she wanted a bowl of the broth that was simmering on the hob. He told her that it was all he had, and had to serve him for several meals. At his refusal she was furious.

"Give me a bowl of the broth," she shouted.

"I tell you it's all I've got," he repeated.

"Give it to me!"

"Och, away with you," he said, exasperated, and taking up a pan of water he had been heating for shaving, began to lather his face.

At that she screwed up her features and started to make faces at him.

"Now stop that, and get away out of my house," he told her.

"Give me some broth then," she spat at him.

"I will not, and that's final. Now, get yourself out."

At this final refusal she screwed her face up terribly, pointing and hissing at him. Disgusted, he flung the pan of hot shaving water all over her. Screaming she fled from the house, ran across the stepping stones and back to the fairy knoll. The miller finished shaving and spent a peaceful evening.

But the following morning he had to go away to market with some flour and sheep. He was away all day. When he returned in the evening his lovely mill was nothing but a heap of rubble. The fairies on the Carrach had taken their revenge.

The poor miller did not know what to do. At length he decided that he would have to rebuild it. So he set to work, using his bare hands, and built the mill right up again. It took him more than a year, and used up all of his savings. When he had finished it was beautiful. He invited all of his friends and neighbours to a party. But that same afternoon, while he was out shopping, the fairies pulled his lovely mill to the ground. They pushed the mill wheel over the cliff, and scattered the stones all up and down the river, in the pools and on the hillsides. When he returned, and his guests arrived, there was nothing but a ruin.

He left the mill then, and made his home a long way off. But

wherever he went, from that day onwards, the miller was followed
by the most terrible bad luck until the end of his days.

An alternative version of the story ends as follows:
The fairy had been asking so many questions that at last the miller
got fed up.
"What's your name?" she asked him, putting on a face.
"Mi fhein," (myself), he replied in irritation.
A little while later she demanded a bowlful of the brochan that
was steaming on the hob ready for his supper. (This was a mixture
of crushed oats and water, similar to brose.) He refused, and when he
had finished washing and was dressed, he took a bowlful himself and
sat at the table. She continued tormenting him until at last in anger
he snatched up the bowl and flung the brochan in her face. Screaming,
she ran back to the fairy knoll.
"Who did that to you?" they asked.
"Mi fhein!" she replied.
"Oh well, if you did it to yourself," they said, "there's nothing we
can do about it. You must be mad."
And so the miller, quite rightly, got off with it.

THE GOOD NURSE

Many years ago two old ladies lived in a little cottage right on the
slopes of the Carrach. It was a real old Highland dwelling with thick
walls, small windows, a thatched peat roof, and hens and ducks in
the field outside. They were sweet, gentle women, well-liked by all
their neighbours. They were on good terms too with the fairies on
the knoll.
One day the younger of the two sisters, who was a widow and the
mother of four grown-up girls, was going to fetch some water from
the well when she heard a thin, high-pitched shouting from the top
of the hill. It was a funny sound, half like a voice and half like music.
She put down the bucket and hurried up as fast as she could.
When she got to the very top she saw two tiny fairies, a boy standing
up and a girl lying unconscious on the grass between fronds of heather.
She was obviously very ill with a fever, her face deathly white with
red, burning cheeks. The boy was calling up to the old lady. It was
strange that although she could not make out a single word she
knew exactly what he was saying to her. He was asking her to take

103

the sick girl down to her house and look after her; there was no more they could do and they feared she was dying.

She said that she would, of course, and in a moment had taken a spotless white handkerchief from her apron pocket and laid the little creature in it. Carrying her very carefully she returned to the cottage.

For a week she nursed her, night and day, as the dreadful fever ran its course. On the seventh night it broke, and in the morning, as the sun touched the bedroom curtains, the little fairy was breathing more easily. Before lunchtime she opened her eyes and looked wonderingly around the cottage bedroom. A week later she was ready to go home.

When the old lady carried her back to the top of the Carrach she was greeted by more than a hundred fairies, all chattering together and calling up to her, some even flying over her head to see the girl in her hands. She placed the little creature on the ground among them and sat down for a few minutes. All of them were thanking her, and the boy she had spoken to earlier handed her a bunch of tiny flowers with an exquisite perfume. For as long as she lived they never withered or faded by so much as a leaf.

104

Then she rose to go, but the girl she had been nursing caught her by the hem of the dress. Still she could not understand the words, but she knew perfectly what the girl was saying. The little fairy was promising that from that time on her daughters, and all their descendants until the end of time, would be wonderful nurses. The old lady was delighted. Her daughters had young children, and at that time a lot of children died in infancy. It was the best present the fairy could have given her.

A week later she received news that one of her grandchildren had been seriously ill. They were given no hope by the doctor, but somehow her daughter had nursed the boy back to health. The doctor said he could not understand it. The old lady thought that perhaps she could, however, and hurried straight to the top of the Carrach with the letter in her hand. It was deserted. She called and called again to let them know, but there was no response, nothing but the heather and the hills, and the wind blowing in from the blue Atlantic.

The Bag of Gold on Island Roan

I.   Betty Macdonald and her brother lived on Island Roan. One day
they were playing near the cliffs watching the sea birds wheeling far
below them when suddenly Donald spotted a small boat almost
hidden by the waves. They watched as it came closer. There were not
many visitors to the island and it was not a boat they knew, so they
were naturally curious. There were three men in it, two dressed like
sailors and one like a soldier.

When the boat reached the end of the island, one of the men in
sailor's uniform jumped out on to the rocks and clambered quickly
to the top of the cliffs. He carried a small bag with him, and he ran
from one end of the island to the other. He ran very fast and though
the children ran after him he was soon out of sight.

When they met up with him he was on his way back. The bag was
gone.

"Where's the bag?" said Betty.

The man had black hair and a brown, laughing face.

"It's where the sun and the sea meet," he said.

"What's in it?" said Donald.

"Gold!"

"Really?" said Donald.

"It's a bag of gold. You'll find it where the sun and the sea meet."

Then he turned away and started running again. A little while
later they saw the boat heading away from the island, and watched
until it was hidden in the waves.

Although the children knew the island from end to end as well as
their own dinner plates they never found any sign of the merry
sailor's visit or his bag of gold: and though people have puzzled
about it for a century and more, no-one has solved the riddle of
'the place where the sun and the sea meet'.

II.   A sailor on board a Spanish ship stole a big bag of sovereigns
from the captain's cabin and escaped in a rowing boat. He must have
had a long row because by the time he was approaching Island Roan
another boat, 'full of fat strong policemen, dressed in blue suits and

with tall hats on their heads', was following him.

He landed just ahead of them, and running over to the seaward side of the island, threw the bag down into a heap of stones and rolled a huge rock on top of it.

When the police caught up with him and asked what he had done with the money he said he had thrown it into the sea on the way across. They took him away and flung him into jail, where he may have died, for he never returned to the island.

The gold is still buried there, and on the longest day of the year the first and last rays of the sun fall upon the stone that hides it.

The Fisherman and the Witch

Many years ago an old woman who lived in Portskerra was believed to be a witch. Very few people called to see her and when they did she was always so sharp-tongued and argumentative that they did not stay for long. Maybe she did not want to be so shrewish, but that was the way it always turned out.

Then one day in the street a fierce argument developed with a young fisherman who had sold her some fish the week before. They both became very angry, she because he would not drop the price still further, and he because at the price he was asking he was almost giving the fish to the poor woman and thought she was being extremely unfair. People from the village gathered around to hear the hot words flying. Eventually the old woman stormed away, but she had gone no more than a few yards when she turned and pointed a threatening finger at him.

"I tell you this, George Henry Macintosh. Before one year is out you are going to be drowned, and they will find your body hanging from a hook."

Everyone heard her. The young fisherman turned his back.

The winter passed and spring drew on, with fine warm weather for the lambing.

One bright morning George Macintosh left his wife and went down to the shore with two friends. Soon they were far out in Melvich Bay. The fishing was good and by lunchtime they had a fine haul of cod.

The other two men never knew how it happened. One moment George was working behind them in the boat and the next there was a splash and he had gone over the side. He was just too far off to grab the gunwale. One of the men snatched up the oars, but instead of giving George an oar to hang on to he tried to back the boat up to him. George, who could not swim, was splashing wildly in the water and reaching out his arms towards them. Then the oars got tangled in the lines, and even as they fought to free them, he was gone.

The currents along the north coast are among the swiftest in Britain and people did not expect George's body to be washed up. Within a few hours, they thought, it would have been swept into the

Pentland Firth. But the three friends must have been fishing out of the main stream, for two or three days later another fisherman out in the bay felt something heavy on his line. When he drew it to the surface he found the body of George Macintosh hanging from his big baited cod-hook.

The Chain (Rope) of Sand

The Kyle of Tongue stretches far inland, and on the east bank, half way up, lies the village of Tongue itself. It is a beautiful setting with the moors behind, the fine peaks of Ben Loyal to the south, and one mile across the ruffled waters of the Kyle a long slope of hill with the hunched shoulders of Ben Hope rising above it. The mouth of the Kyle seems almost closed in beyond the white sands of Melness by the linked chain of the Rabbit Islands and further out the fine cliffs of Island Roan. When the tide flows the sea floods up the deep channel on the Melness shore, and spills across the miles of sand. And when it ebbs, bit by bit the sandbanks appear and the gulls and seals and strands of seaweed settle on the shore.

THE WITCH OF TARBAT

Many years ago when Donald was chief of the Clan Mackay and lord of all the Reay country, he became increasingly irritated, and finally angry, that there was no easy way to cross the Kyle of Tongue. He would stand in the garden of his beautiful House of Tongue and stare across the water to a cottage on the further shore, and kick his heels and walk up and down. He behaved like this because he had a sweetheart in that cottage and it was impossible for him to see her without all sorts of fuss. There were either boats and tides and rocks and sandbanks to bother about, or else he had to saddle a horse and ride a dozen miles, all the way up one side of the Kyle and down the other. It was impossible for him to see her without everyone knowing about it.

"If I could only get a bridge built," he said, and called all his wise men and advisers into council, hoping they might be able to help him.

They shook their heads. "There's nothing we can do," they said. "But perhaps the Witch of Reay can help you."

So to the Witch of Reay he went.

"No, Laird of Reay," she said to him. "I cannot help you."

"But do you not command the fairies of the Reay country?" he asked.

110

"We are friends, it is true," she admitted, "and sometimes they do favours for me. But they are not bridge-building fairies."

"Then what can I do?" he cried.

"I will tell you," she said. "Send a messenger, a man you can trust, to Skain Beg, the wise woman of Tarbat. She has working fairies. They do what she tells them. She can build your bridge for you — if she chooses to."

So the Laird immediately sent Angus Mackay, one of his clansmen, to seek help from the wise woman of Tarbat.

He had a long, long way to walk, by moor and strath and coastal glen. A rowing boat ferried him across the long arm of the sea at Dornoch, and then he was walking far out into the Moray Firth along the wild peninsula. Night was falling for the third time on his journey when at long last he reached Tarbat Ness, and clambering around the rocky headland found the old witch in her dark stone hut.

"Well, well," she said. "What a handsome young man." Her black eyes glittered in the light of a little fire.

Angus shivered, and left the door open behind him, ready to make a bolt for it.

Her thin, crooked fingers toyed with the ears of a black cat in her lap as she talked.

"Well, man of Reay," she said, "and what brings you here to trouble Skain Beg?"

When he told her what the Reay witch had said, she answered coldly, "And perhaps you will tell me, Angus Mackay, why I should help his lordship."

Involuntarily Angus took a step backwards towards the door.

"No, no. You've nothing to fear from Skain Beg," she said. "But I know the Laird of Reay well — and his ancestors back as far as Angus the Absolute. Not a thing did they ever do for me when I was young. Not a thing but drive me out of my house!"

For a long time there was silence, but at length she began nodding her head very slowly, and when she spoke again her voice was softer.

"Ah, but their ladies were often kind. For their sakes I will give you the help you ask for his lordship."

With difficulty she got to her feet. "Now you wait here and I will give you a box to take back to him. When he gets that he will soon be able to bridge the Kyle of Tongue."

Away she went, and soon returned carrying a large box which was made of woven heather and tied with long grasses.

111

"Now you carry this back to Donald Mackay," she said. "But remember this! If you try just once to look inside the box you will rue the day you were born."

"I will. I will," said Angus, backing out of the door as quickly as politeness would allow.

"Will you not stay and have a bite of food with me?" she said. "It's not often I have the chance of such company."

"No, no. Thank you, thank you," he said. "I've got to be getting back. Thank you." As soon as he felt the soft turf under his feet he turned and took to his heels.

Many times he fell that night, but when morning dawned he had put a dozen miles between Skain Beg and himself, and felt free to lie down in the lee of a hay rick and sleep in the sunshine.

Three days later he was climbing over the moors towards Ben Loyal. The box was not heavy, but as he walked along he felt sure there was something strange about it. Indeed at times it felt just as if there was something moving about inside, and he wished very much to know what it was. His fear of Skain Beg seemed no more than a bad dream in such summer sunshine, and many times he nearly gave in to the temptation to have just a quick look.

As he topped the last rise and saw the village below him he realised that this was his last chance.

"Why need I be minding yon auld witch?" he said to himself. "For sure there is something moving in this box. ... I'll just take a peep!"

Holding the box under his arm he very carefully cut the grass fastening with his dirk and eased up one corner of the heather lid.

Well! Angus Mackay got the fright of his life. Just as he put his eye down to peep inside the box, hundreds of little brown fairies came springing and leaping and flying out of the tiny gap. He got such a shock that he dropped the box in the heathery grass and the lid went flying.

In a moment the fairies had clambered all over him. They poked at his ears and in his eyes, they pulled his hair and kicked him all over, screaming all the time, "Give us work, Master! Give us work! We are working fairies!"

"Ooh! Ow! Help!" Angus cried. He was terrified. "Ow! Ooh!" His desperate eyes fell upon Melness Farm on the far side of the glittering Kyle. "There," he roared, "go and pull every piece of heather off Melness Farm. Quick now! Be going!"

112

There was a whirr of brown wings and the next moment they had all gone.

"Whooh! Thank goodness for that!" he exclaimed, and examined himself all over for damage. Then he picked up the box and tied it with fresh grasses so that no-one would ever know it had been opened, and set off the last mile or so into Tongue.

But he had gone no more than a few paces when the fairies were back again. Their task was completed.

"Give us more work! Give us more work!" they screamed.

This time Angus's eyes fell on the top of Ben Loyal.

"Now go and pull all the heather off the top of Ben Loyal," he ordered them, and took to his heels.

But before he had run a hundred yards they were back, pulling at his hair and kicking and poking him until he did not know what to do.

"Stop it!" he roared. "Stop it! Stop it!"

But all the time they kept crying ,"Give us more work! Work! We are working fairies. Give us work!"

By the time Angus arrived back at the House of Tongue he was tormented nearly to death. He told Lord Reay about his terrible journey back with the fairies, and Skain Beg, and what he had to do. Then he ran home and locked the door.

Lord Reay commanded the fairies to build a high wall around the House of Tongue. No sooner were they gone than they were back, the wall was completed.

"Now make me a way across the Kyle of Tongue," he commanded them, seeing that indeed they could do a job well.

Moments later they were back, the causeway was finished, and from the island a boat could finish the crossing in two minutes.

What more could Donald Mackay find for the fairies to do? Time and again he invented little tasks to keep them busy, but in minutes they were back clamouring for more. He was not accustomed to this sort of behaviour and became very angry, but it did no good. The authority of a Highland chief meant nothing to them.

At last he shouted in rage and distress, "Away you go, and make me a chain of sand that will stretch from one side of the Kyle to the other. And don't let me see you until it is finished!"

Off they went. The minutes passed. On tenterhooks he waited: but this time they did not return. Donald Mackay, chief of the Clan Mackay, Lord of the Reay country, poured himself a huge glass of whisky and slumped into an armchair.

113

The fairies never came back. Every time the tide crept in their chain of sand was washed away. And in later years when Lord Reay wanted big jobs doing on his land he would call for the working fairies, but they never returned.

And now, when you hear the sough of the wind across the empty sands, mingling with it you may hear the sigh of fairy voices, for they know that their work can never be finished.

THE DEVIL'S BRIBE

Sir Donald Mackay of Tongue had returned from his studies on the continent without a shadow. The Devil had stolen it from him at the end of a seminar on the black arts: he had been lucky to escape with his life.* From that time onwards he pursued the study very deeply, and in the library, laboratory and quiet chambers of his house in Tongue, became a great master.

News of this came to the ears of the Devil, for people were even saying that Sir Donald's powers were now greater than his own. He remembered the man and was furious, for he was very proud of his skills and reputation, and the idea that a mere mortal could be considered a rival was outrageous. So he challenged Sir Donald to a fight.

For the whole of a long summer's day the battle raged. The mountains smoked, the Kyle of Tongue boiled dry, green and red serpents came hissing from the empty air. It was a terrible spectacle: the women hid themselves and fainted, the men stood by and cheered.

First one had the advantage, and then the other, but at last the Devil, who was doing rather well at the time and seemed about to win, grew over-confident, made a bad mistake, and was soundly beaten. He was absolutely appalled and pleaded with Sir Donald and the men gathered nearby to tell nobody about it. For himself, Sir Donald thought it was rather good, but the Devil was so upset and made such a lot of tempting offers, that at last he agreed to take his shadow back, and a band of fairy slaves to work for him, and tell no-one.

He soon found out, however, that the fairy slaves were a mixed blessing. All the big jobs he wanted doing were completed within two or three days, and it was no good giving them small jobs to do because they were finished almost as soon as they were started. Soon he grew rather frightened of the fairies because they became very angry if they had no work to do. He could not settle to work himself for his mind was perpetually occupied with thinking up jobs for the fairy slaves. Heartily he wished that he had never agreed to take them.

In despair he told the villagers to give the fairies work to do, but in no time at all they had run out of ideas as well.

What could they do? They was no peace. Like midges on a peat bank they would whirr in while people were at their meals, or asleep in the middle of the night, and start poking and pinching and screaming in their ears until they were so tormented that they just had to find them a job for a minute's peace. And it was no good trying to lock them out for they would simply break the window and come streaming in again.

At long last an old woman had the idea of giving the fairies a job

*'... the first Lord Reay, also known as Donald, the Wizard of Reay, had a narrow escape from the Devil. Lord Reay, like many another 17th century nobleman, was a well-travelled man; he had served in the Swedish army, and while visiting Italy met the Devil, who invited him to study the Black Art. At the end of the term it was the Devil's practice to claim the last pupil out of the door as his own. Donald got left behind, but as the Devil pounced he pointed at his shadow and shouted 'De'il tak' the hindmost'. Satan grabbed the shadow and Donald was free to return to Sutherland, where it was soon noticed that he never cast a shadow, even in the brightest sunlight.' — *Folklore, Myths and Legends of Britain.*

that was impossible, and the whole village racked its brains trying to think of something good. The first few impossible tasks they did in the twinkling of an eye, but then a young fellow set them to work to make a rope of sand that would stretch from one side of the Kyle to the other.

Away they went, with a zip, like a flock of humming birds or a swarm of bees. The people waited. A minute crawled by, and then another, and another. Hardly daring to breathe they looked at each other. Still they did not come. The fairies were beaten! A long, ragged cheer spread up the hillsides and from cottage to cottage along the edge of the Kyle.

The whole village was exhausted and retired to bed. For twenty four hours there was no sound on the summer air but the cry of birds, the lap of water on the shore, and gentle snoring from a hundred curtained windows.

Donald, Chief of Mackay, had been fighting on the continent. On the way home he made the acquaintance of a lady, fell in love, and remained with her for a long time. Perhaps she had bewitched him, but nevertheless, at last he remembered his clan and his home, and managed to persuade her that he really did have to return to Scotland.

It was a sad parting. She accompanied him to the port, and to the quay, hanging on to his arm. He embraced her one last time and prepared to climb the gangway, but she held him back for a moment and summoned a servant who had accompanied them on the journey. The servant carried a box which she took with difficulty, for it was heavy, and handed to Donald. It was a box of black wood, studded with brass nails and secured with a bright padlock.

"Take this," she said. "It is a present from me."

He thanked her, and tucked it under his arm.

"It is not right for a man such as you to look after himself," she said.

"But you know I have servants," he said. "I am a chieftain."

"I know," she said, and her eyes filled with tears. "But it is all I have to give you. Take it." She placed a hand on his arm. "But remember; whatever happens, you must not open it until you are safe in your own house."

He nodded. "I promise," he said.

An hour later the beautiful sailing ship moved away from the jetty. She waved until it was a dot on the horizon.

Donald travelled up the west coast, through the Irish Sea and the Western Islands.

He disembarked at Loch Inchard, which was as far as the ship went before turning west to Stornoway, and prepared to walk along the coast and over the hills to Tongue.

It was a long walk, but the sun shone and the days were warm. As he passed through the little villages he was a fine figure with his eagle's plume and plaid and kilt and broadsword. Sometimes he carried the studded box beneath his arm and sometimes he carried it on his shoulder. The less precious belongings were being taken around by boat.

At last he crested the long moorland ridge beyond Loch Hope and saw the Kyle of Tongue lying before him. An hour later he was bathing his feet in the cold salt water. A little old lady who had known him since he was a boy came out of her cottage and gave him a bundle of bread and cheese tied up in a cloth. Just across the water he could see the village of Tongue, with his own Tongue House lying at the neck of the peninsula. Although it was only a mile away he had to walk ten around the head of the Kyle.

An hour later he was climbing along the side of a little hill at the water's edge. He felt hungry, so he put down the box, threw himself in the soft heather, and opened the bundle of bread and cheese.

As he lay there munching and listening to the cry of the curlew and song of the skylark, his eyes kept coming back to the black box beside him. There were only a few miles to go. Surely he was close enough now.

He felt in his sporran for the little silver key and undid the padlock. Then he began to lift the lid. But before it was two inches open it was thrust violently from his fingers, and a hundred fairies sprang out into the sunshine.

"Obair! Obair!" (Work! Work!) they shouted. "Obair! Obair!"

He was startled and astonished. They flew around his head with a great fluttering of wings, and some jumped up and down on the ground.

"Obair! Obair!"

Donald's mouth was a little dry with the bread and cheese.

"Here," he cried. "Fetch me a drink of water."

Like a flock of swallows they sailed to the shore, then up to a sparkling burn that bubbled down the hillside. A moment later they were back, each with a spotless sea-shell brimming with bright water. Donald opened his mouth and they poured them on to his tongue.

He was delighted, and took another bite of bread and cheese.

"Obair! Obair!" they shouted.

Donald looked around. "Yes," he cried. "Pull all the heather out of this cnocan (little hill)."

In a few minutes the shore was thick with heather tufts and the hill stripped bare to the moss and grass. (To this day no heather grows on that hill and it is known as Aon Streapan — 'one twig of heather'.)

Now Donald lay back and set the fairies to do various little tasks, enchanted with his present.

An hour passed.

At length, men being rather contrary creatures, he wondered what they would do if he set them a task that was impossible. He racked his brain to think of something to fox them.

118

The next time they came back he said:

"Now, are you listening? I want to see if you can make me a long siaman out of that sand." ('Siaman' was the home-made rope of roots and long grasses they used to tie down the thatch on houses and barns.)

The tide was out and away they went over the flat sands. But every time the fairies tried to twist it together the sand crumbled in their fingers. Their cries of dismay filled the summer air. They flew further away to see if the sand was better over there; but it was just the same. Hither and thither they flew, becoming more and more distressed; then further and further away.

Donald called them back, said it didn't matter; but either they could not hear him or took no notice. At length they were tiny, tiny dots, way up towards the island, and then he could see them no more.

For an hour he waited, calling, and calling again. He thought of the unhappy woman who had given him the box because it was all she had to show her love, and roundly cursed himself for his stupidity.

The sea filled the deep channels: fingers of water slowly felt their way on to the sandbanks. Donald Mackay locked the empty brass-studded box, picked it up, and settled the plaid on his shoulder. Then, with one last searching look across the Kyle, he set his face towards Kinloch and, as the sun sloped down towards the west, walked the last six miles into Tongue.

The Little Girl Dressed in Red

I. Early one summer morning a man from Bettyhill was making his way over to Skerray to catch the morning tide for the salmon fishing. It was a long way round by Torrisdale sands, even if he had forded the river, so he was taking the normal short cut over Naver Rock.

He had climbed the steep track beside the stream and sand ridge, passed the broch, and was somewhere near the Sandy Loch on top of the hill when he heard a cry that sounded just like a child. He stopped and looked around, but there was nothing to be seen. Thinking it must have been a seagull he went on walking. But again he heard the cry, and this time spotted what looked like a red bundle at the foot of a rock. When he went closer he saw that it was a child, a little girl dressed in red. His first thought was that she must have wandered away from some tinkers who were camping nearby. She was sobbing her heart out and he was very close to her before she spotted him. When she did she stopped crying instantly. He bent to pick the child up or speak to her, but as he did so she began to put on terrible expressions, twisting her face up and hissing at him. He got a fright and jumped back. When he looked down again, there was nothing there.

II. A shepherd, who lived in a cottage on the slopes of Ben Loyal, had discovered that some of his flock were missing. The weather, unusually for the time of year, was misty. Thinking it might clear, however, he pulled on his boots, called the dogs, and set off for the hill.

Though he searched for a long time, all he could find was a lamb, very weak and apparently deserted by its mother. He picked it up, and walked on. The mist, far from clearing, grew thicker. There was no chance of finding his animals in such conditions, so he turned his feet for home. He was descending a long hillside towards a track when he heard a whimpering noise coming from behind a rock. It sounded like a puppy. When he went across, however, he found a baby wrapped in a scarlet shawl, its face red with the cold. His dogs slunk off down the hill and refused to come back. There was some-

120

thing unnatural about it and the shepherd became frightened. Laying the lamb in a sheltered cranny, he ran off down the hill to a cottage a mile away. Friends lived there, and when he told them what had happened they returned with him to see the mysterious child. They found the lamb huddled to the rock, and a small flattened place in the grass and heather where the child had lain, but of the baby in the scarlet shawl there was no sign.

The Ringstone

The Ringstone is a solitary boulder, a massive chunk of rock thirty feet high, coloured pink and white and black. It stands on Torrisdale dunes, a little above the beach. The setting is spectacular; more than a mile of white sands, islands beyond the bay, two salmon rivers, rocky headlands, and a wilderness of dunes rising to a summit of hills.

This is the most popular story of how the Ringstone got its name.

Many years ago there were two giants, the Naver giant, from the river at Bettyhill, and the Aird giant, from the hill above Skerray. Normally they got on quite well, but one afternoon they became involved in a heated argument about some sheep and cattle, and both grew very angry. The Aird giant was standing on top of the hill above Torrisdale Bay with the animals grazing around him, and the Naver giant stormed across the river to the beach below.

"Those are my sheep," he roared up the hill.

"No they're not," the Aird giant said. "At least not all of them."

"You stole them. You're a thief!"

"No I didn't. They came up here themselves. Anyway, you owe me fifty sheep from last year."

"You're not only a thief, you're a liar!" shouted the Naver giant. "If you don't send them down this minute, I'll come up and see to it myself."

At this the Aird giant gave a disparaging laugh and made a rude face, and picking up a great boulder flung it down the hill at his friend.

The Naver giant was speechless with fury, and picking the stone up himself, hurled it back up the hillside, making a great hole in the ground.

The Aird giant saw things had gone far enough.

"I'll send them back if you give me that silver ring you're always wearing," he said.

"Never!" roared his friend, his face all red and angry.

"Suit yourself, then," said the Aird giant, and picking the stone up again he tossed it back down the hill.

For long enough the rock kept flying between them, and in time the giant from Naver grew tired, because he was throwing it uphill all the time.

"Will you give me the ring now?" said the Aird giant.

For answer the Naver giant tried one more time to throw the stone up the hill, but it only got halfway, and rolled back down to the shore.

"Come on," said the giant from Aird, for he wanted to be friends again. "Give me the ring, and I'll let you have it back later."

"No!" said the Naver giant from the bottom of the hill. "I'll never give it to you!" His eyes began to fill with tears.

"Oh, come on; please!" coaxed the Aird giant. "Just for a week."

"Never, never, never!" shouted the giant from Naver, and pulling the ring from his finger he threw it on the ground and jammed the great boulder down on top of it.

Then he sat down on top of the stone and stared out to sea. Every so often he sniffed, and his friend, looking down at his broad back, saw him lift the back of a hand to his eyes.

They never made friends again, and a long time later they both died.

The ring is still buried under the stone, and so far nobody has ever been able to shift it.

The Piper Who Loved Horses

One fine September morning, when the mist was lying in the valley above the river and the air drifting autumn-chill across the red bracken, three young gentlemen, accompanied by a servant, set off into the hills for a couple of days' deer stalking. The servant, a fine young man named Nicholas MacCoinnich, who had served for some years as a piper in the Sutherland Highlanders, led a string of horses. They were loaded with blankets and cooking utensils, for the stalkers planned to pass the night at a bothy far into the hills. When they returned the following day some of the horses would be used to carry the carcases of the deer. Nicholas was very fond of the animals, and as they mounted the hillside in the early morning one of them nuzzled at his shoulder and he patted it on the neck.

The day passed pleasantly, and as the sun moved into the west they dropped down a long shoulder of the moors to the shores of a loch where, near the remains of an old hut circle, stood the solid, stone-built bothy. The young gentlemen threw themselves down on rolls of blankets while Nicholas unloaded the horses and built a fire in the wide hearth. Then, while they passed around the first jug of whisky, Nicholas busied himself with the preparation of a meal.

They ate well and fully, and as the young gentlemen lolled back, replete and half dazed with the combined effect of the whisky, food, fresh air, exercise and heat, Nicholas pulled a set of bagpipes from his roll of blankets and stepping outside, placed them to his lips. He played wonderfully, pacing to and fro on the grass outside the door of the bothy. The light faded and it began to grow cold. Swathes of mist gathered above the loch.

"Hey, Piper!" called one of the young gentlemen. "Play us a jig. Play us a tune you can dance to. Bring the pipes in here. I want to dance!"

Nicholas retreated inside the house and placed the pipes to his lips once more. The merry notes filled the room, tumbling out of the little windows on to the hillside.

"Ah!" cried the young gentleman. "If only there were some lassies here. I want to dance!"

No sooner had he spoken than there was a sound of voices outside and the door opened. Framed in the doorway stood a voluptuous girl, clad in a long, loose-fitting garment that flowed to the floor. Her hair fell over her breast, her black eyes looked boldly at the young men. Behind her stood two other girls, peering over her shoulders.

They entered. The dog's hackles rose: growling and snarling it skirted the young women's feet.

"You want to dance?" cried the first girl. "Piper, play us a reel. And tie up that dog."

Reaching to her head she plucked out a single hair. Instantly it turned into a length of coarse black rope. She flung it to Nicholas. Instinctively he caught hold of it, burning hot in his hand. Already appalled, his eyes widened further. Passing the fire to capture the dog he deliberately stumbled and let the rope fall into the fire. In a flare of red sparks it was gone.

The young gentlemen rose and approached the three girls. They seemed prepared to ignore the air of witchcraft that hung about them. Soon they were chatting eagerly, laughing and jesting. Uneasily Nicholas settled the pipes on his shoulders.

At the first notes the eyes of the dark girl flashed, and catching hold of the young gentleman to whom she had been talking she broke into a headlong, galloping reel. The others followed suit. Like dervishes the six of them danced. Nicholas played and played. The kilts flew high, the girls' dresses swirled to their knees. Looking down Nicholas saw that instead of feet like normal girls, they had hoofs on them, dark shining hoofs that tore the earth floor of the bothy as they whirled and spun. Clearly they were creatures of the Devil. For a moment his piping faltered, then he set to and played as he had never played in his life.

Soon the young gentlemen were exhausted, and tried to retire to rest on their blankets, but the girls would not let them go. Nicholas felt that he must escape from the evil place. As he played on he began edging towards the door. Soon he was standing right beneath the broad stone lintel. He watched and waited. Seizing a moment when the three couples were whirling on the floor he suddenly ceased playing, plucked the sgian dubh (black knife) from his belt and plunged it into the door post. They would never pass cold steel. Then flinging wide the door he sprang out into the night, pulled it shut behind him with a bang, and the next moment was racing away across the moonlit hillside as fast as his legs would carry him.

125

There was a moment's silence, then a hubbub of raised voices and yelping and the smashing of window glass.

Nicholas reached the pasture where his beloved horses were grazing. He called and they came cantering towards him. They seemed restless. He seized the mane of one, a fine, piebald stallion, and prepared to spring on to its back. But suddenly the animal turned from him, rearing in the air and slashing at something invisible with its great hoofs. A second horse, a black mare, did the same. The five horses gathered around Nicholas. He gazed through the circle of their swirling tails and tossing manes. Again the piebald stallion reared back, striking out at the empty air. There was a sharp cry of pain. Nicholas fell on to his knees and crossed himself in fear.

All through the dark hours the horses stayed with him, every now and then whinneying and biting with their long teeth, pressing together to protect him from the invisible attackers. At length the first streaks of a rosy dawn showed in the east. As the light grew the horses fell quiet. Then one lowered its head and took a mouthful of grass. Another turned sideways and looked at Nicholas and walked a few paces off. The air, which had seemed so charged and thundery, was sweet and fresh.

126

Springing on to the piebald's back Nicholas rode as fast as he could to the nearest village, which was many miles off, and told them what had happened. A dozen men returned with him, bearing amulets and charms and bibles to ward off the evil.

As they crossed the pasture they saw the circle of horse-trampled earth where Nicholas had passed the night. In a broad band around it the grass was dead and withered. Apprehensively they approached the door of the bothy. They saw the signs of their occupation the evening before; the rolls of blanket against the walls, the remains of the meal, the flask of whisky, the last wreaths of smoke curling from the fire. They saw too the signs of Nicholas's flight and a struggle; the bagpipes dropped on the floor, the sgian dubh stuck deeply into the door post, the broken window and tufts of dog hair strewn about the floor. Of the three young gentlemen there was no sign. They were never seen again.

The dog, with half of the hair plucked from its body, and still terrified, came slinking into the village three days later.

127

J

The Boar's Scratch

Ben Loyal is called the Queen of Scottish Mountains. If you stand and look for a while you will notice a streak of light coloured rock running down the dark northern face. It is called the boar's scratch. The name is accounted for by the following legend.

Long ago, in the mists of time, a wild boar of incredible size was roaming the countryside of the north causing great destruction. Farms were wrecked, crops ravaged, dogs, cattle and even people carried off and devoured. At length a Fingalian warrior, hearing of the people's terror and distress, came north from Ireland to rid the countryside of the monster.

For days he followed the trail of destruction. Finally, following deep prints in the heather and peat moss, he ran the boar to earth on

128

the slopes of Ben Loyal. There followed a terrible battle, the warrior driving the beast uphill before him to the very summit of the mounttain. At length he had it cornered, its back to the great northern crags. The boar lunged at him with its poisonous tusks, slashed with its razor-sharp hoofs. He took the blows on his great shield, then suddenly, as the monster withdrew for another onslaught, he sprang forward beneath its tusks and drove his sword deep into its heart. The great boar fell to the earth, dying. The warrior watched as it kicked and threshed in its death throes, then rolling backwards vanished over the rim of the precipice.

As it fell the boar's tusks were so sharp and strong that they gouged a great white scar down the face of the mountain.

At length it came to rest, and the people who had assembled below the mountain to watch the fight, gathered around. The warrior was cheered as he strode down the mountainside, his shield torn and buckled, his sword reeking red. When he came up to the dead boar the people warned him to keep clear, that it was still poisonous. He ignored them and sprang on to the monster's flank, the victor. Then he measured it from tail to head with his bare feet. The soles of his feet were scratched by the boar's poisonous bristles. They burned. Within an hour he was fainting. Before nightfall he was dead. Side by side the great boar and the Fingalian warrior lay in the heather at the foot of Ben Loyal.*

*'The Fianna (foot-soldier knights of Fionn — Finn mac Cool) fought several battles with headless giants and magical beasts. When Fionn's wife, Grainne, ran off with the handsome Diarmid, Fionn, having caught them, revenged himself by ordering the youth to hunt down a magical boar and measure it by pacing the length of its spine. A bristle pierced Diarmid's heel, and fatally poisoned him.' *Folklore, Myths and Legends of Britain.*

The Old Woman and the Hind

Late one evening a man was walking home over the hills. He had a long way to go and clearly was not going to reach his house that night, so he looked about for a place to sleep. There was a patch of woodland in the glen below him and soon he had dropped down

into the shelter of the trees. A few minutes later he came to the edge of a clearing. Summery boughs hung low and the bracken was thick. The night was so fine that he was glad to make his bed out of doors. He pulled himself a mattress of dry bracken and lay back, looking up through the leaves at the stars.

It was early when he woke. Sitting up to stretch, he discovered that he was not alone. A little way off in the trees an old woman was standing beside a beautiful hind, stroking its flank. Then she crouched down and began to milk it into a small pail. The man sank low into

130

the bracken and watched. When she was finished she straightened up: but as she stood a twist of blue wool with something glittering in it fell from her pocket to the ground, and before she could pick it up the hind had lowered its beautiful head and eaten it. The old woman was very angry and shouted at the beast in Gaelic that that day it would be shot by Lord Reay as a punishment.

When she had gone the man rose very slowly to his feet. The hind started when it saw him, and in a few leaps had vanished among the trees. He continued his journey, wondering very much.

A few days afterwards he could contain his curiosity no longer and sent his son on horseback to enquire of Lord Reay's keeper whether, in fact, his lordship had killed a hind on that day. The boy was back within a few hours with his answer. Lord Reay had indeed shot a hind, and when the animal was disembowelled a twist of blue wool with a strange silver medallion attached to it was found in its stomach.

The Seal Maid

It was five o'clock on a fine summer's morning and a young fisherman, who had risen early, was repairing his nets on Torrisdale sands. His boat was drawn up beside him and he was waiting until the morning tide should flood sufficiently to float her. Looking up for a moment, while he refilled the wooden netting needle, he was surprised to see six fine seals drag themselves from the waves not a hundred yards away. He wished he had his gun with him, for a fat seal would provide him with enough meat for a month and oil for his lamps. For a minute or two the seals stood, uncertainly, just above the wash of the sea, looking this way and that. They did not see him sitting motionless beside his boat. Satisfied, at length, that the sands were deserted, they set their heads up the beach and began to lollop towards an outcrop of rock close by where the young fisherman was working. Soon they were behind it and hidden from his sight. He dropped the piece of net he was working upon and very quietly crept up behind the rock. Cautiously he raised his head and peered over a narrow barnacled shelf.

The seals were waddling about, brushing their necks together. They seemed very playful. Then, to his astonishment, one after the other each seal put a flipper to its head and pulled off a sleek black cap. (This was the 'ceanna-bhreacan', the magical head-tartan of the seal people.) Instantly the seal turned into a young man or a girl. They were handsome people, slim and dark, with lovely olive skin. Luckily they were concerned with themselves, chattering and stretching their limbs, for suddenly the young fisherman realised that in his surprise he had come right out of hiding. Hardly daring to breathe he crouched back and settled himself to watch for a long time.

He could not take his eyes off one girl. She was beautiful beyond anything he had ever imagined, and he fell completely in love with her. He was enchanted, and then his heart was sore. She was a seal maid; any moment she would take up her ceanna-bhreacan, turn back into a seal, and vanish into the sea. He would never see her again. What could he do?

Running about the beach the seal people drew away from the

rocks. Seizing his opportunity the young fisherman very quietly and secretly slipped down through the boulders, picked up the girl's cap, and scrambled back with it to his hiding place. He was unseen. Carefully he drew the cap through his hands, examining the beautiful misty patterning and delicate fabric. Then he folded it, tucked it away inside his shirt, and once more settled himself to watch.

In a while the young seal people returned to the rock and took up their ceanna-bhreacans. They were laughing, their black eyes shining, the black hair still damp on their heads. They threw their hair back and one after the other pulled on the dark, gossamer caps. Instantly they turned back into seals. The handsome young man with the girl was the last to do so. But she was still searching. She could not find her cap anywhere. Four of the seals gambolled back to the edge of the sea, but the fine fat seal that had been the girl's companion stayed at her side. She searched everywhere, but the cap had just gone. At length she sat down on the rock and started to cry.

The young fisherman crept away again, and keeping the boat between himself and the seals made his way to the foot of the dunes. Then he stood up and began singing, walking forward as if he had just arrived on the beach. As soon as they saw him the four seals turned and vanished among the breaking waves, and a moment later the fine big seal waddled out from behind the rock and followed after them. For long seconds it hovered at the edge of the sea, looking back towards the girl, then it turned and as a big wave creamed in, arrowed forward and was gone.

When the girl saw the young fisherman she was frightened and tried to run away, but he ran after her and caught her. He told her that he knew she was a seal maid, and said he would help her to search for the cap. They searched for an hour, until the village beyond the river was beginning to stir. Then he offered to look after the girl, to take her to his home on the bank of the river, and care for her until her ceanna-bhreacan turned up again, as it surely would. She agreed, there was nothing else she could do. But the cap was never found, for as soon as he returned home the young man wrapped it in tissue paper and oilskin and hid it in a corner of the barn.

The days and the weeks drew by, and in time the seal maid married the young fisherman. He adored her and did everything he could to make her happy. He did not know how she pined and longed to return to the sea, for every day he was away at his nets, and when he returned in the evening she greeted him with a smile and fond embrace. The years passed by and they had four lovely, olive-skinned children.

But the girl's seal mate never forgot her and never deserted her. On the first tide every morning he came to the river in front of the house, and when the water slid back there was always a silver salmon or a bearded cod or half a dozen sweet haddock lying there among the dark weed. She would not go hungry.

One spring morning brought everything to an end. The young fisherman had gone away in his boat and as usual left his wife to look after the house and children and do little jobs about the croft. She decided to tidy out the barn, and was in the midst of pulling out some old hay from the back as bedding for the cattle when something black in the corner caught her eye. She picked it up, and even before she untied the string knew what it was, and her heart beat faster. A moment later her ceanna-bhreacan, stolen and hidden away, was in her hand. The tears ran down her face, for her husband as much as for herself, for she knew how he loved her, and that she and the children were the only things that mattered in the world to him. But now she would be able to return to her people. She looked down at the cap in her hand. For seven years it had been hidden away and now it was withered and dry. Leaving the barn as it was she ran into the house to see that the children were safe and would be in no danger until her husband returned. Five minutes later she was standing at the edge of the river and leaning forward to dip her cap in the cool water. In a moment it was soft and beautiful again. Never caring who might see she tossed back her black hair and pulled the cap over the crown of her head. Instantly she changed back into a seal. With hardly a ripple she slid into the river and vanished.

Later that morning, at high tide, two seals were to be seen gambolling in deep water at the mouth of the river, leaping and splashing, diving and twining round and round one another in tight circles. Then they turned and raced away through the broken water at the bar and disappeared among the waves of Torrisdale Bay.

When the young husband came home he could not find her anywhere. The house was neat and clean, her keys hanging on a nail beside the baby's cradle. He ran to the barn and rummaged in the hay. When he saw the empty piece of oilskin and tissue paper he knew that he would never see her again. He stooped and took the piece of oilskin in his hand. Slowly he walked away, then turned against the stone wall of the barn, buried his head in an arm, and wept.

The seal maid never returned, and five years later the fisherman married again, this time a pretty, brown-haired girl from the village. Though she could never take the place of the seal maid in his affections, he was good to her and she loved him. The seal maid's merry children were soon joined by four brothers and sisters, as fair as they were dark. They were a high-spirited, happy family, and the fisherman and his wife lived together contentedly until the end of their days.

The story is well known, and the following postscript is taken from Alexander Mackay's excellent book *Sketches of Sutherland*, published in 1889, in which he relates a slightly different version of the same Skerray tale. The appearance of the seal people has changed.

The seal never again visited the river, but 'Sliochd-an-Roin', the offspring of the marriage related, were well known for generations in that part of the Reay country. They were a fat, short, dumpy race, and said to have large-sized hands. The epithet Sliochd-an-Roin was invariably applied to them, especially when differences arose, and hard words were bandied, frequently causing serious quarrels, fights and bloodshed. It was one of these quarrels that led to the composing of a song often sung in my boyhood, one stanza of which ran thus:

> Tha sliochd-an-roin cho bagaireach
> 'S nach fuiling iad a chlaistinn,
> Gu'm be Siol nan daoine foghainteach
> A ghabhadh air a maischinn.*

*The verse does not translate easily, but the gist of it is something as follows:
The children of the seal people are wild!
They can't bear to be told who they are.
If they were the children of brave *men*
They would be better looking.

GHOSTS AND SUCH

Old Tom Macleod

It was a dark and stormy night, the rain poured down and a strong wind blew from the east. Old Tom Macleod was making his way home with the mails in his rackety coach.

He was sixty-five years old, and after forty years as the Melness postman was planning to retire in about a month. Six days a week he made the trip around the Kyle to Tongue with the mail and any little messages that people wanted picking up. It was twelve miles. When he made the journey without any breaks, which was rarely, it took him about two hours.

On the night of the storm he was late and his wife, at their little cottage above the shore, was worried about him. Her daughter reassured her that on such a night he would certainly have stayed in Tongue with his sister, and would drive over with the mails in the morning.

But the old man was tough. Steadily he jogged on round the Kyle with the rain beating in his face.

At length, with about four miles to go, he came to a stone bridge crossing a burn, but this night, with all the rain, the burn had become a raging river. A torrent of white water poured down the hillside. Old Tom had been in the bar at Tongue before he left, waiting for the rain to ease and having a whisky to keep the cold out. He did not slow for the bridge, and when one of the horses shied he flicked its flank with the whip and drove it on. In the darkness and rain he did not see the water lapping the road, he did not see the foaming river bearing against the sides of the bridge. Already it had loosened some of the stones, and one parapet had fallen away.

The horses were half way across when the bridge collapsed. Tom was thrown into the water, hit his head on the rocks, and drowned. One horse broke its neck as it fell and the other, dragged under by the dead horse and coach, drowned as well.

The next day some men who were passing saw that the bridge had collapsed. The water had gone down a lot and they could see the

coach and dead horses tangled up at the side of the gully. They found old Tom lying on the bank a little further down.

And now, when the nights are dark and stormy, people claim that they have seen the ghost of the old man, driving his rackety coach down that stretch of road towards the old bridge. The road he took for forty years a man, his ghost has taken for a hundred.

Ghosts from the Sea

THE MAN FROM MELVICH BAY

Bighouse* stands below Melvich on the tidal shore of the River Halladale. It is a dark Highland manor with massive stone walls, gravelled courtyard and a walled garden. The river sweeps round three sides, and a few hundred yards further on debouches into Melvich Bay. Salmon are netted at the mouth of the river, and the boxes are stored in a stone outbuilding at the manor.

Some years ago a man used to live in this box shed at Bighouse, clearing a space among the salmon boxes for a table and chair, and laying his mattress and blankets on the ground. One night, however, a ghost came to haunt him, and he left in a hurry.

The reason for the haunting is quite simple. Going down to the shore one morning he found, lying among the weed and corks washed up by the tide, the drowned body of a man. When the salmon fishers came down later that morning, he told them about it, and they all went to look at the body. None of them knew who the man was. The fishermen thought they should take him up and give him a decent burial in the churchyard, but the man from Bighouse persuaded them that it was easier just to leave the body on the shore

*See 'The Green Lady'.

and let the tide take it out to sea again. So they pulled the dead man down the beach and spread some weed on top of him. When they returned in the evening, he was gone; the sea had washed him away into the depths of Melvich Bay.

In the middle of the night the man from Bighouse woke up and broke out in a sweat. Hands were groping at the window and then at the door of the shed. He lit a lamp, plucked up his courage, and opened the door. There stood the figure of the drowned man, blocking the entrance and looking straight in at him. He backed away, and threw a fishing float at him, but it missed and rattled away in the darkness outside.

For maybe a minute the drowned man stood there, the water running from his clothes, then he turned away and with never a footfall, was gone. The man from Bighouse slammed the door and turned the key in the lock. When he looked down at the flagstones where the man had been standing, they were perfectly dry.

The following morning he left Bighouse and never returned.

Over two hundred years ago in the days of sail there was a great
storm in the north, and a little trading vessel was swept on to the
rocks at Baligill, between Strathy and Portskerra. The entire crew

141

lost their lives and with one exception none of the bodies was ever recovered.

The exception was the body of the captain. Some men down on the shore came upon his corpse one morning. Looking through the pockets they found a great sum of money, or what was a great sum to them, and they pocketed it. Being a bit afraid that if they reported the body the theft might be discovered, they hid it among some rocks and that night carried it up to the moors and buried it in the peat.

From that time on the place was haunted. The ghost of the captain appeared in full uniform with brightly shining buttons, and a halo of silvery light shimmering round about it.

Many years later three men cutting peats at the spot uncovered the skeleton of a man with the remnants of a sea captain's uniform still adhering to it. It was given Christian burial in the graveyard and the ghost of the sea captain was never seen again.

The Dark Stranger

One clear January night two sisters from a house at Baligill, between Strathy and Melvich, went for a walk in the snow. It was freezing hard and there was a full moon that lit up the white moors

for miles around. When they were nearly home again the girls were surprised to see a tall young man leaning against the garden wall of their house. He seemed dark, in the moonlight, and very good looking, and was wearing black evening dress with a tail coat. For a while they stood there, looking at each other, then the older sister spoke to him. "Can I help you?" she said. Still he did not speak, just stood there with a little smile at the corners of his mouth. Then suddenly he winked, smiled broadly, and ran away down the road, turning somersaults in the snow. In a minute he was over a gate and disappearing down a long slope into the valley below. They watched as he grew smaller and smaller and finally vanished from sight behind

143

K

a fold of the hill. Then the two girls went into the cottage, half alarmed and half laughing, and told their grandfather about him. The old man went back out with them, but when they reached the spot where the attractive young man had been standing, there was nothing to see but two little goat-like hoofprints in the snow.

A GAME OF CARDS

One Sunday night, in winter, a knock came to the door of a rough bothy in Skerray where some men were playing cards for money.

One of them picked up a lantern and went to answer it. A dark, neatly dressed stranger stood outside in the falling snow.

"What do you want?" he asked.

"They said I might get a game of cards here," the stranger replied. "Can I join you?"

The Skerray man looked him over.

"Certainly," he said. "Come in."

After they had been playing for a while and passing the whisky around, one of the men accidently dropped some cards on the floor. When he bent to pick them up he saw that the stranger had neat black hoofs on him instead of feet. He looked up, startled, but there was no stranger there. He had vanished.

A few days later this man was found dead in the snow, with deep cloven-hoof marks all around him.

The dark stranger, of course, had been the Devil, drawn to the house by the whisky and the cards on a Sabbath.

144

Drumholliston

Drumholliston, although a hill, is more like a moor. It lies at the eastern march of north Sutherland, a bleak moor and low escarpment that descends from the rolling hills of Sutherland to the flat lands of Caithness. It is crossed by a desolate stretch of road four or five miles in length. To the west lies Melvich, and to the east Reay and Thurso. There are a number of stories concerning this road, some of which doubtless spring from the days when men from the north coast villages went away for months at a time to the herring fishing at Wick. On their return, with their pockets full of money and often enough a celebration drink in their stomachs, they were easy prey for robbers who waited for them behind the peat banks and rough knolls nearby. Drumholliston gained such a reputation for this that the fishermen took to coming home in groups for safety. Since the road was both desolate and much used — for it was the main road of the north — it naturally gathered its share of strange tales.

THREE GHOSTS

Many years ago, when provisions and mail were taken out to all the villages by horse and cart, a roughly dressed man on horseback would appear like a highwayman somewhere along Drumholliston and force them to stop. A few moments later he would vanish, only to reappear at intervals all along the road until they reached the Halladale Bridge. He never crossed the river. Particularly he seemed to like the crisp wintry nights. People said it was the ghost of a highwayman who had been executed a long time before and come back to haunt the road where he had robbed and found excitement during his life. Others claimed it was the ghost of a man who had been desperately looking for help and met with sudden death before he could find it.

One late evening a fisherman, who had been drinking, was making his way home over Drumholliston. Suddenly he had the feeling that there was someone behind him. He turned quickly to catch the person

unawares and found a thin, long-haired man clinging to his back. He could not feel him at all. The fisherman took to his heels and arrived home in Portskerra cold sober. Although he continued working on the fishing boats out of Thurso, he never liked to walk along that road by himself from then onwards. ... We do not know whether he cut down on the whisky.

The Chain Boat Bridge crosses the River Halladale just before Melvich. A number of years ago, if you were downstream from the bridge on a bright moonlight night, you could see what looked like a group of men carrying a coffin across it. Some people said it was just the pattern of girders, but others claimed that you could see them moving. One bright night, however, a man walking down the road towards the bridge saw a dark group of men coming towards him

from the opposite side. He was on the bridge first but they came on too, and when they met near the middle walked straight through him as if he was not there. Rigid with fright he turned and watched them go, and as they drew towards the further end they just thinned out and vanished.

THE SPLIT STONE

The Split Stone stands beside the Drumholliston road about a mile and a half from Melvich. At one time it marked the old county boundary. It is a huge stone split right through the middle as neatly as if someone had done it with an axe. It was, in fact, split by the Devil, and seems to have been a haunt of his, as the following stories show.

One dark evening a woman from Melvich was coming over the moors at Drumholliston. She had been to the store at Reay and was carrying a basket of shopping. Suddenly she had the feeling that she was being followed, and although the basket was heavy she began to run. The thing behind her ran as well. When she reached the big

stone, which was whole then, she was puffed, and turned to look. It was the Devil, half in the shape of an animal. She ran round the stone to the far side. For a minute they stared at each other over the top. Then he began to chase her. She screamed. Round and round the stone they went, first one way and then the other. She was so terrified that he could not catch her, and she kept on throwing things at him out of the basket. Eventually, really angry, he cut straight through the stone to get at her. There was a huge puff of smoke and a piercing shriek. When the Devil could see again the woman was tearing away down the road and too far off for him to catch her.

One stormy night about two hundred years ago a man was returning to Melvich from a sheep sale in Strath Halladale. There was thunder and lightning in the sky. Suddenly there was a great flash and bang beside him that split a huge boulder in half. He got a fright, but went over to look. While he was examining it he heard laughter, and looking up saw the Devil sitting on top of the rock, laughing his head off. Then the Devil jumped down and told the man

to give him a lift on his back. Terrified the fellow crouched down and spread his arms. The Devil sprang up and wound his arms around the man's neck and his legs around his waist. "Run!" he cried. "Run! Run!" The man ran as fast as he could, and the Devil kicked him in

149

the ribs like a horse. At length he could run no further and the Devil jumped down. "Now climb on my back," he cried. The man climbed up and clasped his arms around the shaggy neck. The Devil took his legs under his arms and raced off at a terrific speed. Just before they reached the first house in Melvich the Devil told him to get down. He was to tell nobody what had happened. The man swore he would tell no-one until his dying day.

But many years afterwards, when some friends were in his house for a ceilidh, he told them all about it, and they had a good laugh. Later that same evening there was a knock at the door. He went to answer it. His friends heard a cry and a crash, then laughter and the sound of racing footsteps. They rushed into the hall. The man lay dead on the carpet. There was not a mark on him. They could see no-one outside.

One Sabbath morning Donald, the First Lord Reay, who was also known as the Wizard of Reay*, was making his solitary way eastwards from Tongue. It was a fine morning and he made good progress. As he passed through the villages on his magnificent black stallion the people were on their way to church. Many averted their eyes as he passed, and crossed themselves. Donald laughed and spurred his horse to a splendid canter.

At about eleven o'clock he was ready for a rest in the warm sunshine. Seeing that he was passing the Split Stone he sprang to the ground, turning his horse loose to graze, and took his bread, meat and flask of wine to a patch of soft heather nearby. It was very pleasant, but in a while he began to feel the need of some company and music. He called, and made some passes in the air. With an emerald flash and a whiff of sulphur Satan appeared on top of the Split Stone with a wonderful set of bagpipes under his arm. He waved a friendly hand to Donald and set the pipes to his lips. His wild bacchanalian music filled the Sabbath air; and then he played laments so sweet and seductive that Donald felt the blood flow sensuously within him. The sun was warm on his face, and for a while he slept. When he woke up Satan had gone. Donald stretched luxuriously, called to his horse, sprang on to its back and rode on his way — well fed, well rested, and royally entertained.

*See 'The Devil's Bribe'.

150

The Green Lady

We have not met any people whose claim to have seen the Green Lady of Bighouse we could take seriously, but she is undoubtedly the most recognised presence along the north coast.

Bighouse* is a huge manor built on a small eminence near the mouth of the River Halladale. The river, broad and silver, makes a grand curving sweep around three sides. In the summer, when the walled gardens are in bloom, and the sands and moors sunlit, the building may be most attractive; but in the winter it is gloomy, and exactly the place where you might expect to encounter a ghost, if your mind is that way inclined. The big windows are black and bare, like mirrors reflecting the last traces of daylight; and the heavy dark walls, sliding waters of the river, the distant noise of the sea and soft moan of wind in the chimneys, all contribute to make the trespassing stranger feel uneasy.

The house belongs to a wealthy English family who stay there during the summer, but for the greater part of the year it remains empty. A gardener tends to the immaculate lawns and wintry flower-beds, and a caretaker looks after the house.

The Green Lady, however, stays there all the time. People say she is the spirit of a lady who lived in the house more than a century ago and one night hanged herself in her bedroom. Her hands and face are said to be as white as snow, and she wears a gown of pale green silk. Although her presence is strongest in the room where she died, if you are there in the darkness you may see her green shadow gliding from room to room, drifting through the walls as though they are not there.

Unfortunately the people who told us the story had no idea why she so tragically took her own life. The pupils of Bettyhill School were not short of romantic suggestions. She was a lonely, middle-aged spinster in love with a young fisherman who finally turned and laughed at her: she was mad, driven from her senses by the cruelty of those around her: she was a young governess who had been seduced by the master of the house and was expecting his child: she

*See 'The Man from Melvich Bay'.

151

was a beautiful lady whose hair turned white overnight as she sat with the corpse of her only child, a handsome, spirited boy of seventeen, who had been drowned in the river. We can choose her story to suit ourselves. Perhaps, as often enough, it is more interesting to guess than to know.

Whoever she was, though, for more than a hundred years, through spring, summer, autumn and winter, the ghostly figure of the Green Lady is said to have wandered through this Highland mansion.

The White Horseman

The hillside was deserted except for one man. He stood on a little stone bridge staring up the road in front of him. His face was grey with fear. Suddenly he squeezed to one side against the parapet. The white horseman galloped right past him. A moment later the noise of hoofbeats had faded into silence. It was a death; a sure sign! He turned and made his way home along the edge of the Kyle. The next day his brother Hughie was swept from the deck of the fishing boat he worked on, and drowned.

The story of the ghostly horseman, Donald Gordon, begins with the battle of Bannockburn. In the heat of the fray one flag bearer after another was struck down: the proud pennant lay trampled beneath the horses' feet. The army retreated. Donald Gordon rushed forward, snatched up the banner and held it high. The Scots surged back: the English fled.

Full of victory, Robert Bruce sent for the brave Donald Gordon, but he could not be found. Someone said he had seen him fall, mortally wounded. So Bruce sent a brooch north to Angus Gordon, Donald's brother, in memory of his bravery.

Angus was very proud of it and wore the brooch all the time. After a while, though, he began to get jealous. Here he was always boasting his brother's bravery: he must cut a bit of a poor figure himself! So he began to say that it was he, Angus Gordon, who had been in the battle, and Donald was forgotten.

But Donald was not dead. He had been seriously wounded, and left behind as the army advanced. The care of a good Scotswoman restored him to health. For a long time he stayed with her, looking after her croft, but at last he wanted to go home again.

When he arrived in the village he soon found out about the brooch and the lies his brother had been telling. He was terribly angry and threw his brother out of the house. Angus was too ashamed to ask for help and had nowhere to go. For days he sheltered in a wood a few miles away, but the weather was severe and he took ill. At length he returned to his brother's house to ask his forgiveness. Two days later he died.

153

Donald never forgave himself for turning his brother out. To try to make amends he made it his personal duty to help anyone in need and was soon well known as the best of neighbours and a good Samaritan indeed. He rode a white horse and was a handsome figure on the roads of the north, welcome in every house.

One wintry day while he was out in a boat fishing he fell overboard and was nearly drowned. The hours he spent clinging to his upturned boat in the cold water weakened him and he fell ill. He asked no help, but nursed himself at home. The snow beat around the windows of his cottage. He grew worse and pneumonia set in. A neighbour, having missed him for several days, called at the house and was shocked at his condition. He sent for the doctor, and the doctor sent for the priest. When he realised that he was dying Donald asked the priest to pray for him, since he feared that his soul would never find rest. He died during the night, and two days later was buried beside his brother.

But despite the prayers of the priest he never found the peace he desired. And now, six hundred years later, the ghost of Donald, upon a white horse, can still be seen riding about the countryside on his errands of mercy. From the far side of the grave he rides out to warn people when a death is about to take place.

154

STRANGE OCCURRENCES

The Death Trays

This happened in Portskerra.

It was evening, a lovely moonlit evening in spring. The children were in bed and the family were sitting around the peat fire in the kitchen. There were four of them; a husband and wife, and her aging parents who lived with them. The women were knitting and they were all chatting, all except the old man who was reading a book in his easy chair to one side of the fire.

Suddenly they heard a little tinny rattling, and stopped talking to listen. All was quiet. Thinking it must have been the wind they ignored it and carried on with the conversation. Then they heard it again, only this time loudly, an imperious metallic rattle in the front room. Apprehensively the younger man picked up an oil lamp and went through to see what it was.

The room looked the same as it always did. Nothing had fallen, nothing was out of place. Puzzled, he gazed around. There seemed nothing that could have caused the noise except two silver trays on the polished table by the window, and clearly they had not since they were still neatly propped up against the middle of the window sill. He assumed that a draught from the window must have blown them, and they had slipped a fraction; but then he realised that there was no wind, it was a dead calm outside.

He looked back through the living room door and told his wife that he had no idea what it was. Not satisfied, she laid aside her knitting and went to have a look for herself. But she found nothing either. When she gave the trays a rattle they made exactly the same noise as they had all heard. It was eerie, but there was nothing to be done about it. In a while they went to bed.

The next morning the young wife was up first. She made some tea and took a cup up to her mother and father. She shook the old man gently to wake him, but he would not wake up. He was dead.

On the day of the funeral they had some trouble getting the coffin out of the door because of the position of the furniture, and so had to take it through to the other room and slide it through the window. This took the body of the dead man only inches above the two silver trays. The coffin was heavy, and a corner caught the edge of the trays so that they rattled loudly, but did not fall.

And later that day, when people came back to the house after the funeral, the two trays were used to serve them with food and drink.

A Ball of Light

One winter's night, when the snow was thick on the ground and a brilliant moon shining in the sky, a man set out to walk home to Melvich from a friend's house in Strathy. He could see for miles around but then, in the space of a few minutes, a heavy bank of clouds drifted over the moon and it began to snow. The landscape

vanished, the visible world shrank to a vague circle two or three feet round about him. In those days the road was no more than a broad track across the moor and soon he was far off it and stumbling forward into the snowy hills. It was frightening and dangerous to be lost in the hills, particularly on a night like that, with no possibility of shelter. For more than an hour he trudged on, falling into peat banks, wrenching his ankles on hidden boulders. The snow was deep and as he grew tired he began to panic. Then suddenly a strange ball of light appeared in front of him, hanging in the air about four feet

157

from the ground and lighting up the snowflakes that swirled past it. He stared at it a bit scared, then went forward to look closer, but as he walked towards it the light moved away in front of him. They were superstitious times and people told stories of such apparitions. Feeling very nervous, he walked after it. For nearly an hour the light moved on in front of him. Then suddenly it vanished, just was not there any more. In the darkness and the snow, which was as thick as ever, the man had no idea where he was; even less than when he first saw the light. He was hopelessly lost. Then he saw a wall not ten feet away from him, and a barrel shrouded in snow, and realised that he was standing right at the end of his own house.

Alec and his Father

Mr. and Mrs. Innes were a middle aged couple who lived in Naver. He ran a very successful croft, his wife was cheerful and homely, they had excellent neighbours. By all rights they should have been content; but they were not. They had no children although they both wanted a son or daughter very much. Mr. Innes, particularly, wanted a son, and his wife was very unhappy that she was unable to give him one.

At length they had to accept that Mrs. Innes would never have any children, and after a lot of discussion decided to adopt a boy. They named him Alec and brought him up in every respect as their own son. They were a happy family.

When he was twenty-two Alec married a girl from Strathy. Now he needed a croft of his own and had to leave home. The Ineses were sad to see him go, for they were getting on in years by this time. It was only twelve miles, however, and he came through from his new home in Strathy as often as he could. They were pleased to see him so happy.

One evening in November, two years after he was married, Alec was sitting over the fire day-dreaming. His wife, who was expecting her second child, had gone to bed early. Suddenly he started violently and stared hard into the peat fire. Shapes stirred in the glowing cinders.

He sprang to his feet. "My father!" he shouted upstairs to his wife. "I must go!"

Stopping only to seize a coat and hat he strode out to the barn and saddled the horse. Then, a lantern swinging from his hand, he rode off into the rain.

When he reached his old home in Naver the door was not locked. He went through into the living room and found his mother sitting at the fire.

"Alec!" she exclaimed. "I thought it was your father."

"Where is he?" Alec said.

His mother looked at him anxiously. His face was distressed, his clothes sodden. "Are you alright, Alec? Come on, boy, sit down and get a warm."

159

L

"Never mind that," he said impatiently. "My father, where is he?"

"He was in Skerray with the bull," she said. "I'm expecting him back any minute."

Alec ran out of the house and pulled himself on to the horse's wet back. Steadily he rode down the track his father would be taking across the sands. The lantern, swinging from his hand, threw dizzy patches of light on the ground.

At the edge of Torrisdale Beach, high above the murmuring sea, he found what he had dreaded and expected. Lying on the hard wet sand was the body of his father. Alec picked the old man up, and holding him in the saddle before him, rode slowly home.

Lights in the Dark

One winter's night Mr. Duncan of Scullomie felt he could do with a breath of fresh air. The wind was rising and it was cold so he put on a warm coat and muffler and was soon stepping out briskly along the road. The moon would not be up for a while but the sky was starlit and he could see the way well enough. In a few minutes he was going down the track that leads to the harbour.

As he walked along the track above the shore he heard a rattle of pebbles down at the water's edge, and a jingle of chains as though a boat was being pulled up. He shone his torch all around but there was nothing to be seen.

He walked along the harbour wall and in a little while climbed back up the track to the road. He paused at the top, panting a little, and looked back over the bay towards the islands. As he stood there he saw the light of a torch coming up the track towards him. He waited as it drew closer. There was no sound of a footfall, and when the light was only a few feet away from him it glimmered, faded, and was gone. Even in the darkness he could see that there was no-one there.

Although at the time Mr. Duncan did not know it, that same evening an old man had died on Island Roan.

During the night the wind rose still more and by the time daylight came the sea was getting rough. Despite this, however, they managed to ferry a coffin across to the island from Skerray. But the next day, when the body should have been carried back to the mainland for burial, it blew a full gale and the sea was too high for boats to venture out. By late the following afternoon, however, it had calmed, and the islanders were able to load the coffin on to a boat and set off. But when they got to Skerray, where the island boats normally landed, they found that the sea was still too high for them to venture through the channel. The only other place they could land the coffin was at Scullomie, in the mouth of the Kyle of Tongue, two miles around the rocky coast.

When they arrived it was almost dark. Mr. Duncan had gone down with some other men to help with the unloading. The open boat

161

pulled in towards the shore. A man in seaboots caught the prow, then the islanders jumped out and they all gathered along the gunwales. As they pulled the boat up the beach Mr. Duncan heard the jingling of some chains in the bows and the rattle of pebbles under their feet.

It took a little while to get everything properly arranged, and by the time they were ready to climb the track total darkness had fallen. Six men hoisted the coffin to their shoulders and preceded by a man with a lantern, carried it up the track to the road. A car was waiting, and as they reached it the man with the lantern blew it out and helped them to lower the coffin and slide it in the back.

The noises, the light, were exactly as Mr. Duncan had heard and seen them two nights earlier.

THE LIGHT AT SEA

One evening as a lady from Armadale was walking home from a friend's house she saw an unusual light out at sea. It twinkled brightly, like a star, and as she continued down the road it floated in towards the shore and vanished beneath the cliffs. Then she thought she must surely have just imagined that it was out at sea, because it was coming up the road towards her. Fifty yards short of her own house the light turned off the road up a neighbour's path and vanished inside the barn. She had never seen anything like it and was quite frightened. A few moments later the twinkling light reappeared, went back down the path and floated up the road towards her own house. She watched it turn in the front gate, waver along the side of the barn, and disappear through the door. This time it did not come out again.

162

When she got home she told her husband and he took a lantern out to have a look in the barn, but there was no sign of anything unusual. The following day she asked the neighbours. They had seen nothing.

Some weeks later, however, a seine net boat sank close in-shore and bodies were washed up on the rocks. Two came in at Armadale and men from the village brought them over to the shore by boat because all the rocks have high cliffs behind them. They laid the drowned fisherman on two rolled-up sails and carried them up the road to the neighbour's barn to wait for transport. It was a dirty place, however, and not very suitable, so they took them on to the lady's own barn and laid them in the clean hay. As they went through the door she realised that the dead men had followed exactly in the track of the strange light she had seen a little while before.

THE WHITE FLASH

One Saturday night there was a dance at the village hall in Melness. Down the road, not very far away, an old lady lay on her death bed.

A little before midnight the dance came to an end. Laughing and jostling, two young fellows called goodnight to their friends and set off walking home in the darkness. They were passing the old lady's house when one of them saw a bright white flash at the window. He caught his friend by the arm.

"Did you see that?" he said.

"What?" his friend asked.

"That flash."

"Oh, come on!"

But when he got home the young man told his mother about it.
"It's a bad sign, that," she said.

And the next day when he was on his way to church he heard that the old lady had died in the night, a few minutes before midnight; just at the time he saw the flash.

THE LADDER ON THE SHED

A long hillside runs down from the thousand foot summit of the Watch Hill to the winding Kyle of Tongue. It is covered with heather and rocks and whins. A dark wood, probably the most northerly on the British mainland, reaches to the shore. Far down the hillside, at the edge of the wood, stand the four cottages and old school that make up Rhitongue.

One winter's teatime Mrs. Mackay left her husband and son by the fire and went out to the byre to milk the cow. It was very dark. When she was on her way back with the bucket of milk in her hand, she was amazed and frightened to see the stone wall of an outbuilding bathed in strange light. Her husband kept a ladder there, hanging from two nails, and a white light glimmered around it like St. Elmo's fire. Quickly she hurried inside and told her husband and son to go and look, but when they got there the light was gone.

Two days later a big storm broke and a boat was wrecked in Tongue Bay. Policemen and volunteers searched the shore for bodies and one was found washed up the Kyle and caught in a deep cleft of rock below Rhitongue. Although a man managed to climb down and they had ropes, they were having trouble in getting the body up until someone suggested a ladder. Mr. Mackay's ladder was taken from the wall of his shed and used to bring the dead sailor up from the rocks.

Mrs. Mackay was perfectly convinced that the light she had seen was an omen of death.

CANDLE ON THE NAVER

It is well known that the Vikings sent their dead leaders out to sea in blazing long-boats, funeral pyres that released their souls and bodies into the Great Ocean. A symbolic custom, representing a similar idea, was practised in Strathnaver in days gone by. At a death a flame, usually a candle, was placed in a small, roughly carved boat,

and set adrift on the current of the river, drifting down towards the
sea. Later, boys enjoying the spectacle would set candles in jam jars
on pieces of wood and float them away in the darkness. Sometimes
they did this as a prank, and people seeing the light would think that
there had been a death. When there was not, it was said instead that a
death was soon to follow. Superstitious, of course; but today it is
claimed that lights definitely *have* been seen — on the River Naver
preceding a death and on Loch Naver preceding a drowning.

The following story is told of a water-bailiff: Returning home one
night after a tour of the likely spots for poachers, he saw a white
light down at the river, which passed out of sight behind a knoll.
Drawing a small club from his pocket to tackle the poachers he crept
up, then rushed out from his cover calling on them to stay where they
were. The riverside was silent and deserted; but slowly a light came
drifting down the river, softly shining. In the light that it cast he
could see the ripples of the water beneath it. There was no raft, no
boat. Rather scared he watched it descend to a short rapids. Smoothly
it flowed down the tumbled water, passed out of sight for a moment
behind the bank, then reappeared, and drifted away down the valley.

165

Headlights at the Athan Dearg

Just after the Scullomie turning the main road from Tongue to Borgie Bridge makes a long, curving sweep over the moors around Loch Buidhe (the yellow loch). Then it drops in a little twisting turn over a burn and climbs again to the crest of the moors. Just before the crossing a side road forks left and runs away parallel to the stream and just above the edge of the flat, boggy valley towards Skerray. Most of these roads are single track with passing places, and the region around the intersection is known locally as the Athan Dearg (the little red ford).*

Quite a lot of people driving around here at night have seen lights

*This name is interesting, because 'dearg' is a much brighter red than the rusty red of 'ruadh' which is commonly given to lochs and burns and crags. It may come, as usual, from the peat in the shallow water, but possibly on some occasion, as for example the Viking retreat to Fiscary, there was a battle and the water ran red.

that cannot be explained: it still happens today. They see the lights of a car coming towards them and as usual draw into a passing place and dip their headlights, waiting for it to pass. The lights of the other car come on towards them — and then just vanish, as if the car has gone into a dip, or taken a turning, or switched off its headlights. When at length they continue there is no car at all, no other turning, nowhere that a car could have gone.

The lights are not seen in the same place or from the same place, not even on the same road or in the same direction, so they can not possibly be a trick of the eyes or a freak reflection. They are a complete mystery.

One could name a number of people who have seen them: a Church of Scotland minister, who went back the following day to examine the road for himself; a visitor who, of course, knew nothing about the lights; a gentleman from Tongue who is on the roads a lot and has seen them several times.

The Phantom Cortege

Dusk was falling. Dark reflections lay mirrored in the silent lochs and the hills stood clustered together. James Mackay leaned on the gate of his old cottage in Melness and filled his lungs with the fresh sea air. Slowly the light faded from the sky and the colour drained into dark pools above the western horizon. Often he stood there enjoying the peace at the end of the day, but what happened that night stayed in his mind for the rest of his life.

In the dusk, far down the road, small lights were swaying to and fro. Slowly they drew towards him until, at length, he could discern men carrying lanterns. The body of a dead man rested on their shoulders. He recognised them as men from the village, but strangely none of them spoke, in fact there was not so much as a whisper of sound from the whole procession. In the light of a lantern dangling from one man's hand he recognised, to his horror, that he was himself one of the bearers. The cortege proceeded along the road.

In a few minutes it came to the next house. The lady who lived there watched it pass. A minute later it had disappeared around the bend towards Peter Campbell's house.

James went along to see his neighbour. She was as alarmed and bewildered as he was. The old folk had told tales of this sort of thing, but neither of them had ever expected to see it themselves. What could it mean? Surely no-one was going to die. She poured two good nips of whisky to steady their nerves.

That same morning Peter Campbell had left Heilam on the shores of Loch Eribol to walk home across the hills. He never arrived. His family was not expecting him and so it was several days before he was missed. A search party went out to look for him. Mist was lying in pockets on the hills but at length they found him, sprawled out among the heather. He was dead.

They picked the body up and carried it down into Melness. As they went along the road towards Peter's house, James Mackay made a terrifying discovery. The procession was exactly the same in every detail as that he had witnessed a few nights previously. He himself was walking in the same position with Peter's arm over his shoulder.

They passed his cottage and walked on up the road. The only difference was that now there was the noise of boots on the gravel and the sound of men's subdued voices.

The Dog with Red Eyes

A long time ago an old man who had the gift of second sight lived alone in a little house at Clasheddy in Skerray. His nephew, a young man named George Macdonald, lived in a cottage close beside him.

One night as George was walking home from the lobster fishing, taking the short cut across the side of the hill, he heard the clink and rattle of chains coming up behind him. When he looked round he was terrified to see a dog with big red eyes, chains around its neck and fire in its mouth. He ran off up the hill with the dog right behind him. When he came to a little burn he jumped straight across and kept on running, but when the dog reached the burn it vanished. As soon as George realised he was being followed no more he very bravely retraced his steps and found the chains lying on the bank of the stream. He did not like to touch them and went on home. Later he returned with a lantern to have a better look, but they had gone.

The following night as he was walking home he saw a stag drawing a light cart along the road in front of him. He ran to catch it up but the stag trotted on ahead, always keeping just twenty or thirty yards away. When it came to the burn that ran down the hillside, stag and cart disappeared right in front of his eyes.

After his evening meal he went into his uncle's house and told him what he had seen. The old man was not surprised. He told him that the next night a ball of fire would come rolling down the long hillside. It would strike a great boulder on the bank of the same stream, and vanish with a flash. After that there would be no more apparitions.

Sure enough, the following evening George saw the wonderful sight, and when he went in to tell his uncle about it he found the old man lying dead on the floor.

OCCASIONAL TALES

The Carrying Party

Snow lay deeply on the ground. Tiny on the open hillside the party of men trudged up the long slope above Loch Hope. In the middle six men sweated under the weight of the coffin.

"By heaven, he's some weight," grunted one of them.

"I'll be glad when we get to Moine House, I tell you," panted a second, slipping and hanging on to the brass handle for support. "I can do with a dram."

"Here, you lot," called another. "It's your turn again."

An hour later they stopped outside the lonely cottage at the crest of the hill and lowered the coffin into the snow against the railings. As they did so an old woman appeared in the doorway. She gave a fangy grin and waved them towards the gate.

"Come on, boys. Come on in and rest your backs."

Willingly they followed her through to the sitting room. It was plainly furnished — a long deal table set around with lots of wooden chairs — for the house was well known as the local shebeen. Within a couple of minutes they were seated around, smacking their lips and gasping as the fiery spirit scorched the backs of their throats.

An hour later they were all happy. One man was singing, another was telling terrible stories about the dead man outside, a third had his arm about the waist of the old crone's daughter.

A while later a few of them rose.

"Well, boys," said one of them, "we'd best be getting along."

"Ach, he's in no hurry," said a little bald man, who was an elder of the kirk, still sitting at the table. "Sit yourself down again."

The man who had first spoken staggered a little and put out an arm for support.

"No, no. We'll be getting along. It's a few miles yet into Melness."

"Aye, well. You go on ahead and we'll catch you up in a few minutes."

Tucking a few small bottles into their coat and inside pockets, the men went out into the cold afternoon. Half an hour later, laughing and slow-footed, the remainder followed them.

171

The sky above Ben Hope was turning pink with the evening. Soon the first splinters of stars appeared high overhead. It promised to be a blindingly cold night.

By the time the second group arrived at the dead man's house in Melness it had been dark for an hour. Stamping the snow from their feet they followed his sister through into the living room. It was already half full with the first members of the carrying party. They were eating scones and pancakes and drinking hot cups of tea. There was no sign of the bottles of whisky, though some of their eyes were very heavy. The dead man's sister reached into the dresser for cups and plates and went through to the kitchen for more scones and tea. When they had all been served she stood back beside the fire and looked at the new arrivals expectantly. They looked from one to the other, puzzled at her meaning.

"Where have you put him?" she asked at length, her eyes anxious.

They stopped chewing: the teacups froze, halfway to their lips. One group looked at the other.

"Why he's ... "

"Didn't you ... ?"

Far away, on top of the hill, a fox paused, sniffing daintily at the strange box lying against the railings of the shebeen. With a twitch of its brush it lifted a leg against one corner, then trotted away around the end of the house. The coffin lay, forgotten in the snow, beneath the gaze of the half moon.

Manu Forti

The crest of the Clan Mackay is officially defined as 'A right hand holding up a dagger, paleways, proper'. The motto is 'Manu Forti'— With a Strong Hand. Before it was Latinised by the College of Heralds in 1628, for the First Lord Reay, it was in the Gaelic: 'Bi Tren'—Be Valiant. Both mottoes, in the tradition of Highland

history and clan warfare, and with regard to the reputation of the Clan Mackay as being among the finest warriors of them all, are challenging and apt.

A legend, however, apocryphal in the Highlands, has attached itself to the crest. It tells of two chieftains, one a Mackay, who were rowing to the shore at Reay. The time was a little before dawn. Massed warriors watched their progress from the beach, for it was a race. The first to place his hand upon the sand should claim as much land as he could walk over between sunrise and sunset.

173

Neck and neck they rowed, arms straining, backs knotting. As they drew close to the shore they were tiring, the sweat stood out on their foreheads. The Chief of Mackay found his challenger inching ahead. Then they were among the breakers. The other chieftain was establishing a definite lead. In desperation the Chief of Mackay tossed aside the oars and pulled the dirk from his belt. Laying his wrist across the thwart he severed the hand from his arm with a few strong slashes of the sharp blade. Standing then, he flung it ahead of the leading boat. Even as the other chieftain shipped his oars and sprang over the side into the shallow water, the severed hand flew ahead of him and landed on the clean sand. The Chief of Mackay was the victor. Nearly fainting, he wrapped his plaid around the bloody stump of his arm and paddled the last few yards to the shore. The Highland warriors surged forward, flinging their bonnets into the air and raising a loud cheer of salutation.

The morning sun was just tipping the edge of the sea as the chieftain set out on his long walk. By the time it had set at the end of the long summer day he had travelled the length of the north coast as far as Durness, being permitted to take the ferry across the Kyle of Tongue and Loch Eriboll. That land became the Land of Reay, the proud inheritance of the Clan Mackay.

Emily Macintosh and the Tinker *

Miss Macintosh was seventy. Neatly dressed in a tweed coat and green felt hat, with a flame-coloured silk scarf about her throat, she made her way home on Sunday evening. It was cool for June and there was a wind from the bay. As she approached her cottage she saw the hayfield beyond the garden. The long grass would need cutting soon. She smiled, thinking of her dear friend Sam Blacklock, the tinker, and his family, who would soon be up again. They would cut it for her, as they had for the past . . . forty years. Could it be so long? Forty years? She shook her head wonderingly. As clearly as if it had been yesterday she recalled the events of their first meeting.

It was a Sunday afternoon in August. At half past three, as always, she was walking up the road to her brother's, where she always took Sunday tea. Already, at thirty, she was known in the village as Miss Macintosh, an acknowledged spinster. She was small, with grey eyes and pretty brown hair; painfully shy. No-one but her few close friends ever called her Emily.

As she drew towards the village shop she saw, with some disapproval, three men come lurching down the road towards her. They were drunk. Their arms were around each other's shoulders and they were singing snatches of song, talking loudly and laughing. They were not men she knew, and from their appearance and dress were tinkers, north for the summer. As they drew level with Miss Macintosh one, a tall, thin fellow with a scarlet handkerchief flying from his waist, pulled apart from his comrades and made a deep bow, doffing his cap. "Goo — good afternoon," he said solemnly. Miss Macintosh averted her eyes and walked on. Drunk, in the middle of Sunday afternoon; it was shocking.

Two days later, as she was dusting in her little cottage, there was a knock at the front door. She went to answer it, and through the lace

*Alone of the stories in the book this tale is not traditional. It is a composite tale, uniting the following traditional elements: the lady who was known as 'the tinkers' friend'; the mysterious and prophetic dream voice heard at the edge of the sea; 'the Giants' Bed'; the tinkers in the north.

M

that covered the glass saw the tall, dark-haired tinker standing on the doorstep. She paused, a little nervously, then pulled herself together and went to open the door.

"Good morning, Ma'am," said the man. Clearly he did not remember her. "Do you have any jobs that need doing; any pots to mend, knives to sharpen, walls that need re-building? Any odd jobs about the place?"

She shook her head, wishing him gone. "No, I don't think so," she said dismissingly. "Not just now, thank you." She began to close the door.

"Thank you, Ma'am," the tinker said, removing his cap. "Perhaps another time."

"Yes, perhaps," she said; "another time," and stepped back into the hall. As she shut the door her heart was fluttering.

Only when he had gone was she able to think, did she remember all the jobs that needed doing, that she was unable to do herself. The dry stone walls were falling in a couple of places, the barn roof leaked, and most of all the hay wanted scything. Of course she could always ask the neighbour's boy, or her brother, but she hated asking favours; and if she asked a local man, whom she knew, it was so awkward paying him. She thought again of the tall tinker. Although he had been drunk, and there was a wild look about him, he seemed a decent enough fellow. She determined to ask him if he would cut the hay. She had little money, the other jobs would have to wait.

It took more than a little courage to approach him, particularly as he was not alone, but it was soon done. The following Monday morning she had her breakfast early, and was ready for him when he arrived a little before eight o'clock. She took him out to the barn, where her father's scythe hung on the wall, red with rust. He looked around, from the mildewed rack of tools above the old work bench to the stars of daylight winking through the roof. She followed his eyes, painfully aware how things were going to pieces without the hands of a man about the place. The tinker looked down at her for a moment, then reached for the scythe and picked up a blackening whet-stone from the edge of the work bench.

He worked steadily. The scythe hissed through the sweet grass, laying even swathes in his wake. The air became fragrant. The horse Miss Macintosh kept for her little trap watched him over the paddock fence. He went across and stroked its neck, breathing into its nostrils, making friends.

Miss Macintosh worked in her sheltered, high-walled garden, weeding between the delphiniums and hollyhocks as tall as herself, removing the dead blooms from the roses, lifting a border of daffodil bulbs, tying bunches of lavender for her linen chest and wardrobe. When she had done enough she picked a large bunch of sweet peas and carried it into the kitchen.

From the window she watched the tinker work. Suddenly she remembered the time and looked down at her watch. It was time to make the dinner. She wondered if it would be safe to leave him for a few minutes. The tinkers had such reputations. She decided she would take the chance. Carefully closing the windows and locking the doors she slipped down the front path to the village shop. She would make him a meal; he could have it in the kitchen.

He was very pleased and sat at the table in his waistcoat and shirt sleeves, seeming to Miss Macintosh very big and brown and quite overpowering.

By five o'clock the hayfield was more than half finished. He hung up the scythe and replaced the whet-stone at the side of the work bench. He said that he would be back the following morning.

Relieved to see him gone and that everything had so far gone so well, Miss Macintosh made her tea and prepared to spend the evening crocheting and reading her book. As she sat down she remembered that she had not yet arranged the sweet peas still soaking in the kitchen. She would do them later.

The tinker, Sam Blacklock, went ferretting for his supper, and then he went to the bar. The summer evening was still bright when he returned down the road with his tinker friends. On such fine evenings they slept out of doors, and favoured a sheltered hollow above the rocks, known locally as the Giants' Bed.* There they could make their fires, gather wood from the seashore, spread their stolen sheaves of straw on the earth in peace. There they interfered with no-one, and were left alone.

In the middle of the night Sam Blacklock was woken by a strange, reedy whispering; a voice that rose from the cliffs about him, compounded with the soft roar of the sea, and breathed back from

*The Giants' Bed, traditionally the place where the tall tinkers slept, is situated on a long spur of moor and rock at the mouth of the Cleich Burn behind Portskerra. The cliffs there are both spectacular and dangerous. Just above the Giants' Bed stands a strange, pink, conglomerate stack known locally as 'Cailleach Coirce' (or 'Killy Korky'). From certain points on the cliff this resembles a witch, and she is said to stalk the cliff-tops looking for over-adventurous children, to catch them and stick pins in the backs of their legs.

177

the night sky. Startled he sat up. But the night was silent. He looked at his companions. Dead to the world they slept on. Smoothly he rose to his feet and brushed the straw from his clothes. Something was wrong. In the house where he had been working all day . . . something was wrong. Something had happened to Miss Macintosh.

Leaving his friends sleeping he turned to the track and climbed up the side of the ridge to the cliff top. It was a clear night. He looked up at the stars: it was one o'clock in the morning.

In ten minutes he was walking up the road towards the house. A dog barked in a barn as he passed by; a cat, a grey wraith, fled across the road and vanished over a wall.

When he reached Miss Macintosh's cottage everything was still. The windows were dark, the door closed. Dimly he made out the shapes of the tall flowers in the garden. What was he doing there? Apprehensively he gazed around. Surely it had been a dream. What would she think when he knocked and everything was alright? But yet that voice! Drawing a deep breath he unlatched the gate, walked up the garden path, and knocked firmly on the front door. There was no reply. He waited, then knocked again, loudly, and stepped back, looking from window to window. Still there was no reply. A third time he knocked, and called. The house remained unnervingly silent.

A minute later he stood at the back door. Pulling the sleeve of his jacket over his fist he punched a hole in the glass of the kitchen window and reached through for the catch. Pushing the window up he clambered to the sill and squeezed his long body through into the kitchen. It was very dark. He opened the back door and pushed it wide to let in the starlight, but it made little difference. Reaching into his pocket he pulled out a box of matches and struck one. It flared. Blinking against the bright flame he looked around. Everything seemed perfectly in order. Carefully he felt his way into the hall and living room. He struck another match.

Miss Macintosh lay on the floor perfectly still. Clearly she had fallen, for sweet peas and fragments of china were strewn on the carpet around her, a chair lay toppled on the floor, plates had been swept from the top shelf of the polished dresser. She had struck her head on the sharp edge of the hearth, for it was badly gashed and her temple was bruised and swollen.

Sam Blacklock threw the guttering match into the hearth and struck another one. The lamp had burned dry and he had to go

178

searching for oil. When at last it burned up he set it on the hearth rug to attend to her. She was very cold. He felt for a pulse and at length found it, irregular and weak. Carefully he lifted her in his arms; she was as light as a feather. He carried her through to the

neat bedroom and laid her in the bed, pulling the blankets to her chin. His hands and jacket sleeve looked very dirty against the clean coverlet.

Then he ran out of the back door and climbed over the dry-stone wall into the paddock. He called softly and the horse came to him. Springing on to its back he rode away up the road to fetch the doctor.

Miss Macintosh was taken to the hospital. She was seriously hurt. For days she remained unconscious, and for a time they thought she might die. But although she was so slightly built she was tough, and a week later was on the mend. She asked earnestly about Sam Blacklock, but no-one was able to give her any news.

When she returned home three weeks later he had gone. The tinkers had moved on. A note lay on the kitchen table beside a jar of withered wildflowers. In awkward handwriting it said:

I hoap you are beter
Sam Blacklock.

Her hay had been cut and turned, the stone dykes were repaired, her barn roof no longer let in the daylight.

When he returned the following summer he brought with him his dark young wife and baby daughter. Miss Macintosh invited them into the parlour for tea. When she offered to pay for the work he had done he said nothing, but politely declined. He asked, instead, if he might park his wooden caravan at the far end of her field and graze his horse in the pasture. She was only too pleased they should want to stay.

And from that time on Miss Macintosh and Sam Blacklock's family became the best of friends. She was an aunt to the children and knitted them warm scarves and jumpers during the winter. Through Sam she came to know the other worthy tinkers of the north, and as a friend was never in any danger from their lawless ways. Her hay and peats were always cut, her fences kept in good repair. And as the years went by Miss Macintosh and her tinkers became well-known, spirited and fondly regarded characters of the north.

The Minister's Wife

It is still the practice in the north when someone has died for friends and neighbours to call and view the body.

In Strathy the minister's young wife had died, and it was noticed that, as she lay in her coffin, two lovely rings that she had always worn still remained on her fingers. It was, of course, mentioned in conversation and two ruthless men, who I hope were not friends of the family, heard about it and planned to steal them from the grave.

On the night of the funeral they made their way down to the graveyard armed with shovels. They lifted the flowers from the mound of earth and got busy. Soon the coffin lay bare and one of them set to work with a screwdriver. A few minutes later he passed up the coffin lid to his companion, who propped it against a gravestone. It would make a neat little table. A crumble of earth fell in upon the white shroud.

It was awkward down in the hole trying to pull the rings from her fingers. They were very tight, and no matter how the robber tugged and twisted, he could not get them off.

"Here, use a file," said his comrade. "And for heaven's sake get a move on."

It took ages, for he did not like to catch the flesh and had to keep the light shaded. Time and again they thought they heard someone coming.

The second man was very frightened, and perhaps this was what made him brutal. Unseen by the other he pulled out a big clasp-knife, and jumped down into the grave.

"Here, let me have a go," he said, seizing the woman's arm. "There'll be someone coming in a minute."

A few moments later he had severed the finger, and the rings fell off into his hand. He pushed them into a waistcoat pocket.

It was dreadful work, but his feelings then can have been nothing to what he felt when, even as he looked down, the young woman's corpse stirred, moaned, and struggled up to a sitting position in the coffin.

181

Utterly horrified, the two men dropped everything and ran for their lives.

She had been buried alive.

Now she dragged herself out of the grave and somehow managed to struggle home across the fields.

The minister was in his study when he heard the dull thumping on

the front door. The maid went to answer it. Then there was a cry and a noise. Rising from his desk he went to see.

There stood his wife. She looked ill and white and dirty. Her shroud was all covered with earth and blood, and blood ran from the severed stump of her finger to the floor. As well as they were able they comforted her and put her to bed, then sent for the doctor.

The following morning the sexton, having pocketed the perfectly good file and clasp-knife, filled in her almost empty grave.

The minister's young wife lived for many years after this and, it is said, had five of a family.

The Shoemaker's Revenge

Matthew Mackay was a miser. Not that the old man lacked money, he had plenty, but he hated to part with it. One day, though, to his great chagrin, he looked down at his leaky, patched, curled up, dried out boots, and decided that he really did have to buy another pair. So, after double-checking that he carried no money with him, he walked over to Bettyhill where there was a young shoemaker by the name of Ben Og McSwale.

For ages he searched through the piles of boots, looking for the very cheapest pair that would do. At last he found a pair of strong tackety boots that would last for years and years and only cost eight shillings. He waited while the young shoemaker wrapped them in a good piece of brown paper and tied them with a strong piece of string, then promising to send the money with the post the next week, he tucked them under his arm and walked back to Swordly.

Weeks passed by and Ben Og received no word of payment. He sent a reminder, but there was no reply. He was a poor fellow, with a wife and child to support, and needed the money, so at last he set off for Swordly himself to demand it from the miser. But Matthew Mackay rubbed his hands together in distress and claimed that he had no more than a few pennies in the house.

Ben Og was really angry, and when he got home he told his good friend the postman about it. Now he was a shrewd sort of fellow, with a reputation for practical jokes. Together they worked out a plan.

The following day the postman carried a huge, brown-paper parcel with him. It was registered, part-cash on delivery, ten per cent, which came to just eight shillings; and it was addressed to Matthew Mackay. The old man did not want to part with the money, and pleaded with the postman to let him have it and he would pay him later. The postman refused and the miser became greatly agitated. The thought of getting a four pound parcel for eight shillings was too much to resist. Making sure that he could not be observed, he went to the loose floorboard in his bedroom and took the eight shillings from his hidden hoard beneath. Grudgingly he counted the pennies

into the postman's hand, then snatched the parcel from under his arm and banged the door in his face.

The postman cycled back to Bettyhill and gave the money to his friend the young shoemaker.

Carefully the old miser removed the string and wrappings from the parcel and laid them aside to be stored away. But in a minute a little wrinkling of his nose made his heart beat faster. Feverishly he tore off the remaining sheet of paper and opened the cardboard box inside. Pooh! No accidental and expensive gift lay before him, but two large and crusty pats of cow dung; and a note which read:

Receipt: To one pair of tackety boots,
Eight shillings,
Received with thanks,
B. McSwale.

Uisge Beatha *

THE WHISKY WORM

Hardly anybody makes his own whisky now, but in the old days it was quite common, and there are many stories about it. The spirit they produced was very strong and often tasted terrible, but the real drinkers could put up with it easily enough. The police were always after the moonshiners who made it, partly because it was bad for the health, but more because it was illegal and they were dodging the heavy government duty.

One of the main pieces of apparatus in the distilling process was the whisky worm, a long coil of copper tubing in which the spirit vapours were condensed.

A man from Armadale was well known to be a distiller, and to be good at it, but the police and the excise men were never able to catch him out or prove anything against him. He was always very generous, and most of what he made was either given away to friends, or sold for next to nothing. But then he realised that there was money to be made and he started to sell the whisky in earnest, putting the price quite high; and, of course, somebody reported him.

The next time he was coming home from Caithness with some sacks of barley for malting, the police followed him, and when they got to Armadale went in and searched the house. But the Armadale fellow was one jump ahead of them. While they were still in the hall he nipped into the kitchen, snatched up the whisky worm from the draining board beside the sink, and dropped it into a big jug of milk that was standing on the kitchen table. Though they hunted and hunted they never found it; or any of his other paraphernalia; or the bottles that were hidden behind the byre.

A week later, when the night was stormy and nobody was wandering about, the steam was rising into the long copper worm and falling, drop by distilled drop, into the jug of clear spirit that stood beneath.

*Uisge beatha — the water of life.

185

A hundred years ago in Portskerra a number of men ignored the law and made their own whisky. They grew barley on the crofts, and spread it on their barn floors for malting. Several used a bothy in the hills for the distilling.

It was situated on the Cleite Burn* between Baligill and Portskerra. The steep hills on either side squeeze right in on top of what are now the ruins of the old place. It must have been about the most hidden and closed-in building in Sutherland. To be sure that the distilling was kept secret most men went at night, carrying the malted barley on their backs across the half mile of moor.

One particular night a Portskerra man, who already had a drink in him and probably took another one with him for company, went to the bothy to get some work done. He had just got everything set up and bubbling nicely when there was a knocking and pushing at the door. He thought it must be the excise men and was so terrified that he did not know what to do. At last he opened the door a wee bit and looked out. Two bright shining eyes blinked and stared at him out of the darkness. He got such a shock that he snatched up an old hammer from the table beside the door and flung it towards them. Then he slammed the door shut and bolted it and sat down on the old bench by the stove, trembling like a leaf.

It was a long time before he could pluck up enough courage to have a look. Taking the lamp from the table he opened the door very slowly and peered out. No monster, no excise man lay dead on the doorstep. But there lay a sheep, stretched out cold. It was his own pet lamb that had followed him to the bothy.

BUCKETS OF WHISKY

Around the turn of the century there was, in Strath Halladale, an underground bothy which for many years had been a most successful haunt of the whisky distillers. At length the excise men came to hear about it and planned a surprise raid. Luckily the local men heard them coming, for they were falling about in the heather like a team of bad horses. They were able to make their escape across the moonlit moors easily enough, but were compelled to leave behind them a number of kegs of valuable raw spirit. From behind tussocks

*Cleite Burn: Allt na Cleite — 'The Rocky Burn' or 'The Burn with a Hut'.

of heather they watched the excise men load the kegs on to a little cart and set off with them back up the road towards Melvich.

Usually when they were in those parts the excise men put up at the inn, so the distillers, loathe to lose their whisky, set off across the moors towards Melvich, taking a short cut to try to arrive at the inn before them.

Somehow they made it. Doubled up, wheezing, and pouring with sweat, they stood at the corner of the inn and watched the little cart swing in from the road. In the deceptive moonlight the excise men did not notice their condition, and were only too glad of the offer when two of the distillers volunteered to help carry the kegs to a safe lock-up in the hay loft above the stables.

During the night, while the excise officers were in bed, sleeping off the effects of their celebration at the good haul, the distillers crept into the stables armed with augers, lengths of pipe and buckets. They had taken good note of where the kegs were lying. Now they drilled through the ceiling and into the bottom of the kegs, pushed up the pipes, and drained away their whisky into the buckets. The spirit that spilled out at the edges and trickled through the hole they took too, for though it was mixed with dust, hayseed and shavings, it could easily be filtered and re-distilled. Laughing and chuckling, their sleeves and shoulders wet with the heady spirit, they made away in the moonlight with the precious buckets of whisky.

When the excise men woke in the morning, to their great chagrin they found the holes and the empty kegs. They plugged up the holes in the ceiling, lest they should become laughing stocks, made the empty kegs into a bonfire, and told their superiors that the distillers must have been given prior warning, since they had got clean away.

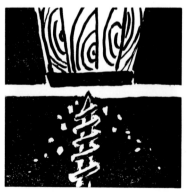

187

Harry Leod *

Harry Leod was lazy, very poor, and a bachelor. Well, those facts could apply to a thousand men, but in addition to all that, Harry Leod was a sheep thief. He lived in a small croft cottage on a tributary of the Strathy Burn, about two miles into the hills above the village. It was a poor sort of a place, roughly furnished, uncleaned, with a few thin animals wandering around outside.

Most of the time he did little, just slept, or called around to see working neighbours, or lounged over a few glasses with his cronies in the local inn. But sometimes, when the night was dark but pleasant enough, he used to take a heavy piece of wood for a club and go prowling around the better crofts in search of a sheep. When he found one that he could creep up on or corner, he would club and kill it, and then carry the carcass home on his back. The next morning there would be a new patch of smoothed-over brown soil on the poor grass of his field where he had buried the head and innards. The carcass itself he hid in a deep hole he had dug in the floor of the barn: it was cool and secret, for he covered the top with a heavy flagstone. For a few days he would live richly, stuffing himself with lamb or mutton, and when the carcass began to go off his half-starved dogs would have a feast in their turn.

Although the other crofters were managing their crofts much better than Harry Leod, and led generally more well-fed and tidy lives, they were little better off financially, and could ill afford to lose one of their best sheep every so often. They certainly noticed that the animals had gone, but no-one suspected this scruffy and idle neighbour. One night, however, a crofter who was on his way home from the river with a couple of salmon in a sack saw someone lurking near a dry-stone wall at the corner of his field. He crept up close and was just in time to see Harry Leod shouldering a dead sheep. He reported him and Harry's croft was searched. They found the carcass in the

*The story of this sheep thief is well known, and he is commonly referred to as 'Harry Leod'. His Christian name, however, may not have been Harry, for some people believe that 'Harry Leod' is a corruption of the Gaelic 'Airidh Leoid', which means 'the Shieling of Leod (Macleod)'.

hole and the buried offal in the field. Then they dug in other places and found more, and more, tell-tale remains.

He was taken to court and, of course, convicted. Sheep stealing was, and indeed still is, a serious crime, and Harry Leod was deported to Australia. He never returned.

To this day you can see the ruins of his house, and the hole in the barn floor where he hid the sheep.

The Resurrection in Clachan Churchyard

Long ago there was a lot of fishing on the north coast of Sutherland. There are piers all the way along, at Melness, Tongue, Scullomie, Skerray, Bettyhill, Farr, Kirtomy, and so on, which are hardly used today. The main centres, however, were always east and and west; Scrabster, Wick, Helmsdale; Ullapool, Kinlochbervie, Lochinver.

At Wick there were usually a lot of 'West Coasters', (men from anywhere west of Thurso), and between these men and the 'Wickers' there was always a lot of trouble. They did not even use the same bars.

A man called John Morrison, from Skerray, was a fisherman at Wick, and he was due a bit of holiday. Just as he was getting ready for the coach, trouble flared up between the two groups and there was a pitched battle, which became known locally as 'The Battle of the Black Stairs'. The battle cry of the West Coasters 'Highland Rifles'* rang out. John Morrison heard it and, shouting the same himself, rushed out of the cabin to join in the fight.

When it was over they had a few drinks to celebrate and then he went back to the boat to get himself dressed for going home.

It is over fifty miles from Wick to Skerray, so the journey by coach took quite a while. They stopped at every inn, and so by the time he was half way there, John Morrison was rather tight and either missed the coach or let it go on. But eventually, somehow, he got to Clachan, near Bettyhill. He was tired and drunk, and for several hours it had been dark as well. Wanting a bed for the night he decided to visit a friend who stayed in Clachan, at the house by the bridge. He thumped on the door and called aloud. There was no reply. Again he knocked. His friend heard the hammering and ignored it, for it was long after midnight and John had obviously been drinking.

When he got no answer John Morrison looked around for any sheltered spot where he might snooze in peace. Everywhere seemed

*'Highland Rifles' — the old regiment battle cry.

rocky and bare save for the Clachan churchyard across the burn. Soon he had crossed the wooden bridge and gone in through the side gate. The grass was sodden with dew. He looked around for a dry spot and his eyes fell upon a raised flag stone. Taking his good jacket off to save it, he rolled it up as a pillow, crawled underneath the ancient, lichen-covered slab, and fell asleep on the crumbling earth of the grave.

When he woke up it was daylight. He crawled out from beneath the gravestone in his white shirt, now hanging out of his trousers, and stood there stretching and wondering where on earth he was.

It was very early, and a young maid from the manse nearby was out shaking the mats. She saw the white figure crawl slowly out of the grave and rushed back screaming into the house:"An aiseirigh! An aiseirigh!* The dead are rising from their graves!"

John Morrison was startled, his brain still very fuddled with drink and sleep, and began roaring, "Highland Rifles! Highland Rifles!" But then, as it obviously wasn't a battle, he looked around him and for the first time saw that he was in the graveyard.

"Well," he said. "It's a poor show for Bettyhill if *I'm* the only one rising up at the Day of Judgement."

*An aiseirigh — the resurrection.

192

The Cobbler's Ghost

At eleven o'clock on Sunday morning Angus Donald walked into the kitchen and dropped his wife's shoes on the end of the table.

"Och, you're not doing that today, are you?" she said.

"Well, you wanted them repaired, didn't you?" he answered. "You've been on at me long enough."

"Aye, but not on the Sabbath," she said. "Do them tomorrow night."

"Better the day, better the deed," he replied, pulling a last and hammer from the bottom of the cupboard.

"I wish you wouldn't," she said, drying her hands on the hem of her apron, and looking anxious.

"Hush now, and put out my Sunday shirt," he said.

Ten minutes later he had trimmed and glued a new sole on the damaged shoe. Pop . . . pop . . . pop . . . his hammer went on the new leather, tracing a line of tiny nails around the welt.

"That's it, then," he said, dropping the tools back in the bottom of the cupboard, and taking the cup of tea she handed him. "Did you get a new packet of pan drops? He preaches an awful long sermon sometimes."

At half past eleven that night Angus was wakened by his wife poking him in the back.

"Angus . . . Angus! Wake up!" she hissed. "Wake up!!"

"Shut up," he mumbled.

"Wake up!" she insisted. "Listen!"

And then he heard it too. A soft tapping noise downstairs. In an instant he was wide awake.

"What is it?" he said.

"I'll tell you what it is," she said. "It's you with your repairing shoes on the Sabbath. You've brought old Joppie back to haunt us."

"Don't be stupid," he said. "He's been dead ten years now."

"Maybe," she whispered. "But isn't that just the noise he was always making with his tap — tap — tapping?"

"Aye. But more likely it's hoofs they'll be having where he's gone."

"Never mind that. You just go down and see what it is."

193

Very quietly Angus Donald swung his feet out of bed on to the cold linoleum and crept to the head of the stairs. A light burned at the crack of the kitchen door. A minute later he had tip-toed downstairs and was standing beside it, listening to the soft popping noise within.

"Don't be so stupid," he said to himself as his heart thumped in his chest. "It's nothing at all."

Very slowly he pushed the door open and peered through. No ghost was to be seen. But he found they had forgotten to turn off the tilly lamp and it was nearly out, going pop . . . pop pop . . . pop, as the pressure died.

He laughed at how superstitious they both were, and turned off the tilly. Then he thought of his wife upstairs and gave a smile. Uttering a great roar of fright he raced back up the stairs, jumped into bed, and huddled shivering under the blankets.

"Oh Mary!" he gasped. "You should have seen him! Old Joppie to the life! Blood all over him, nailing a great pair of red-hot boots . . . and his head lying there on the table beside him. . . . And the eyes! . . . It was awful!"

The Press Gang Visits Kirtomy

A man named Iain Beg Mackay* lived in the little house at the end of the track that leads down to Kirtomy shore. He made his own whisky, which was illegal, and was always frightened that he would get caught.

One day he saw a strange ship anchored in Kirtomy Bay and a boatful of men rowing ashore. He thought it might be the police or

the excise men coming to look around, so he hurried up to the house and hid all the evidence of his whisky making in the peat stack. Then he went out to see who the men were and keep them away from his own house if he could.

For a while they talked, and then began to make their way back down the track towards the shore. When at last Iain Beg turned to go home, they grabbed him and began to march him along with them. He struggled and shouted, but a couple of thumps were enough to silence him and after that he went meekly enough.

But when his wife one of those women who are real Highland

*Iain Beg: Little Iain

195

warriors, saw her husband being led away, she ran after them. She caught up a stick and began beating them with it so that they had to cover their heads, but they did not let go of her husband. When they reached the shore she dropped the stick and picked up a heavy stalk of seaweed. So violently did she attack them with this weapon that she cut one man's face open to the ear and drove them off. When they were in the boat she picked up stones from the beach and hurled them after it.

And so this spirited woman saved her husband.

The men from the press gang were ashamed and when they got back to the ship they wanted some revenge. So they loaded the cannon and took a few shots at Iain Beg's house. None of them hit, though one landed in the peat stack and broke all his bottles of whisky.

The Fighting Men of Strathy

Maor na Srathaidh was the Laird of Strathy, and Donald, Chief of Mackay, had given him the job of rounding up a troop of local men to fight as mercenaries on the continent. The Thirty Years' War was

in progress and Donald saw that it would be to his advantage to put the great fighting prowess of the Mackays to some use. After all, it was their chief asset.

However, while it is one thing to fight fiercely for your rights, your clan, and even, possibly, your country, it is quite another to risk death in a foreign land for no reason but a dubious glory and the tiny wages of a soldier. This was apparently how the men of Strathy felt, for when Maor na Srathaidh appealed to them they were quite unmoved, and no-one volunteered.

He gave them a week to think about it, then again exhorted them to consider the great advantages and glory that would ensue. Again he got no response whatever, except from a drunken half-wit.

What could he do? Donald was becoming impatient.

Finally he hit upon a desperate scheme. He invited all the men of the village to a feast in a large barn a little way up the strath. For days workmen were busy making preparations, but the villagers did not see what they were doing.

The day arrived, and the men of the village, tidily dressed, jostled in through the door of the barn. They did not notice at once that there was no sign of food and drink, but as the last man passed inside, Maor na Srathaidh slammed the door behind them and bolted and padlocked it from top to bottom.

When the men looked around them they saw that they were trapped. The workmen had barred the windows, strengthened the door and roof, removed every last piece of wood or metal that might be used to pick a way out.

For days Maor na Srathaidh kept them locked there, until they were on the point of dying from thirst. Only then did he offer to let them out, but on condition. They must sign an official paper volunteering to fight with Donald Mackay's mercenaries on the continent. When enough men had signed, he let them all out.

A few days later they joined up with the rest of Donald Mackay's troops and served, as always, with great distinction.

As for Maor na Srathaidh, I do not know what happened to him. Probably he was murdered.

A Dishonourable Profession

One night two men set off from somewhere east of Melvich to rob a new grave in Kirkton graveyard. They wrapped straw round their cart wheels to muffle the noise they made on the stones as they went up the rough track past the little cottages. They dug up the coffin, tipped out the body, buried the coffin again and tidied up the pile of earth and flowers. Then they set off home with the body rolling around in the back of the cart.

When they came to the main road they felt they could do with a drink so they turned left instead of right and drove on up to the inn at Melvich. When they got there they left the cart in a secluded corner and slipped a nosebag on the horse to keep him quiet. Just in case anyone looked in while they were away they dressed the body in a cloak and hat and propped it up on the driver's seat with a whip in its hand.

A few minutes later, while they were still in the inn, a young local fellow who was passing called out a greeting to the dark figure on the cart.

" ' Evening."

When he got no answer he was annoyed, and stopped and called out again.

" ' Evening!"

When he still got no reply he thought the driver was deliberately ignoring him and went over and gave the fellow a poke with the pitchfork he was carrying. To his astonishment the figure fell backwards off the seat revealing a pair of bare, white legs.

He got a terrible fright and started to run away. But when he had gone a few yards he stopped again, and waited. Everything was quiet, so plucking up his courage he crept up to the cart and peeped over the edge.

When he realised what had happened he did not know what to do, so he went to get a friend who lived in a cottage close by. On the way back he had his great idea. Between them they lifted the body out of the cart and hid it behind a hedge. Then he dressed himself in the

199

cloak and hat, took the whip in his hand, and sat down on the seat where the corpse had been.

In a little while the two body snatchers came out of the inn with a few whiskies inside them and climbed back on to the cart. They did not bother to shove the body into the back but simply wedged it between themselves and set off home.

After they had been going for a time the young Melvich fellow nudged one of the men under the arm. The man glared over at his companion but said nothing. They had already been quarrelling. Then he nudged the other one.

"What do you think you're playing at?" the man snapped.

"What do you mean?" his friend said.

"You know perfectly well what I mean."

They argued for a while but soon fell silent. The horse and cart rattled on along the rough moonlit road. Suddenly the Melvich fellow felt one of them squeezing his arm. Then a hand was feeling all over his back.

"Hey, George," the man said slowly. "I know it sounds, er, funny, but I reckon this chap's getting warm."

When he heard this the young fellow from Melvich slowly turned round and looked the man straight in the face in the moonlight.

"Aye," he said in a low voice. "And if you'd been in Hell as long as I have you'd be feeling pretty warm yourself."

The two men roared with fright and jumped down from the cart and ran away into the darkness.

The young fellow laughed and drove himself back to Melvich. His friend had fetched the minister and they returned the body to the grave.

No-one came to collect the very good horse and cart, and at last the young fellow sold them. He got enough money for them to buy himself a small croft, where he settled down and spent the rest of his life.

200

Long ago in Melvich there was a man named Smaddan, whose greatest pleasure in life was to see a funeral procession go by. For he lived by digging corpses from their graves and selling them.

Normally he would wait until he had a couple, keeping them in a cool shed dug into the hillside at the back of his house, and then he would carry them into Wick on the back of a cart and sell them to a man who had a ready market for nice fresh corpses down the country. The people of the village were frightened of Smaddan, and when he went out into the darkness with his shovel they locked their doors and drew the curtains.

One night a woman who had been in Reay for the day missed the coach so she started walking. When she reached the lonely stretch of road over the hills at Drumholliston, a cart came up behind and the driver stopped to offer her a lift. She thought he was rather strange because every time she looked across at him he drew his face down into the collar of his coat and kept his hat pulled well down over his eyes. In the shadowy light of the lantern she could not make him out at all. Two or three times she tried to make conversation, but his replies were so brief that even before they had reached the crest of the moors there was no sound but the rattle of the wheels on the rough road.

When they came to the inn at the top of the village he stopped to let the woman off. There was not a soul in sight: the moon flitted between shreds of tattered cloud.

"Well, I'm glad I never met Smaddan," she said.

The driver drew his face from the collar of his coat and gave her a smile to make your blood run cold.

"You can tell them you came home in Smaddan's cart!" he said.

When the woman saw him she nearly fainted and ran away to the nearest house.

Smaddan laughed, and drove away.

The Woman with a Hungry Cow

A very poor woman who lived in Skerray owned a small croft cottage and a cow. It was a very thin cow, for there was little grass around the house. She certainly could not afford to buy food for the beast and she did not like to beg from her neighbours.

So early one morning, while it was still dark, she slipped out of the house and made her way down the road towards the graveyard. When she got there she found that the latch of the gate was rusted and so stiff that she could not open it. So she looked all around to make sure that no-one was watching her, then lifted her skirts and with much puffing and panting hauled herself over the high wall. The grass was long. She had the corran (sickle) with her, and soon was laying long swathes of sweet grass to feed to her hungry cow. When she had cut enough she packed it into a sack she had brought and prepared to leave.

At the same time a crofter who had risen early was setting out to milk his cow in a nearby field. As he drew level with the graveyard wall he was startled by a loud 'thump' just behind him. He stopped and peered around, but in the half light he could not see the bag of grass the old woman had pushed over on to the rough verge.Then there came a rustling and a panting and a pair of wrinkled hands appeared, clutching a sickle and clawing at the top of the wall. They were followed by a wild head of grey hair. It was enough for the man. Thinking the dead were rising from their graves he gave a cry of horror, took to his heels, and fled away up the road.

When all was quiet again, the old woman peeped over the wall to see that the coast was clear, climbed down, picked up the bag of grass, and set off chuckling over the fields to feed her hungry cow.

The Lonely House *

Three miles south of Tongue the lonely road to Altnaharra and Lairg drops from the crest of the moors through a view of lochs and mountains to the shore of Loch Loyal. For six miles then it runs along the edge of the loch, with the lovely peaks of Ben Loyal standing above; then the loch comes to an end and there is only the mountain and the moor, and the broad, slow stream that drains the glen. A mile further on the road makes a big, swinging turn over the bridge that crosses this stream, passes the lonely shepherd's house of Inchkinloch, and climbs once more to the summit of the moors. This long hill, treacherous in snow, is known locally as the Stank. From the crest the empty moorland road, with limitless views of mountains and rolling hills, slowly descends for six more miles to the little village of Altnaharra at the head of Loch Naver.

The following events, which are true, took place at the shepherd's house of Inchkinloch in the winter of 1941. At the time the shepherd who lived there was Mr. George Mackay. Also in the house were his wife and one son, a young man in his early twenties who was the under shepherd. Mr. Mackay's other children were all grown up and away from home.

It was the middle of January and there had been heavy falls of snow with exceptionally low temperatures. Going outside in the early morning Mr. Mackay could see that there was more snow on the way. Some of the sheep were still on the hill, so when he and his son had eaten their breakfasts they got ready to bring in as many as were still accessible. His wife made them each a packet of food and thermos of tea, and soon, with the telescope and dogs, they were away into the snowy hills.

The sky darkened, and by the late morning it was snowing quite heavily. When Mrs. Mackay looked from her kitchen window, and opened the door upon the swirling flakes, she saw that the visibility was becoming limited and the wreaths were building up still higher along the front of the house. It was bitterly cold. Although she

*This is a true story and should be in no way linked with some of the other tales in this section.

205

realised that her husband and son were experienced and knew the hills well, she began to feel anxious. It was not her usual day for baking, but to take her mind off them she made a batch of scones. It did not take very long. Once they were in the oven, however, she thought she would make a cake as well since she had all the things out and her pantry was, perhaps, a little on the empty side. After that she made oatcakes, bread, Scottish pancakes, another batch of scones. It took most of the day. After all, she thought in justification, it would always be eaten. But she had never baked so much. She even made butter and crowdie.

In the late afternoon her husband and son returned. They were plastered with snow and very tired, shepherds though they were. The job was done, the sheep were safe; now they were looking forward to a sit down by the fire and a good hot meal. When they went into the kitchen they were astonished to see the amounts of food Mrs. Mackay had made in their absence. There seemed to be plates and white cloths full of bread and scones all over the kitchen. Mr. Mackay was even more surprised when he remembered that it was not her usual baking day. Still, she explained how it was, though now they were back she didn't know what had come over her to make so much.

In a little while the two men had their meal, and they settled down to pass the evening as usual. The snow, which had eased for a while, came on heavily again, and by the time they went to bed a real blizzard was raging around the house.

They were awakened at two o'clock in the morning by a loud hammering on the door. They were so far from the nearest neighbour that it could only be someone who was stuck on the road in the snow. Mr. Mackay pulled on a jacket and trousers and went down to see who it was. When he got to the door, however, he found that far from being just someone, or even two or three people, it was a party of sixteen. Some of them were smothered in snow, with their eyebrows and ears iced, and they were all freezing.

They had endured a dreadful journey. Half of them were the road squad, who had been cutting a way through the deep wreaths and drifts; the others were a funeral party from Lochinver with the remains of a gentleman who had died and was to be buried near his family in the churchyard at Tongue. The appalling weather added to the natural distress of the occasion. Their first bus had been blocked by snow at the top of the Crask hill, the worst in that part of the country, several miles beyond Altnaharra. In a blizzard, with the wind whipping the snow into a blinding sheet, they had carried the coffin for more then a quarter of a mile through deep drifts to two waiting lorries, one open and one with a canvas hood which belonged to the road squad. The snow whirled in upon them and it took several hours to reach Altnaharra. There, in the darkness, they transferred at six o'clock in the evening to the Tongue bus, with the lorries following on behind. One lorry broke down; in blinding conditions the other went off the road. The coffin was transferred to the bus. There was no heating. The road men, with nothing but shovels, sometimes vanishing in the whirling snow, had to cut their way through drift after drift. They had no option; in those days there were no snow ploughs or rescue helicopters. They had been out since the early morning. It took them eight hours to cut a way through to Inchkinloch.

In a few minutes Mr. and Mrs. Mackay were dressed and downstairs and making the refugees comfortable. In those days the peat fire was never allowed to go out, but covered with a wet peat and ashes at bedtime so that it was ready to poke into life in the morning. In a few minutes, therefore, Mr. Mackay had a huge fire roaring up the chimney. Mrs. Mackay put on the kettle to make tea and went to her food cupboard. What had been comparatively empty the previous morning was now full to over-flowing. Her guests, many of them roadmen and all hungry, were able to eat until they were filled.

An hour and a half later, warmed through, rested, and feeling much better, they were able to continue their journey. It was six o'clock in the morning when they arrived in Tongue.

Of that huge baking there was hardly a scrap left, and later in the morning Mrs. Mackay had to set to and make some more. She was very impressed by what had happened and as time went on, being a good-living woman, could only believe that the Lord had had a hand in it somehow.

The following summer the minister from Lochinver, the Reverend Angus Mackenzie, who had been one of the funeral party, called to see Mr. and Mrs. Mackay, taking with him his usual gift to friends of a parcel of fresh fish from the fishing boats in Lochinver harbour. They recalled the wild night. He had been intrigued ever since by the way in which she had managed to feed so many people when there were only the three of them, and she explained how it had come about. He was impressed by her story, and in a radio programme some time later he recounted the incident. He concluded his account with a question. Are we, perhaps, 'so far from the centre of things' as the visitors who come up in the summer are always telling us?

THE CLEARANCE
OF STRATHNAVER

Introduction

In a succession of evictions during the first quarter of the nine-teenth century the lovely valley of Strathnaver was emptied of its inhabitants. From Kildonan too, and Strathoykell, indeed the whole heart of the county and the Highlands of Scotland, the people were removed by force from the homes and crofts of their ancestors and cast adrift on the winds of change that were sweeping the country. They might go where they pleased, anywhere so long as it was away from the hills of their homeland, for they were being given over to sheep. It was an act of economic expediency carried out within the law by planners and men of vested interest, an act of total disregard for all human and moral rights. To understand how it came about it is necessary to go back seventy years.

The second half of the eighteenth century is distinguished as the start of the agrarian and industrial revolutions. The peasant farmers of rural England were being driven from their cottages and small patches of ground to make way for larger and more economic farm units. Their story has much in common with that of their Scottish counterparts fifty years later. With nowhere else to go, they most often made their way to the developing cities with their wretched slums and unspeakable working conditions. There they found the only employment that was to be offered, in the new factories and wool and cotton mills. New trading overseas, the fast machine spinning and weaving, the money that the industries themselves were making, had created a great new demand for cotton and woollen goods.

At the same time as this industrial development there were corresponding developments in the fields of science and agriculture. Careful husbandry was producing new strains of cattle and horses, and, of particular importance to the Scottish Highlands, new strains of sheep. The great Cheviot sheep, which could withstand the rigours of the Scottish winter and still produce a lamb and good yield of wool, began to nibble its way across the more accessible moors.

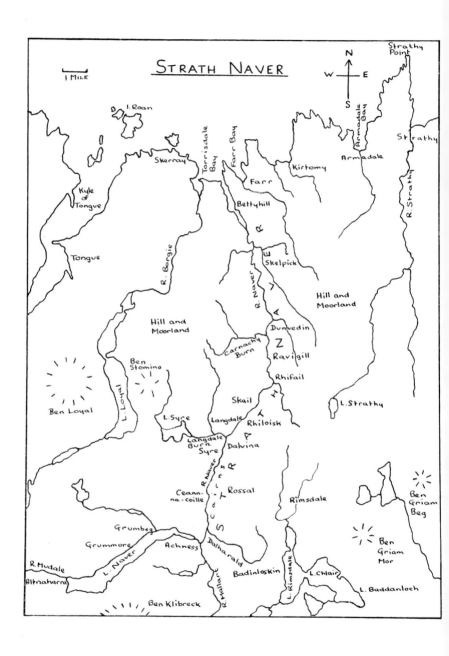

In 1746, a few years before all this, the Battle of Culloden had destroyed for ever the old Scottish clan system. The men and women who inhabited the hills and glens of the Highlands were left with no leadership and no rights of their own in a time of sweeping change. By 1800 a new generation of landowners and expatriate chiefs had grown up, men to whom the old days were history. Titled and wealthy, they moved among the English and Lowland Scots as some of the brightest lights — and none more brilliant than the Dukes and Duchesses of Sutherland, catholic in their interests — trading, coal, steel, wool, cotton — and in the early years of the nineteenth century the wealthiest and greatest landowners in Britain. A most privileged class of men.

Right at the other end of the social spectrum, though one step up from the labourers by dint of 'possessing' land, were the crofters who inhabited the Highland estates. Untitled and poor, they still lived in houses built from rock and sod, neither read nor wrote, and spoke a 'foreign' tongue. Their property consisted of a postage stamp patch of arable land for corn and potatoes and a few thin, black cattle that roamed the open moors. They lived, in fact, as they had lived in the old days, but the justification was gone, the fierce spirit was dying. Now the young men fought for the English king, summoned by a chieftain who lived in a fine house in Edinburgh or London.

In that new age of development and improvement they were clearly an anachronism. Not only the landowners, but speculators too, began to see what profits might be wrought from the bleak and unproductive hills of the Highlands.

Sutherland is the most remote of the Scottish mainland counties, and perhaps was the most out of touch and undeveloped of them all. To the traveller who pressed on it was like journeying to another age or another country. There were no roads, no inns, the empty hills rolled on as they had since time immemorial. Financially they yielded a mere £15,000 per annum, little more than a bagatelle to a man whose income was twenty times that, and might spend twice as much on paintings in a morning or two at Sotheby's. The potential, however, was unknown. Certainly it would be several times that amount with the advent of the great sheep.

And so, under the influence of the age, the promise of unknown profits, and the advice of experts, to whom ideas were more than men, permission was given for more than a thousand Sutherland families to be removed from their homes and ancestral lands. Five hundred years of faith and the prowess of fighting men were now irrelevant. You cannot stop progress! And to be fair, land had been made available for them at the edge of the sea, and the sea was teeming with fish. But what land; land with no timber, thin soil, salt-laden air, exposed to all the gales that blew; no safe harbours; and a sea that must be the most dangerous on the British coast. In conception the idea sounds alright, but in reality it was little more than a sop.

Doubtless the landlords did not intend ill of the people who inhabited their lands, but in sanctioning the schemes they did for more than half a century, and empowering their factors to use whatever means they thought necessary, without enquiring too closely into them, they surely displayed a neglect and casual cruelty which is both culpable and shameful, for one of a landowner's prime duties was the care and well-being of his tenants.

Strathnaver was the scene of some of the greatest ruthlessness. Though the process of removal continued over a number of years, there were two major evictions, in 1814 and 1819, in the course of which something in excess of two thousand people were removed to the coast. Lands which from time immemorial had been occupied by men, and for many centuries by members of the Clan Mackay, were totally emptied and given over to the raising of sheep.

Several months before the first great eviction, in 1814, the tenants were informed that they were to quit their cottages by a certain date and remove to the coast. Knowing nothing good of that land and nothing whatever of fishing, having no wood for houses, and thinking that nothing like this edict could surely come to pass, the people remained. But on the appointed day the factor, accompanied by sheriff's officers, constables, and such men as could be persuaded physically to carry out the task, arrived to see that the cottages were, indeed, emptied, and the people removed.

What happened we leave the following accounts, taken from a number of sources, to describe. In reading them we must not forget the extent to which Strathnaver and the northern Highlands were cut off from the rest of Britain. Arguably it was just this separation that allowed the authorities to do whatever they chose with no regard to the outside world; although, of course, the climate of the times in any case gave them carte blanche, for these were the years of children in the mines, Tom the chimney sweep, the satanic mills. We must remember, too, that by the time it came to the point of discussion in the press, and the making of some kind of social record, the last ruthless clearance of Strathnaver in 1819 had been over for more than twenty years. At the time of the burnings, and the emergence of such figures as James Loch, William Young and Patrick Sellar, the people were on their own. Their cries went unheeded for a quarter of a century.

The accounts tell mainly of what happened to the people, but we must not forget the other side. There was undoubtedly an enormous improvement in the county's agricultural economy. Roads and bridges were built, bogs drained, pastures improved, inns provided for the traveller. Enormous sums of money were poured into modernising the county, raising it from the mists and methods of a world now dead, that had no place in such a modern, energetic age.

But now, as we gaze upon the still empty strath, and recall how ironically brief were the great years of the sheep, we ask for whom was it done? For one man? For the few? For the land? For the age itself? And how long will it last?

How great was the real suffering? And how great the historical insult? Does the end justify the means? Can the clearance of Strathnaver be justified?

Key Personages

The Duke and Duchess of Sutherland (Marquess and Marchioness of Stafford).

James Loch: Commissioner of the Marquess of Stafford's estates in Sutherland and throughout Britain. Architect of the Policy of Improvement, and its greatest force. An energetic practical economist and agriculturalist. Ruthlessly pursued his end, which was the development of the county as he visualised it.

Rev. David Mackenzie: minister of Mission at Achness and later the Parish of Farr. From his pulpit and outside translated and supported the edicts of the improvers to his parishioners.

Patrick Sellar: advocate of Morayshire. Invited by Marquess of Stafford to examine Sutherland estate with regard to improvement. Entered Sutherland in 1809, aged 29, with little money. Within ten years one of the richest sheep farmers in the north. Organised and led the clearance of most of Strathnaver, farming the emptied land. Brought to trial in 1816 for 'Culpable Homicide, Oppression and Real Injury' — honourably discharged.

William Young: of Morayshire. Originally a corn-chandler. Became Lord Stafford's first Commissioner for the Sutherland estate. Later Chief Factor under James Loch for the whole of Lord Stafford's estates. Planned early clearances. Became a successful sheep farmer.

Donald Macleod: stonemason from Rossall, Strathnaver. A young man during the clearance of 1814. Fearlessly condemned the outrages perpetrated upon the poor people of the Highlands. Hounded by the authorities. His wife driven from her mind in a series of evictions. Left Sutherland for Edinburgh 1831. Published critical letters in the *Edinburgh Weekly Chronicle* 1840-41. 1850's emigrated to Canada.

Rev. Donald Sage: young minister of Mission in Achness, Strathnaver, after the Rev. David Mackenzie. Son of minister of Kildonan (Mr. Sage 'of evergreen memory'). Supported people as he could during clearances. Whole parish laid desolate in 1819.

The Clearance of Strathnaver *

1. The most notorious single episode (in the history of the Highland clearances) was the clearance of Strathnaver in 1814.

(*T. C. Smout*)

2. Strathnaver is a green glen through which the River Naver slowly winds northwards from Loch Naver to the Atlantic Ocean. It is a fine, broad river, rich in trout and salmon. From the hills on either side tributary streams run down through banks of heather and birch trees, levelling out to join the parent river on the green, level pastures of the valley bottom. It is the richest land in that part of the country.

The houses, in 1814, were grouped into more than a dozen small townships. Some stood on the shore of beautiful Loch Naver, looking across the water to the smooth flank and fine crest of Ben Klibreck. The greater number, however, were situated on the hillsides down the length of the strath. The old place-names — townships and clusters of cottages — describe the scene: Syre — the plentiful land; Ceann na coille — the head of the wood; Achness — the field of the waterfall; Dalharrald — Harrald's field (echoes of the Norse invasion); Carnachadh — the field full of cairns; Skail — the farmstead; Rhiloisk — the parched plain; Achoul — the field in the nook; Mallard — the river from the high brow of the hill; Dalvina — the fine, smooth dale.

At its northern end the River Naver flows into the Atlantic Ocean through the broad, white sands of Torrisdale Bay. (*A.T.*)

3. The people who lived there in 1814 were Mackays, by name or allegiance, though the Countess Elizabeth was their lord. † They lived in long stone houses roofed with sod. One end of the house was a byre, the other was living accommodation. There was no window-glass, the floors were uneven earth, and the smoke of the open hearths found its uncertain way through holes in the roof. The

---

*For continuity in this necessarily condensed account we have not distinguished between the major clearance of 1814 and that of 1819. The manner of their execution was almost identical.

†See footnote: 'Dhruim na Cupa'.

215

stone walls were sometimes plastered on the inside and plugged with clay to make them draught-proof. Scattered about such primitive buildings were dry-stone barns, outhouses and drying kilns . . .

(Many of the houses were walled with alternate layers of stone and turf. Some of the poorest houses were constructed entirely of turfs — of earth or peat — around a skeleton bog-wood frame. The latter were commonly renewed every three years, the smoke-impregnated turfs being used to fertilise the land.   A.T.)   (John Prebble)

4.   The peasantry in general throughout the county had held their farms in the valleys or on the hillsides from time immemorial; they were members of the clan, and knew no other country but Sutherland. They each possessed from two or four to twenty milk cows — in some cases as many as thirty — with a proportionate following of younger cattle; and the tenants of the separate valleys or other well defined districts grazed their cattle in common. They cultivated, each for his own family, a sufficient extent of barley and oats, along with potatoes . . .

In midsummer, when the grass was rich on the mountain slopes, and the cows yielded a copious quantity of milk, they migrated and lived in temporary huts called shielings, where for six weeks they made butter and cheese. It was somewhat like the harvesting in the Low country. It was a change and period of enjoyment and rejoicing.

There were then no Game Laws, and no objection was taken to a shot at a stag or a moorfowl. The rivers and sea teemed with fish as they do now, and afforded a plentiful supply of food. Hence in general the people lived comfortably and well in their way. They provided for their own poor and dependents, although, no doubt, from want of forethought they experienced distress in backward seasons and long winters. They built their own houses and provided their own clothes. . . . The proceeds of the sale of their cattle paid their rents.

. . . they were strict in their religious observances.

(Joseph Mitchell)

5. Never were there a happier or more contented people, or a people more strongly attached to the soil.   *(Hugh Miller)*

6. I remember you would see a mile or half a mile between every town if you were going up the strath. There were four or five families in each of these towns, and bonnie haughs between the towns, and hill pastures for miles, as far as they could wish to go. The people had plenty of flocks of goats, sheep, horses and cattle, and they were living happy, with flesh and fish and butter, and cheese and fowl and potatoes and kail and milk too. There was no want of anything with them, and they had the Gospel preached to them at both ends of the strath.   *(Angus Mackay)*

7. Sutherland had never been as Donald Macleod (and others) painted it, a pleasant Arcadia of rosy prosperity, plump girls and happy bakers. On the contrary, it had for long been a county of poverty and emigration.   *(T. C. Smout)*

8. (The people of Sutherland are) almost torpid with idleness, and most wretched; their hovels most miserable, made of poles wattled and covered with thin sods. There is not corn raised sufficient to supply half the wants of the inhabitants . . . yet there is much improvable land here in a state of nature: but till famine pinches they will not bestir themselves . . . Numbers of the miserables of this county were now migrating . . .   *(Thomas Pennant, 1772)*

9.   The men being impatient of regular and constant work, all the heavy labour was abandoned to the women, who were employed occasionally, even in dragging the harrow to cover the seed. To build their hut, or get in their peats for fuel, the men were ever ready to assist; but most of their time, when not in pursuit of game, or illegal distillation, was spent in indolence and sloth. They were contented with the most simple and poorest fare. They deemed no comfort worth the possession which was to be purchased at the price of regular work.

(The people suffered from) every species of deceit and idleness, by which they contracted habits and ideas quite incompatible with the customs of regular society and civilised life, adding greatly to those defects which characterize persons living in a loose and unformed state of society.   (*James Loch*)

10.   (The 93rd Regiment had been formed in 1800. Also known as the Sutherland Highlanders, the greater part of this justly famed regiment was formed of men from the valleys of Sutherland which were, within the next twenty years, to be cleared of their inhabitants. A large proportion enlisted at Syre in Strathnaver, some hundreds coming from the Strath itself. A stone by the Strathnaver village hall commemorates the spot and the occasion. Colonel Stewart (David Stewart of Garth) wrote thus of the men and morals so criticised by James Loch.   A.T.)

There are few regiments in his Majesty's service which, in all those qualities requisite to constitute good soldiers, and valuable members of society, excel this respectable body of men. None of the Highland corps is superior to the 93rd Regiment. I do not make comparisons in point of bravery, for if properly led they are all brave. But it is in those well regulated habits, of which so much has been already said, that the Sutherland Highlanders have for twenty years preserved an unvaried line of conduct. The light infantry company of this corps has been nineteen years without having a man punished. This single fact may be taken as sufficient evidence of good morals.

. . . Being anxious to enjoy the advantages of religious instruction agreeably to the tenets of their national church, and there being no religious service in the garrison except the customary one of reading prayers to the soldiers on parade, the men of the 93rd Regiment formed themselves into a congregation, appointed elders of their own number, engaged and paid a stipend (collected from the soldiers) to a clergyman of the Church of Scotland . . . and had Divine Service performed agreeably to the ritual of the established Church.

(*Colonel Stewart*)

11.   The marriage of the countess brought a new set of eyes upon it (Sutherland) . . . It seemed a rude, wild country, where all was wrong, and all had to be set right — a sort of Russia on a small scale. . . . Even the vast wealth and great liberality of the Stafford family militated against their hapless county! It enabled them to treat it as a mere subject of an interesting experiment, in which gain to themselves was really no object.   (*Hugh Miller*)

12.   . . . the coast of Sutherland abounded with many different kinds of fish, not only sufficient for the consumption of the country but affording a supply to any extent, for more distant markets, or for exportation when cured and salted. . . . It seemed as if it had been pointed out by Nature, that the system for this remote district . . . was to convert the mountainous districts into sheep walks, and to remove the inhabitants to the coast.   (*James Loch*)

13.   In 1809 Patrick Sellar and William Young of Morayshire were invited by the Marquess of Stafford to examine his Sutherland estate with regard to 'improvement'. They were in their twenties, full of enthusiasm and new ideas. They went about their work with great energy, and soon Young became the Marquess of Stafford's commissioner for the estate, and Sellar became his factor. By their advice, and through the 'Policy of Improvement' which had been designed by James Loch, it was decided in 1813 that east Strathnaver should be made into a large sheep farm. Plans were drawn up, but there was no auction: on Whitsunday, 1814, Patrick Sellar took possession. The proposed method of farming necessitated the removal of the inhabitants to the poor land that James Loch and the Marquess had designated, and thought suitable, on the north coast. As both farmer and factor Patrick Sellar was enabled to use whatever means he thought necessary: he had, under the ultimate jurisdiction of the Marquess, complete power, and by his misuse of it Sellar ultimately became notorious.

It would be wrong, however, simply to write him off as the villain of the piece. In many ways Sellar exemplified the thinking of the new age, that was only now arriving in the Highlands. Perhaps, had he travelled overseas instead of to the north of Scotland, he would be remembered as a bold pioneer instead of as a tyrant, have become lauded instead of vilified. For he was just the sort of man who was at the same time taming the colonies, laying solid economic foundations, creating the greatness of the British empire. His mistake was to do it so near to home, for his actions have been placed under a microscope.

He was an educated man who, even in the remote northern Highlands, managed to keep abreast of the great questions of the day, the political scene, the new science, the literature. He raised a family of nine children who succeeded brilliantly. He was an outstanding farmer, and became a great influence through his "shrewdness, intelligence and energy" among the other sheep farmers of the north.

(*A.T.*)

14. On 15 January, the first rent-day of 1814, and in bitter snow-driven weather, Sellar arrived in Achness. With Mr. Mackenzie the minister as his host, ally and interpreter, he gave notice to those tenants whom he wished to quit his property at Whitsuntide. Others were told that their time for removal would come later, and still more of the people were warned that within four years Mr. Young proposed to clear the whole of Strathnaver from Altnaharra to Dunvedin and place it under sheep.   (*John Prebble*)

15. Summonses of ejectment were issued and despatched all over the district. These must have amounted to upwards of a thousand, as the population of the Mission alone was 1,600 souls, and many more than those of the Mission were ejected. ... They were handed in at every house and hovel alike, be the occupiers of them who or what they might — minister, catechist, or elder, tenant, or sub-tenant, out-servant, or cottar — all were made to feel the irresponsible power of the proprietor.   (*Donald Sage*)

16. On Wednesday, 15 December, 1813, twenty-seven tenants-at-will from Strathnaver, some of them with their families, gathered before the Inn at Golspie (forty miles away from their homes) under the direction of their minister, Mr. David Mackenzie. He was the missionary at Achness in their glen, and for such work as this day's the Staffords would shortly reward him with the great parish of Farr, a splendid manse for his home, a glebe consisting of the best land in the area, and a fine church from the pulpit of which he would translate and support each successive eviction order issued by his patrons. He was here this day to translate Mr. Young's Lowland English into the Gaelic of his parishioners, and to urge upon them

that it was God's will that they should obey those whom He had placed above them. (*John Prebble*)

17.   The seventeen parish ministers (in Sutherland), with the single exception of the Rev. Mr. Sage, took the side of the powers that were, exhorting the people to submit and to stifle their cries of distress, telling them that all their sufferings (their original poverty, their eviction, and the succeeding famine and disease) came from the hand of their Heavenly Father as a punishment for their past transgressions. (*Alexander Mackenzie*)

18.   From the great pulpit that had been placed in his church in 1774 he (Rev. David Mackenzie) translated and expounded the successive eviction orders to those who had sometimes walked as far as 20 miles to hear the Christian message. (*Ian Grimble*)

19.   While the Reverend David Mackenzie threatened the people with hell-fire for the slightest disobedience, Sellar seems to have been studying them with interest. (*John Prebble*)

20.   In the month of March, 1814, a great number of the inhabitants of the parishes of Farr and Kildonan were summoned to give up

221

their farms at the May term following, and, in order to ensure and hasten their removal with their cattle, in a few days after, the greatest part of the heath pasture was set fire to and burnt, by order of Mr. Sellar, the factor, who had taken these lands for himself. ... In the spring, especially when fodder is scarce, as was the case in the above year, the Highland cattle depend almost solely on the heather.

(Donald Macleod)

21.   By this cruel proceeding (burning the pasture) the cattle were left without food during the spring, and it was impossible to dispose of them at a fair price, the price having fallen after the war — (the Napoleonic war in which the young men from the strath, still away fighting for their country, had and were yet to so distinguish themselves). *(Alexander Mackenzie)*

22.   At Rhimisdale, a small township crowded with small tenants, a corn-mill was set on fire in order effectually to scare the people from the place before the term for eviction arrived. Firing or injuring a corn-mill, on which the sustenance of the lieges so much depends, is or was by our ancient Scottish statutes punishable by imprisonment, or civil banishment ... *(Donald Sage)*

23.   To my poor and defenceless flock the dark hour of trial came at last in right earnest. It was in the month of April, and about in the middle of it, that they were all — man, woman and child — from the heights of Farr to the mouth of the Naver, on one day, to quit their tenements and go — many of them knew not whither. For a few, some miserable patches of ground along the shores were doled out as lots, without aught in the shape of the poorest hut to shelter them. Upon these lots it was intended that they should build houses at their own expense, and cultivate the ground, at the same time occupying themselves as fishermen, although the great majority of them had never set foot on a boat in their lives. Thither, therefore, they were driven at a week's warning. As for the rest most of them knew not whither to go, unless their neighbours on the shore provided them with a temporary shelter; for, on the day of their removal, they would not be allowed to remain, even on the bleakest moor, and in the open air, for a distance of twenty miles around. *(Donald Sage)*

24.   In Strathnaver we assembled, for the last time, at the place of Langdale, where I had frequently preached before, on a beautiful green sward overhung by Robert Gordon's antique, romantic little

cottage on an eminence close beside us. The still-flowing waters of the Naver swept past us a few yards to the eastward. The Sabbath morning was unusually fine, and mountain, hill, and dale, water and woodland, among which we had so long dwelt, and with which all our associations of 'home' and 'native land' were so fondly linked, appeared to unite their attractions to bid us farewell. My preparations for the pulpit had always cost me much anxiety, but in view of this sore scene of parting, they caused me pain almost beyond endurance. I selected a text which had a pointed reference to the peculiarity of our circumstances, but my difficulty was how to restrain my feelings till I should illustrate and enforce the great truths which it involved with reference to eternity. The service began. The very aspect of the congregation was of itself a sermon, and a most impressive one. Old Achoul sat right opposite to me. As my eye fell upon his venerable countenance, bearing the impress of eighty-seven winters, I was deeply affected, and could scarcely articulate the psalm. I preached and the people listened, but every sentence uttered and heard was in opposition to the tide of our natural feelings, which, setting in against us, mounted at every step of our progress higher and higher. At last all restraints were compelled to give way. The preacher ceased to speak, the people to listen. All lifted up their voices and wept, mingling their tears together. It was indeed the place of parting, and the hour. The greater number parted never again to behold each other in the land of the living. (*Donald Sage*)

25. (Patrick Sellar, it appears, chose his time carefully, waiting until the beginning of June, when minimum resistance might be anticipated. A.T.)

The able-bodied men were by this time away after their cattle or otherwise engaged at a distance, so that the immediate sufferers of the general house-burning that now commenced were the aged and infirm, the women and children. (*Donald Macleod*)

26. The middle of the week brought on the day of the Strathnaver Clearance. It was a Tuesday. At an early hour on that day Mr. Sellar, accompanied by the Fiscal, and escorted by a strong body of constables, sheriff-officers and others, commenced work at Grummore, the first inhabited township to the west of the Achness district. Their plan of operations was to clear the cottages of their inmates, giving them about half-an-hour to pack up and carry off their furniture, and then set the cottages on fire. To this plan they

223

ruthlessly adhered, without the slightest regard to any obstacle that might arise while carrying it into execution. (*Donald Sage*)

27. It was ... the natural consequence of the measures which were adopted, that few men of liberal feelings could be induced to undertake their execution. The respectable gentlemen, who, in so many cases, had formerly been entrusted with the management of Highland property, resigned, and their places were supplied by persons cast in a coarser mould, and, generally, strangers to the country, who, detesting the people, and ignorant of their character, capability, and language, quickly surmounted every obstacle, and hurried on the change, without reflecting on the stress of which it might be productive ... (*General Stewart*)

28. The houses had all been built, not by the landlord ... but by the tenants or by their ancestors, and, consequently, were their property by right if not by law. They were timbered chiefly with bog fir, which makes excellent roofing but is very inflammable: by immemorial usage this species of timber was considered the property of the tenant on whose lands it was found. (In Sutherland there was very little timber save for small birch copses, unsuitable for building. The bog-fir, remnant of the old Caledonian Forest, was dug from deep in the peat moss, where it had lain preserved for centuries, and carted down to the village for sawing up. It was difficult to replace; impossible if they were to be removed from the land. A.T.)
(*Donald Macleod*)

29. Our family was very reluctant to leave and stayed for some time, but the burning party came round and set fire to our house at both ends, reducing to ashes whatever remained within the walls. The people had to escape for their lives, some of them losing all their clothes except what they had on their backs. The people were told they could go where they liked, provided they did not encumber the land that was by rights their own. The people were driven away like dogs who deserved no better, and that, too, without any reason in the world. (*Betsy Mackay*)

30. George Munro, the miller at Farr, who had six of his family down with fever, had to remove them in that state to a damp kiln, while his home was given to the flames. (From the kiln they were able to watch the house burning. A.T.)
(*Alexander Mackenzie*)

31. Robert Mackay, whose whole family was sick with fever, carried his daughters on his back for twenty-five miles, "first by carrying one and laying her down in the open air, and, returning did the same with the other till he reached the seashore".

(*John Prebble*)

32. ... parts of the parishes of Golspie, Rogart, Farr, and the whole of Kildonan were in a blaze. Strong parties with faggots and other combustible materials were set to work; three hundred houses were given ruthlessly to the flames, and their occupants pushed out in the open air without food or shelter. (*Alexander Mackenzie*)

33. In such a scene of general devastation it is almost useless to particularise the cases of individuals; the suffering was great and universal. I shall, however, notice a very few of the extreme cases of which I was myself an eye-witness. John Mackay's wife, Ravigill, in attempting to pull down her house, in the absence of her husband, to preserve the timber, fell through the roof. She was in consequence taken in premature labour, and in that state was exposed to the open air and to the view of all the by-standers. Donald Munro, Garvott, lying in a fever, was turned out of his house and exposed to the elements. Donald Macbeath, an infirm and bed-ridden old man, had the house unroofed over him, and was in that state exposed to the wind and rain until death put a period to his sufferings. I was present at the pulling down and burning of the house of William Chisholm, Badinloskin, in which was lying his wife's mother, an old bed-ridden woman of nearly 100 years of age, none of the family being present. I informed the persons about to set fire to the house of this circumstance, and prevailed on them to wait until Mr. Sellar came. On his arrival, I told him of the poor old woman being in a condition unfit for removal, when he replied, "Damn her, the old witch, she has lived too long — let her burn." Fire was immediately set to the house, and the blankets in which she was carried out were in flames before she could be got out. She was placed in a little shed, and it was with great difficulty they were prevented from firing it also. The old woman's daughter arrived while the house was on fire, and assisted the neighbours in removing her mother out of the flames and smoke, presenting a picture of horror which I shall never forget, but cannot attempt to describe. She died within five days.

(*Donald Macleod*)

34. The tinker (Chisholm) said that one of Sellar's men had refused to carry the sick woman from the cottage, saying, "He would not attempt it, even though they should take off his coat, as he would not be an accessory to murder." Sellar then ordered the cottage to be burned, laying faggots against it himself. Janet Mackay, Chisholm's sister-in-law, arrived then, and dragged her mother out in a blanket. The old woman cried, "God receive my soul! What fire is this about me?" She never spoke a word more, said Chisholm.

(*John Prebble*)

35. Grace Macdonald, a girl of nineteen living by Langdale, took shelter up the brae with her family when the township was burnt, and waited there a day and a night, watching Sellar's men sporting about the flames. When a terrified cat sprang from a burning house it was seized and thrown back, and thrown back again until it died there.

(*John Prebble*)

36. Had you the opportunity, madam, (Harriet Beecher Stowe, qv.), of seeing the scenes which I, and hundreds more, have seen — the wild ferocious appearance of the infamous *gang* who constituted the burning party, covered over face and hands with soot and ashes of the burning houses, cemented by torch-grease and their own sweat, kept continually drunk or half-drunk while at work; and to observe the hellish amusements some of them would get up to for themselves and for an additional pleasure to their leaders! The people's houses were generally built upon declivities, and in many

227

cases not far from pretty steep precipices. They preserved their meal in tight-made boxes, or chests, as they were called, and when this fiendish party found any quantity of meal, they would carry it between them to the brink, and dispatch it down the precipice amidst shrieks and yells. It was considered grand sport to see the box breaking to atoms and the meal mixed with the air.

(*Donald Macleod*)

37. Where the letters of Donald Macleod burn with anger, the private journal of Donald Sage displays pity and sorrow: where Donald Macleod rails at the inhumanity, Donald Sage more quietly refers to the unmerited plight and distress of his parishioners. In passages unfortunately too long to include in this account, he describes their characters and situation, upon which, for no reason of theirs, the dictatorial hand of the proprietor fell, totally destroying their homes, and casting them unprotected to the edge of the sea. Among them is Henny Munro, the cheerful, brisk and godly soldier's widow, who was told that if she did not remove her 'trumpery', (her furniture and all her worldly possessions), within half an hour, it would be burned. She was not strong enough to drag it more than a few yards from the gable wall, where the flames from her burning house blew towards it and reduced all that she possessed to ashes. Another is the brave, aging, 'good-wife of Rhimisdale' in whose house Sage used to conduct prayer meetings. Crippled through illness, and in acute pain from any movement of her limbs, she was compelled to spend her entire life in a chair. None the less she was a spirited Christian and Sage confessed himself greatly refreshed by her conversation. Already she had been evicted from Rimsdale, and friends and neighbours had built her a house at Ceann na coille (the head of the wood), for she was much respected and loved. Now she was to be evicted again. Hers was one of the first houses the burning party came to in the township. Pleas were made that she should be allowed to remain, at least until a conveyance was fetched, but they were rejected and the neighbours were informed that if friends did not carry her from the house immediately she would be removed by the constables. Her family informed her of the situation and she permitted them to lay her on a blanket. This caused her great pain, but she managed to smile through it. Everyone present was very distressed. Then four strong boys, themselves in tears, carried her from the house and it was set fire to. In the blanket she was carried

ten miles to the sea, and the movement caused her such pain that she was unable to keep her tears and cries back. They continued nearly to the end of her journey, when from sheer exhaustion she fell asleep. As a result of the eviction she contracted a fever from which she died a few weeks later. (*A.T.*)

38.   I cannot remember the number, but I would say there were about twenty (houses burned at Rossal). There were four other townships near this, each with about the same number of houses, all of which were burnt on the same day. My father, when his own house was set on fire, tried to save a few pieces of wood out of the burning house, which he carried to the river about half a mile away, and there formed a raft of it. His intention was to float the wood down the stream and built a kind of hut somewhere to shelter his weak family, but the burning party came that way and, seeing the timber, set fire to it, and soon reduced the whole to ashes.

(*George Macdonald*)

39.   In previous removals the evicted had been allowed to take their house-timbers with them for use in the building of new houses. Now it was learnt that the moss-fir was henceforth to be burned when it was torn from the cottages. The people were to be paid the value of the wood, or the value which Sellar set upon it, but this was no compensation at all in a land so sparsely timbered as Sutherland. . . . The timber of three hundred buildings burned in the thin May sunshine. (*John Prebble*)

40.   The consternation and confusion were extreme; little or no time was given for the removal of persons or property; the people striving to remove the sick and the helpless before the fire should reach them; next, struggling to save the most valuable of their effects. The cries of the women and children, the roaring of the affrighted cattle, hunted at the same time by the yelling dogs of the shepherds amid the smoke and fire, altogether presented a scene that completely baffles description — it required to be seen to be believed. A dense cloud of smoke enveloped the whole country by day, and even extended far out to sea; at night an awfully grand but terrific scene presented itself — all the houses in an extensive district in flames at once. I myself ascended a height about eleven o'clock in the evening, and counted two hundred and fifty blazing houses, many of the owners of which were my relations, and all of whom I personally knew, but whose present condition — whether in or out of the flames — I

229

could not tell. The conflagration lasted six days, till the whole of the dwellings were reduced to ashes or smoking ruins.

(Donald Macleod)

41. During these proceedings I was resident at my father's house, but I had occasion on the week immediately ensuing to visit the manse of Tongue. On my way thither, I passed through the scene of the campaign of burning. The spectacle presented was hideous and ghastly! The banks of the lake and the river, formerly studded with cottages, now met the eye as a scene of desolation. Of all the houses, the thatched roofs were gone, but the walls, built of alternate layers of turf and stone, remained. The flames of the preceding week still slumbered in their ruins, and sent up into the air spiral columns of smoke; whilst here a gable, and there a long side-wall, undermined by the fire burning within them, might be seen tumbling to the ground, from which a cloud of smoke, and then a dusky flame, slowly sprang up. The sooty rafters of the cottages, as they were being consumed, filled the air with a heavy and most offensive odour.

(Donald Sage)

42. For days after the burning was over the homeless people remained in the glen. They sat on the hillsides among what they had been able to salvage from the ruins. They put canvas over their heads for protection against the night rain. *(John Prebble)*

43. The people were pushed further and further down to the coast. They suffered very much for the want of houses and threw up earthen walls with blankets over the top, and four or five families lived like this throughout the winter while the last of their cattle died. They were removed as many as four or five times until they could go no further. *(Donald Macleod)*

44. As to those ridiculous stories about the Duchess of Sutherland, which have found their way into many of the prints in America, one has only to be here, moving in society, to see how excessively absurd they are. ... Everywhere that I have moved through Scotland and England I have heard her kindness of heart, her affability of manner, and her attention to the feelings of others spoken of as marked characteristics.

Imagine, then, what people must think when they find in respectable American prints the absurd story of her turning her tenants out into the snow, and ordering the cottages to be set on fire over their heads because they would not go out. *(Harriet Beecher Stowe)*

230

45.   I agree with you (Harriet Beecher Stowe) that the Duchess of Sutherland is a beautiful accomplished lady who would shudder at the idea of taking a faggot or a burning torch in her hand to set fire to the cottages of her tenants, and so would her predecessor, the first Duchess of Sutherland, likewise would the late and present Dukes of Sutherland. Yet it was done in their name, under their authority, to their knowledge, and with their sanction. The dukes and duchesses of Sutherland, and those of their depopulating order, had not, nor have they any call to defile their pure hands; no, no, they had, and have plenty of willing tools at their beck to perform their dirty work.   (*Donald Macleod*)

46.   In the early days of 1815 petitions alleging cruelty, injury and oppression, and specifically citing Patrick Sellar, were brought to the attention of the Sheriff of Sutherland. After what seems a certain prevarication, the matter was placed in the hands of Sheriff-Substitute MacKid. He pursued his enquiries rigorously, and at the end of May, 1815, Sellar was imprisoned in the Tollbooth at Dornoch, bail being refused. His release was ultimately effected only by means of an order from the Court of Judiciary in Edinburgh. The trial took place in Inverness on 23rd April, 1816. The charges, 'Culpable homicide, as also Oppression and Real Injury', involving the capital crime of arson and possibly murder, took nearly two hours to read out. The trial lasted all day, but by evening every charge, according to the Judge, Lord Pitmilly's summing up, was to be disregarded, save that of the death of Chisholm's mother-in-law; and so far as that was concerned, if they were in any doubt the established characters of Sellar and Chisholm should be taken into account. It only took fifteen minutes for the jury, consisting of eight landed proprietors, two merchants, two tacksmen, one lawyer, one farmer and a gentleman author, to reach a unanimous verdict of not guilty. Sellar was dismissed, with the following words from Lord Pitmilly. "Mr Sellar, it is now my duty to dismiss you from the bar; and you have the satisfaction of thinking that you are discharged by the unanimous opinion of the Jury and the Court. I am sure that, although your feelings must have been agitated, you cannot regret that this trial took place; and I am hopeful it will have due effect on the minds of the country, which have been so much and so improperly agitated." Though honourably discharged, his days in the Tollbooth and the slur upon his character had not left Sellar unmarked. He immediately

turned the tables, pursuing his legal accuser, MacKid, with all the powers at his disposal, ultimately extracting a cringing retraction of all the accusations and driving MacKid, a broken man, from the county.   (*A.T.*)

47.   . . . the final issue of it was only what might have been expected when a case came to be determined between the *poor*, as the party offended, and the *rich*, as the lordly and heartless aggressor. Sellar was acquitted.   (*Donald Sage*)

48.   . . . in many ways it was a pyrrhic victory. . . many people were persuaded that the trial had been a travesty of justice: mainly on the grounds that the jury had been composed of 'gentlemen', while the key witnesses were Gaelic speakers who were not given a fair hearing. It was taken to be the case that landlord influence had triumphed over the truth.   (*Eric Richards*)

49.   Sellar was subsequently removed from the estate administration, but he remained the largest sheep-farmer in Sutherland. Thereafter his dealings with the estate were frequently cool, often hostile.

(*Eric Richards*)

50. Donald Macleod wrote: "The removal of Messrs Young and Sellar, particularly the latter . . . from the power they had exercised so despotically, was hailed with the greatest joy by the people, to whom their names were a terror." Their appearance in any neighbourhood had been a great cause of alarm. One woman had been so frightened that she had partly lost her reason, and thenceforward, whenever any stranger came among them she would clasp her arms about her body, roll her eyes, and cry out in fear, "Oh! sin Sellar!" — (Oh! there's Sellar!) *(A.T.)*

51. Patrick Sellar was a blunt, energetic man: in his nature there could be no understanding and no respect for the common people of Strathnaver. To unite his observations upon them may be to give too strong a picture; nevertheless, in letters over a number of years he referred to them variously as: 'the aborigines'; 'a parcel of beggars with no stock, but cunning and lazy'; 'the most lying, psalm-singing, unprincipled peasantry in the Queen's dominions'; 'a great deal of trash'; 'subtenants, turf-cutters, and whisky smugglers, who poach the game, destroy the woods, destroy the surface of the ground'; being among 'the unwashed part of mankind'; and most cruel of all, 'the redundant population'. *(A.T.)*

52. Sellar's commercial success was purchased at high cost to his public reputation: his name is perhaps unrivalled in the ranks of Highland villany. *(Eric Richards)*

53. We have heard of the famished people blackening the shores, like the crew of some vessel wrecked on an inhospitable coast, that they might sustain life by the shell-fish and sea-weed laid bare by the ebb. Many of their allotments . . . were barren in the extreme — unsheltered by bush or tree, and exposed to the sweeping sea-winds, and in time of tempest, to the blighting spray; and it was found a matter of the extremest difficulty to keep the few cattle which they had retained, from wandering, especially in the night-time, into the better sheltered and more fertile interior.

The poor animals . . . were getting continually impounded; and vexatious fines, in the form of trespass money, came thus to be wrung from the already impoverished Highlanders. Many who had no money were obliged to relieve themselves by depositing some of their few portable articles of value, such as bed or body clothes, or, more distressing still, watches, and rings, and pins (small and treasured heirlooms; sometimes medals, awarded for gallantry in the Napoleonic wars. A.T.) *(Hugh Miller)*

54. It was nothing strange to see the pinfolds, of twenty or thirty yards square, filled up to the entrance with horses, cows, sheep and goats ... *(Donald Macleod)*

55. The people occasionally struck back at the Great Cheviot flocks, now and then stealing a young ewe or killing a ram. The gentry formed themselves into an Association for the Suppression of Sheep-stealing in Sutherland, and transported any man found guilty of it. Stafford offered £30 for information that would lead to the conviction of an offender, and one of the Northumbrians, Atkinson or Marshall, was prepared to pay £1,000 for the capture of the ringleaders. The money was never claimed. *(John Prebble)*

56. The 'allotments' were generally situated on the sea coast ... the spots allowed them could not be called land, being composed of narrow stripes, promontories, cliffs and precipices ... bogs and deep morasses. The whole was quite useless to their superiors, and evidently never designed by nature for the habitation of man or beast... The patches of soil where anything could be grown, were so few and scanty that when any dispute arose about the property of them, the owner could almost carry them in a creel on his back and deposit them in another place. ... In most years, indeed, when any mentionable crop was realised, it was generally destroyed before it could come to maturity, by sea-blast and mildew ... the sea scattering its spray upon the adjoining spots of land, to the utter destruction of anything that may be growing on them.

(Donald Macleod)

57. And these *one or two acre lots* are represented as *improvements!* ... over the whole of this district where the sea-shore is accessible, the coast is thickly studded with thatched cottages, crowded with starving inhabitants ... Ancient respectable tenants ... are reduced to extreme misery. ... when the herring fishery (the only fishery prosecuted on this coast) succeeds, they generally satisfy the landlords, whatever privations they may suffer, but when the fishing fails, they fall in arrears, and are sequestrated, and their stock sold to pay the rents, their lots given to others, and they and their family turned adrift on the world. *(Alexander Mackenzie)*

58. Their first efforts as fishermen were what might be expected from a rural people unaccustomed to the sea. The shores of Suther-

land, for immense tracts together, are iron-bound, and much exposed. ... There could not be more perilous seas for the unpractised boatman to take his first lessons on; but though the casualties were numerous and the loss of life great, many of the younger Highlanders became expert fishermen.   (*Hugh Miller*)

59. The people's joy at the removal of Young and Sellar was short-lived, for their successors merely continued the same process of eviction, which continued through the intervening years until the final clearances of 1819 and 1820.

The weather of the early years was exceptionally bad with long, severe winters, floods, and very poor harvests. Sellar wrote: "one of my guides was lost and actually lost several of his toes by the frost." Donald Macleod wrote: "(there was) no shelter left, except on the other bank of the river, now overflowing its banks from the continual rains; so that, after all their labour and privations, the people lost nearly the whole of their crops, as they had already lost their cattle, and were thus entirely ruined."

In the summer of 1816 Sellar busied himself with removing, "in the same unfeeling manner", the last forty families who remained on his land on the east bank of the river, being very careful, however, in view of his recent trial, to burn no houses until the inhabitants had departed. He told them that they might return later to harvest their crops, but before that time came he released four thousand sheep on the land, and the harvest was largely destroyed. The winter came early, as Donald Macleod reported: "The winter commenced by the snow falling in great quantities in the month of October, and continuing with great rigour, so that the difficulty — almost impossibility — of the people, without barns or shelter of any kind, securing their crops, may be easily conceived. I have seen scores of these poor outcasts employed for weeks together, with the snow from two to four feet deep, watching their corn from being devoured by the hungry sheep of the incoming tenants; carrying *on their backs* — horses being unavailable in such a case, across a country without roads — on an average of twenty miles, to their new allotments on the sea-coast, any portion of their grain and potatoes they could secure under such dreadful circumstances. ... they had to subsist entirely on potatoes dug out of the snow; cooking them as they could, in the open air, among the ruins of their once comfortable dwellings! ... Even Mr. Loch ... has been constrained to admit the extreme distress of the people."   (*A.T.*)

60. Their wretchedness was so great that, after pawning everything they possessed to the fishermen on the coast, such as had no cattle were reduced to come down from the hills in hundreds for the purpose of gathering cockles on the shore. Those who lived in the more remote situations of the county were obliged to subsist upon broth made of nettles, thickened with a little oatmeal. Those who had cattle had recourse to the still more wretched expedient of bleeding them, and mixing the blood with oatmeal, which they afterwards cut into slices and fried. Those who had a little money came down and slept all night upon the beach, in order to watch the boats returning from the fishing, that they might be in time to obtain a part of what had been caught. (*James Loch*)

61. ... many severe diseases made their appearance; such as had been hitherto almost unknown among the Highland population; viz., typhus fever, consumption, and pulmonary complaints in all their varieties, bloody flux, bowel complaints, eruptions, rheumatisms ...

Many vices, hitherto almost unknown began to make their appearance ... squabbling, drunkenness. ... Religion also, from the conduct of the clergy, began to lose its hold on their minds.

(*Donald Macleod*)

62. The mild nature and religious training of the Highlanders prevented a resort to that determined resistance and revenge (which only twenty-five years earlier had led the French peasants into revolution). Their ignorance of the English language, and the want of natural leaders, made it impossible for them to make their grievances known to the outside world. They were, therefore, maltreated with impunity. (*Alexander Mackenzie*)

63. (The Duchess of Sutherland) ordered bed and body clothes to all who were in need of them, but, as usual, all was entrusted to the ministers and factors, and they managed the business with the same selfishness, injustice and partiality that had marked their conduct on former occasions. Many of the most needy got nothing, and others next to nothing. For an instance of the latter, several families, consisting of seven or eight, and in great distress, got only a yard and a half of coarse blue flannel, each family. Those, however, who were the favourites and toadies ... Generally speaking, the poor people were nothing benefited by her ladyship's charitable intentions.

(*Donald Macleod*)

64. There are no fewer than seventeen who are known by the name of water bailiffs in the county, who receive yearly salaries ... protecting the operations of the Loch policy, watching day and night the freshwater lakes, rivers, and creeks, teeming with the finest salmon and trout fish in the world, guarding (them) from the famishing people, even during the years of famine and dire distress, when many had to subsist upon weeds, sea-ware, and shell-fish, yet guarded and preserved for the amusement of English anglers. (*Donald Macleod*)

65. Large sums were spent ... by the Sutherland estate on roads, bridges, fishing harbours, inns and steadings. (Most of the fishing was on the east and west coasts, though many years later a few small jetties and harbours were built in the north. Several of the local hotels, however, date from little coaching inns built at that time. *A.T.*)
(*T. C. Smout*)

66. The church, no longer found necessary, was razed to the ground, and its timbers conveyed to construct one of the Sutherland 'improvements' — the Inn at Altnaharra, while the minister's house was converted into a dwelling for a foxhunter. A woman, well-known in the parish, travelling through the desolated Strath next year after the evictions, was asked on her return home for her news, when she replied: "O, chan eil ach sgiala bronach! sgiala bronach!" "Oh, only sad news, sad news! I have seen the timber of our well attended kirk covering the inn at Altnaharra; I have seen the kirkyard where our friends are mouldering filled with tarry sheep, and Mr. Sage's study turned into a kennel for Robert Gunn's dogs, and I have seen a crow's nest in James Gordon's chimney head;" after which she fell into a paroxysm of grief. (*Alexander Mackenzie*)

67. The services of Donald Sage in the open air were attended by large congregations, sometimes of two or three hundred people. They were uplifting, and greatly appreciated by a simple and religious people. Ten years later Donald Macleod, himself a religious man, attended a service in a parish church nearby. He was shocked to find the church a small, poor building, and the congregation shrunk to eight shepherds, with their twenty or thirty dogs, the minister and three of his family. At the singing of the psalm the dogs became restless and "raised a most infernal chorus of howling". They were attacked by their masters with crooks, the following disturbances, with yelping and more howling, continuing all the way through the service. (*A.T.*)

237

68.   The land upon which the people were settled was still controlled by the factors, and rent was still due to the proprietor. James Loch considered himself entitled, as architect of the new Sutherland, to lay down laws governing the habitation of the new coastal cottages, built by the evicted families themselves. Whenever a son succeeded his father the rent was to be increased. Should any child marry, then he or she must leave the parental home. This, in fact, meant that permission to marry must be obtained from the factor, if the couple wished to remain in Sutherland, since only he could grant them an empty cottage in which to live, or the ground upon which to build a new one. Commonly the permission was withheld, since many landowners wished to rid the countryside of its 'excess population' as quickly as possible. Such as married without permission were forced to leave the county. As a *Times* commissioner reported: "They may travel the length and breadth of Sutherlandshire but not a cottage will they find, or a place where they will be suffered to remain."

For centuries it had been the custom of the Highlanders to marry young. Of this tendency James Loch wrote: "It is a principle in every respect most praiseworthy, and which strongly upholds the moral character of a people, when the subsistence of the family is obtained through the exertion and labour of the parents. But when their maintenance must be left to the gratuitous support of others, it degenerates into a selfish gratification of passion." They are remarkable words in view of the fact that he was, by his policy, directly responsible for removing that 'subsistence of the family' and 'labour of the parents' of which he speaks.

Loch himself was the owner of three fine houses, two in Scotland and one in England.   (*A.T.*)

69.   Patrick Sellar occupied four Sutherland farms: Morvich, near Golspie, 1810; east Strathnaver (2), 1814; west Strathnaver, 1819. "Mr. Sellar had three large farms, one of which was twenty-five miles long, and in some places nine or ten miles broad, situated in the barony of Strathnaver" — Donald Macleod.

On Monday, 13 June, 1814, Patrick Sellar commenced the clearance of east Strathnaver, from the heights to within one mile of the sea. The area so cleared, 85,000 acres, had already been divided into three sheep farms, Rhiloisk, Rhifail and Skelpick. On Whitsunday of that year, Sellar had taken occupation of the first two, an area of approximately 50,000 acres, extending from Dunvedin to Ben Griam Mor, south of Loch Rimsdale, and the River Mallart. The third farm was let to the Border shepherd, John Paterson, who later was to occupy the heights of Kildonan, Armadale and Bighouse.

On Tuesday, 17 April, 1819, Sellar commenced the clearance of west Strathnaver, a distance of approximately twenty-five miles, from the River Mudale to the sea. The pattern was the same. On Whitsunday of that year he took occupation of the whole area (excluding the salmon fishing station at Invernaver), being 75,000 acres. This was his largest farm, extending from the mouth of the River Naver to Loch Loyal, Mudale and Loch Naver; and adjoining his other Strathnaver farm as far north as Dunvedin. (See accompanying map.) (*A.T.*)

70. Many who had been turned off the fertile straths and been dumped on small plots of shallow, acid land moved out to Caithness and other counties. (*T. C. Smout*)

71. Donald Macleod was pursued by the servants of Lord Stafford, who wanted him out of the county for his outspoken criticism. He was summoned for debt and brought to what, if one is to believe his own account of it, was a travesty of a trial, in which evidence that conclusively proved his innocence was totally ignored, demands and vituperation took the place of enquiry, and the complainant was also the prosecutor and judge. The case was declared undecided.

Three years later, in October 1830, while Macleod was working in Caithness and many miles from home, his family was again forcibly evicted. (It was sixteen years since the campaign of burnings and his first bitter eviction from Rossall.) On this occasion a party of eight men, having turned his wife and four young children out of doors, flung the furniture after them, doused the fire, nailed up the doors and windows, and threatened the neighbourhood with similar treatment if anyone offered to help or shelter them. His wife made a rough wall out of the furniture to protect her children from the wind, and set out in the night to fetch her husband, forty miles away. She had just reached Caithness when with the combined effort and distress her strength gave out. She was given shelter in Sandside by William Innes, a tacksman, protected by his lease from the power of the factors. Macleod found her there the following day, but when he went for his four children they had gone. In the night, because of the wind and cold, his oldest child, who was seven, had taken the infant on his back, and with the other two holding on to his kilt had led them in the darkness 'through rough and smooth, bog and mire' until they arrived at the house of a great aunt. This woman's husband was so justifiably afraid of the factors that when the children arrived he left, hoping that by so doing he and his wife might be spared from their wrath and summary eviction.

For a year the family found safety on William Innes's land, but then, when once again Macleod was working away from home, his wife was so frightened by the threats of a factor that she fled to the home of Macleod's mother in Bettyhill. Yet again she was evicted, and this time, walking thirty miles with the children in bitter weather, the population once more warned to offer them no assistance, her health broke and her mind gave way. She remained a physically and mentally ill woman for the rest of her days.

The purpose of the campaign of persecution was achieved: Donald Macleod took his family south to Edinburgh.   (*A.T.*)

72.   It came to be Sellar's view that there were too many people altogether in Sutherland. ... Sellar considered emigration the logical and only practical remedy to the population problem. ... He saw no other solution to the famine problem of 1816-17. There were, he figured, between 12,000 and 15,000 people on the Sutherland estate, who would be "destitute of three or four months food".

(*Eric Richards*)

73.   The sailing of an emigrant vessel was a deeply emotional experience, for those leaving and for those who remained. The Highlanders were like children, uninhibited in their feelings and wildly demonstrative in their grief. Men and women wept without restraint. They flung themselves on the earth they were leaving, clinging to it so fiercely that sailors had to prise them free and carry them bodily to the boats.   (*John Prebble*)

74.   Hands were wrung and wrung again, bumpers of whisky tossed wildly off amidst cheers and shouts; the women were forced almost fainting into the boats; and the crowd upon the shore burst into a long, loud cheer. Again and again that cheer was raised and responded to from the boat, while bonnets were thrown into the air, handkerchiefs were waved, and last words of adieu shouted to the receding shore, while, high above all, the wild notes of the pipes were heard pouring forth that by far the finest of pibroch tunes, Cha till mi tuille — I shall Return No More!   (*Inverness Courier*)

75.   The families evicted from Strathnaver and the other Highland glens were not the first to go to America. Emigration had commenced in the middle of the eighteenth century as a trickle: by the middle of the nineteenth century it had become a flood.

The men were desperate. Dishonest and misleading advertisements promised fresh starts and wonderful opportunities in virgin lands.

Landowners and their agents, only too aware of their plight, were ever ready to advance wages. Men signed indentures in good faith, too often signing themselves and their families into servitude in countries that proved to be far from the golden lands they were depicted. Shipowners and merchants too were ever ready to milk what they could from the trusting and worldly-innocent Highlanders.

Conditions aboard ship were appalling. Families were herded together in conditions so dreadful that it is difficult to believe the reports. The Highland Society spoke of "circumstances of suffering ... shocking to humanity." The new ruling of 1828 "legalised crowding past belief." Under this ruling the lower deck of a vessel of 400 tons, a space about 32 yards long, eight yards broad, and five-and-a-half feet in height, was considered adequate accommodation for 300 adults and their baggage. A report to the new Colonial Secretary, Huskisson, observed: "I really do believe that there are not many instances of slave trading from Africa to America exhibiting so disgusting a picture." Under the new law, what was considered acceptable for 489 slaves could be made to do for 700 emigrants. A number of people died on every crossing, either from typhoid or other fever, dysentery, or possibly cholera. Occasionally the losses were appalling. Ship masters demanded exorbitantly high prices for food aboard ship: frequently there was a shortage of food and water. As late as 1854 *The Times* reported: "After a few days have been spent in the pestilential atmosphere created by the festering mass of squalid humanity imprisoned between the damp and steaming decks, the scourge bursts out, and to the miseries of filth, foul air and darkness is added the Cholera. Amid hundreds of men, women and children, dressing and undressing, washing, quarrelling, fighting, cooking and drinking, one hears the groans and screams of a patient in the last agonies of this plague."

Nevertheless the migration continued, the numbers swelling year by year. From the western harbours of Scotland farmers and labourers set out for those districts destined to become the nucleus of British North America. Their arrival was seldom what they had been led to expect: no houses, frequently no shelter even, virgin forest, unbroken wilderness, Indian raids, actual starvation, and winters the like of which they had never even heard. They persevered — there was nothing else they could do — and finally they triumphed. Where the land had been considered more than its inhabitants, now this same 'parcel of beggars', 'lying, psalm-singing, unprincipled peasantry', 'great deal of trash', tamed the land, founded whole new societies, and always treasuring the memory of their homeland, transported its values and culture to the farthest corners of the empire.   (*A.T.*)

76.   Governmental efforts to humanise the emigrant traffic were, to Sellar, meddling and misguided. He regarded the introduction of minimum food requirements on migrant vessels as an absurd

obstruction to the exodus from the Highlands — Highlanders did not need so much meat as regulated, they could live on oatmeal.

(Sutherland papers — Sellar to Lady Stafford, 10 April, 1817.)

(Eric Richards)

77. The first year was hard, a winter to be suffered, a country to be broken, bands of Indians and half-breeds to be fought; ... They carried muskets in their hands as they walked behind their ploughs; they fought Metis and Cree to defend the Red River Colony, and they called their land Kildonan.

... in 1815 there was another emigration from Sutherland to the Red River Valley, this time from Upper Kildonan and Farr. Their going had not disturbed Mr. Loch. "The idle and lazy alone think of emigration," he said. *(John Prebble)*

78. (The following entry refers to the whole of the Marquess of Stafford's Sutherland estate.)

Between the years 1811 and 1820, fifteen thousand inhabitants of this northern district were ejected from their snug inland farms ... the interior of the county was thus improved into a desert. ... The county has not been depopulated — its population has been merely arranged after a new fashion. The late Duchess found it spread equally over the interior and the sea-coast, and in very comfortable circumstances; — she left it compressed into a wretched selvage of poverty and suffering ... *(Hugh Miller)*

79. ... it has been reckoned that quite five hundred families and two thousand persons were ousted from the 215,000 acres in Strathnaver between 1809 and 1819 to form five large farms.

(A. Polson)

80. Upon the top of the hill, Cnocan-a-choillich, you can set a compass, with 25 miles of a radius upon it, and go round with it fully-stretched, but, mark what I say, within this broad circumference you will not find a single human habitation, or one acre of land under cultivation, save that occupied by shepherds belonging to some sheep farmers. With regard to this very district Mr. Donald Macleod in his book, which I sent you, says, "And I recollect when 2,000 able-bodied young men could be raised within the same circuit in 48 hours!" *(Donald Ross — to Harriet Beecher Stowe)*

81. In too many instances the Highlands have been drained, not of their superfluity of population, but of the whole mass of the inhabitants, dispossessed by an unrelenting avarice, which will one day be found to have been as shortsighted as it is selfish and unjust. ... if the hour of need should come, the pibroch may sound through the deserted region, but the summons will remain unanswered.

(Sir Walter Scott)

82. In March, 1854, Britain declared war on Russia. By the end of the year, heavily outnumbered, by six to one at one stage, the British troops were engaged in the long and bitter battle of Inkerman. The Highland regiments, so conspicuous in the past, were now equally conspicuous by their absence. Increasingly people began asking: "Where are the Highlanders?"

Among the Highland regiments none was more justly famous for its discipline and fighting prowess than the 93rd. The men of Sutherland, who formed this regiment, had in the past responded magnificently to the call for their services. In 1854, however, when it was hoped to raise a new battalion, in six weeks of recruitment James Loch failed to secure a single enlistment. The Duke of Sutherland came north from London to Dunrobin Castle to enquire the reason, and personally addressed a large gathering to exhort them to arms. He failed signally; and was replied to by an old man:

" ... Your Grace's mother and predecessors applied to our fathers for men upon former occasions and our fathers responded to their call. They have made us liberal promises, which neither them nor you performed. We are, we think, a little wiser than our fathers, and we estimate your promises of today at the value of theirs; besides you should bear in mind that your predecessors and yourself expelled us in a most cruel and unjust manner from the land which our fathers held in lien from your family. ... I do assure your Grace that it is the prevailing opinion in this country, that should the Czar of Russia take possession of Dunrobin Castle and Stafford House next term, that we could not expect worse treatment at his hands than we have experienced at the hands of your family for the last fifty years."

According to Donald Macleod a solitary man did enlist at this assembly, foolishly believing that by so doing "his bread was baked for life, but no sooner was he away to Fort George to join his regiment than his place of abode was pulled down, his wife and family turned out . . ."

Donald Ross wrote: In Sutherland not one single soldier can be raised. Captain Craigie, R.N., the Duke's Factor, a Free Church Minister and a Moderate Minister, have been piping for days for volunteers and recruits; and yet, after many threats on the part of the Factor, and sweet music on the part of the parsons, the military spirit of the poor Sutherland serfs could not be raised to fighting power. The men told the parsons: "We have no country to fight for. You robbed us of our country and gave it to the sheep. Therefore, since you have preferred sheep to men, let sheep defend you." (*A.T.*)

83. (The existing 93rd Regiment was already under orders for Scutari. Within a few weeks it was in the Crimea. Very soon, as the only Highland regiment in the battle, these men of Sutherland were to achieve greatness and immortality as the 'thin red line tipped with steel' at the battle of Balaclava.

Before this, however, the young men who had refused to volunteer called a public meeting and drew up a statement for the newspapers to explain their attitude. A.T.)

We have no country to fight for, as our glens and straths are laid desolate, and we have no wives nor children to defend as we are forbidden to have them. We are not allowed to marry without the consent of the factor, the ground officer being always ready to report every case of marriage, and the result would be banishment from the county. Our lands have been taken from us and given to sheep farmers, and we are denied any portion of them, and when we apply for such, or even a site for a house, we are told that we should leave the country. For these wrongs and oppressions, as well as for others which we have long and patiently endured, we are resolved that there shall be no volunteers or recruits from Sutherlandshire. Yet we assert that we are as willing as our forefathers were to peril life and limb in defence of our Queen and country were our wrongs and long-endured oppression redressed, wrongs which will be remembered in Sutherlandshire by every true Highlander as long as grass grows and water runs.   (*The Young Men of Sutherland*)

84. Strathnaver was resigned to the sheep and the deer, the new farms and the wilderness. New walls went up around the few parcels of land that were to be planted with oats and turnips; the great white sheep produced its lamb every spring, and in the summer the bales of wool travelled south over the improved roads to feed the hungry mills. In their new stone houses the farmers flourished; but on the slopes of the hills and much of the valley floor, where the old roads had run and where thousands of clansmen had lived for centuries, the green fields and plots of arable land vanished beneath weeds and whins and rank grass, the old earth dykes and standing walls of the destroyed houses crumbled and fell, the long heather moved down to the valley bottoms. Nature resumed sway, the strath took on the air of desolation it has worn ever since.   (*A.T.*)

85. (1886) I remember my grandmother, a sadly-depressed woman with a world of sorrow in her faded blue eyes, as if the shadow of the past were always upon her spirit. I never saw her smile, and when I asked my mother for the cause she told me that that look of pain came upon my grandmother's face with the fires of Strathnaver. Even when my mother was in her last illness, in May 1882, when the present was fading from her memory, she appeared again as a girl of twelve in Strathnaver, continually asking, "Whose house is burning now?" and crying out now and again, "Save the people!"   (*Annie Mackay*)

Sources

Ian Grimble: Scottish historian. *The Trial of Patrick Sellar*, 1962. *The Inverness Courier*.

James Loch: *An Account of the Improvements on the Estate of Sutherland belonging to the Marquess and Marchioness of Stafford*, 1820.

George Macdonald: From Rossall, Strathnaver. Aged fifteen, he drove his father's cattle north to safety during the burning. Days later he returned to see the ruins of his home and township.

Angus Mackay: From Strathnaver. His family evicted when he was eleven years old.

Annie Mackay: Daughter of a girl evicted from Strathnaver.

Betsy Mackay: From Skail, Strathnaver. She was sixteen when her family was evicted.

Alexander Mackenzie: Scottish writer and historian. *The History of the Highland Clearances*, 1883.

Donald Macleod: *History of the Destitution in Sutherlandshire*, 1841. *Gloomy Memories in the Highlands of Scotland*, 1857.

Hugh Miller: Stonemason and amateur geologist of distinction. Published widely. *Scenes and Legends of the North of Scotland*, 1853.

Joseph Mitchell: Distinguished railway engineer. *Reminiscences of my Life in the Highlands*, 1884.

Thomas Pennant: Eighteenth century naturalist and traveller.

A. Polson: *The Book of — Sutherland and Caithness*.

John Prebble: Novelist and Scottish historian. *The Highland Clearances*, 1963; an outstanding study.

Eric Richards: Scottish historian. Essay *The Mind of Patrick Sellar*, 1971.

Donald Ross: Glasgow lawyer. Various publications 1854-1856.

Rev. Donald Sage: His private journal, detailing Highland life and manners, published posthumously as *Memorabilia Domestica*, 1889.

Sir Walter Scott.

T. C. Smout: Scottish historian. *A History of the Scottish People 1560-1830*, 1969.

Colonel David Stewart of Garth: Officer of the 42nd Regiment (the Black Watch). Later major-general and governor of St Lucia. *Sketches of the Highlanders*, 1821.

Harriet Beecher Stowe: American authoress of *Uncle Tom's Cabin*. *Sunny Memories of Foreign Lands*, 1854 — containing an account of her views, and experiences as guest of the Duchess of Sutherland.

K. A. Walpole: Historian. Essay *The Humanitarian Movement of the Early Nineteenth Century to Remedy Abuses on Emigrant Vessels to America*, 1931.

The Re-population of Strathnaver

There are, perhaps, three Strathnavers. First there is the historical Province of Strathnaver, which covered the greater part of what is now north Sutherland; then there is the Strathnaver to which these 'Clearances' refer, being really the total catchment area of the River Naver; and finally there is lower Strathnaver, which was re-populated between 1900 and 1903, a comparatively small area on the west bank of the river.

Life in the lonely cottages and clachans near the shore was hard, and even within two or three generations they were falling empty. Built in desperation, they were left behind as people had time to readjust. Today you will find the shells or tumbled ruins in remote coastal glens where it looks almost as if the foot of man has never trod. And the de-population is still going on; the clachans are emptying, the village populations falling year by year. There is more money about than ever before, but even as a village sprouts its row of council houses, and retired couples and parents smarten and build on to their own property, the young people are moving away, for there is little employment beyond labouring. And in the remote straths and on the outskirts of the villages you will find the more recent ruins; the slowly decaying cottage, fondly held on to for a nephew who might one day return, the house for summer letting, and increasingly the nice property, bought by a well-to-do visitor, modernised with a grant, and now curtained and empty for ten months of the year.

The villages are on the coast: inland the land remains empty. It is well described by Ian Grimble.

"Inland, except for such rare areas of resettlement as the lower Naver valley, it is a no-man's land over which the sporting visitors roam in the summer time.

Mile on mile of desolation,
League on league without an end.

So Swinburne described his journey through it. In ever-extending districts of these vast hinterlands the Forestry Commission is now active, fencing, ploughing, and building the roads for new plantations.

Soon the ruins of Rossall, where Chisholm lived and Donald Macleod was reared and the Rev. Donald Sage listened to the long-silenced ballads of Ossian, soon these scenes of heartbreak will be ringed with trees. Life will never return to them and they will be hidden from the windows of Patrick Sellar's house at Syre."*

In 1900, however, when the first people came back, there was no forestry. Strathnaver was divided into a number of huge hill farms: Syre, Rhifail, Klibreck, Mudale, Altnaharra, and so on; a broad valley of rough pasture fringed with birch trees, and hundreds of square miles of empty moorland. In that year the House of Sutherland handed over to the Board of Agriculture that part of Syre Farm which lay between the Carnachy Burn and the Langdale Burn, on the west bank of the river.

People were invited from the now established coastal villages, and further afield, to apply to the Board of Agriculture for one of the six or so farms into which they had divided the area. But the units were too big, the price, low as it was, too high: they did not realise how poor the people were. There were no takers. The area was re-divided, this time into thirty crofts.

There was nothing but land. A peg driven into the valley floor, another driven into the rocky hillside — these marked your boundaries. All the Board of Agriculture had done was to erect a fence around the whole district; the rest was up to you.

With so much hard work ahead, the majority of the buyers were young couples, people who had their lives ahead of them. There was not a rush of takers, it was three years before the last croft was purchased.

In most cases the young men started with a steading; a barn and a byre. They lived in the barns, painted, often plastered, and even decorated with wallpaper, until they had built their houses. Many of the stones they gathered from the ruins of the old dwellings pulled down by Patrick Sellar, from underneath the grass and weeds, where they had lain for the last eighty years.

As has already been said, they did not have much money, and before many years had passed the majority found it impossible to provide what was necessary for fencing, stock, implements, the high tax of the owner-occupier, and regular payments on a twenty-five or thirty year mortgage. Consequently they had to appeal to the

*Ian Grimble: *The Trial of Patrick Sellar*, 1962.

Board to take over the land once more, and lease it to them instead. The whole area was treated as one unit. It is still leased today.

The children were born and grew up, but there was a maximum population the thirty crofts could support. Despite its share of the 14,000 acres of hill grazing, one croft could not provide a living for more than one family, even if they had been permitted to build a second house. No more land was forthcoming. As the young men needed work, therefore, or married and had to find a home of their own, they moved away.

The population was at its highest about the time of the First World War. It was, as people remember, a little over two hundred. Many went away to fight, and quite a number died.

Today the population is fifty. In the whole strath, counting the shepherds, workers, the small village of Altnaharra, and the owners, most of whom are away at their city houses and other estates for the greater part of the year, it is maybe one hundred and fifty, not many, compared with the two thousand or two thousand five hundred who lived there in the years before the clearances.

251

Today the emptiness is cherished by those who travel north for their holidays, caravanners and fishermen, botanists and ornithologists. But to the people who live there, who see the strath in its winter flood as well as summer sunshine, the solitude is not an unalloyed pleasure. Strathnaver is becoming a lonely place. There are few young people, there is little work. And though the road is well maintained, many of the old houses have been modernised, and most families own a car, television and refrigerator, these are merely the appurtenances of modern living. The population of lower Strathnaver is declining, and until new powers and new ideas are introduced it will continue to do so. Yet will it be possible, in this modern world, to build houses, provide employment, and leave the land unspoiled?

For the strath itself, despite all that has happened, is as beautiful as ever. The sheltered waters of Loch Naver mirror Ben Klibreck, herons flap down the river at dusk, gorse and heather decorate the slopes of moor above the birch trees. It is the world outside, and people, that have changed.